LADY ROSAMUND
AND THE
PLAGUE
OF
SUITORS

LADY ROSAMUND
AND THE
PLAGUE
OF
SUITORS

BARBARA MONAJEM

LEVEL
BEST BOOKS

Historia
ESTABLISHED 2019

Praise for the Rosie & McBrae Regency Mysteries

Praise for Lady Rosamund and the Poison Pen:

"An intriguing and clever work that will appeal to fans of Regency-era fiction."—*Kirkus Reviews*

"Barbara Monajem's *Lady Rosamund and the Poison Pen* is a delightfully spicy mystery, peppered with sharp wit and memorable characters, especially the titular Lady Rosamund. Rosie is a woman who seems to know her own mind...or does she? Battling her greatest fear, Rosie must discover the true identity of the mysterious caricaturist Corvus, and outsmart the author of the poison pen letters before it's too late. Indifferent to the tongue-clucking of her peers, Rosie is full of surprises. Fans of historical mystery are in for an entertaining treat."—Kelly Oliver, Award-winning, bestselling author of the Fiona Figg Mysteries.

Praise for Lady Rosamund and the Horned God:

"Lady Rosamund and the Horned God is an excellent historical mystery—well researched and well written! As a psychotherapist, I was particularly intrigued by Lady Rosamund's OCD tendencies (accurately presented, by the way), and her realistic terror of being locked away in an asylum as mad should others become aware of her behaviors. OCD and most other psychological disorders have existed for centuries. Portraying how one suffering from it might have coped in a society unforgiving of "oddness" gives the Lady Rosamund stories a unique twist."—Kassandra Lamb, author of the Kate Huntington Mysteries and the Marcia Banks & Buddy Cozy Mysteries

Chapter One

A member of the House of Medway must never give way to fear. Or so I told myself sternly as my coach rumbled the last few miles toward London.

It is mortifying to confess that my fear was not of highwaymen, which are not unheard of upon some stretches of the Great North Road. My coachman and groom were armed (as was I, but only my father and I knew that), and in any event, I can afford to lose my diamond drops and a few guineas.

Perhaps anxiety is a better descriptor of my sentiments as we approached the metropolis. I had left London after the death of my husband some months earlier to spend the summer with my father in Westmoreland—but now, as autumn drew in, I was on my way home. My father, the Earl of Medway, decided to come south to visit friends, so he accompanied me for most of the journey. Now, on the last leg home, I looked forward to my London friends and all the entertainments the metropolis offers.

Unfortunately, I was still in mourning. I would have to be circumspect about which events to attend—the quieter sort, nothing too frivolous, and definitely no balls. My mother lives in Kent, but she has many London friends (and enemies) who would be swift to write to her about any social solecism I commit. She might even send my brother Julius to spy on me, for mourning multiplies the number of solecisms just waiting to be committed.

But that wasn't my only anxiety, because—

The coach slowed, and I woke from my uneasy reverie to the sound of whinnying and shouted curses. A coach heading north was stuck in the mud at the roadside, teetering toward the ditch. Two men struggled to manage the frightened horses.

John Coachman slowed our vehicle to ascertain whether help was required. One of the two men—a huge bear of a fellow with a catskin waistcoat, a red neckerchief, and a broken nose—snarled at us and cried, "(Expletive expletive), we're in the (expletive) now!"

Well! That is hardly the proper way to greet a nobleman's coach, nor to express oneself in the presence of a lady. Perhaps he didn't see me through the window, but he could certainly see the crest on the door. In any event, John Coachman immediately took offense and kept going.

"What a rude fellow," said Mary Jane, my maid. We continued around a bend, Mary Jane muttering about unmannerly behavior on the roads. I gazed out the window, pondering my second source of anxiety, when I spied a woman running ahead of us along the verge.

She turned, stark terror on her face, and leapt into the ditch. She scurried up the other side and ran pell-mell across a field towards a nearby wood.

In that one instant when she faced us, I recognized her. The fugitive was none other than my brother's mistress, Esme Concord!

I pounded on the roof of the coach, and when it kept going, I put down the window and called, "John, stop this instant!" He is my father's coachman and a stubborn old fellow, but he knew better than to disobey a direct order.

The coach came to a halt, and I gathered my skirts and leapt out the door without waiting for the groom to let down the steps. Mary Jane's cries of dismay pursued me, but I ignored them.

"Miss Concord!" I called. "Please wait. It's I, Rosamund Phipps." I slid into the ditch and ploughed up the other side. She was halfway to the wood, but at that she paused. She wore neither pelisse nor hat, and her hair fell loose down her back. Heavens! She's not a lady, but I'm sure she wouldn't choose to travel in such dishabille.

"Lady Rosamund, I—" She glanced fearfully up the road in the direction from which we had come. It didn't take much to guess that her flight had something to do with the coach we had just passed.

Well! Whatever had happened, it was clearly my duty to help her. My mother would disagree, but surely my brother would want me to succor his mistress. I beckoned. "Quickly, come with me. I'll take you home."

She shook her head, glancing again up the road. "I *can't* go home."

"Come!" I commanded, hurrying toward her. "Don't be foolish. I don't know whose coach that was, but you're definitely safer with me." Good Lord, now that I saw her more clearly, I realized she had a bruise on her temple. "You're injured! You may explain it all once we're on our way."

With a dry sob, she capitulated, and wisely. We were almost at the coach when a shot rang out! I bundled her inside and scrambled after her. "Hang on, lad," John shouted, whipping the horses into motion. The groom clung precariously as we raced away down the road. A minute later, we slowed so he could climb up next to John.

"Are you unhurt, John?" I called as we moved forward again at a spanking pace.

"I'm well, my lady," he said in a grumpy tone that meant he wished he hadn't stopped in the first place but was at the same time proud that he had. He is expected to consider my welfare before anyone else's. However, he is also supposed to obey me. At times, this must be tricky. Luckily, he didn't anticipate any danger to us, for he wouldn't want to leave a helpless woman on the road with an armed man shooting at her any more than I would. Neither would Mary Jane, however much she disapproved of this particular female.

Poor girl, her teeth were chattering. It wasn't particularly chilly, but it had rained earlier, and her feet were soaked, her thin slippers covered in mud. I suspected, however, that her shivers had more to do with fright than cold. I felt quite shaky myself.

I put my shawl around her shoulders, and Mary Jane, who had moved to the rear-facing seat, silently helped her off with her slippers and draped one of the carriage rugs over her knees. (Although this silence was entirely proper in a servant, it was unusual in Mary Jane, who seldom hesitates to tell me precisely what she thinks.)

Miss Concord thanked her while I dug beneath the seat for a flask of brandy. "Here. This will help calm you and warm you up, too."

She took a gulp, coughed, and took another. "Thank you," she murmured.

She wasn't shaking quite so much now. "I apologize for inconveniencing you. I didn't know he would shoot at me." She glanced at the stone-faced Mary Jane and quickly back at me, her lip quivering.

"You suffered far greater inconvenience than we did," I told her, scowling at Mary Jane. She is not an unkind person, but she was having a fit of the horrors, imagining what my mother would think—whilst my glare told her, I hope, that my mother could go to the devil.

"Tell me what happened," I said. She hesitated, and I asked, "Whose coach was that?"

"Lord Worsten's," she said, biting her lip hard.

"That tedious prig?" I cried, and she burst into tears.

"There, there." I put my arm around her and passed her my handkerchief. "I apologize if you are enamored of him, but if so, why would you run away?"

"I'm not enamored—in fact, I loathe him. He abducted me!"

"Heavens, how ghastly." Lord Worsten is one of my brother's cronies. He may be a prig, but I would never have suspected him of such infamy. However, maybe stealing another man's mistress is *de rigueur* in some circles.

"I was in my garden in Kensington—"

Mary Jane couldn't help but take offense, because the house and its garden belong not to Miss Concord, but to my brother Julius, Lord Derwent. (Unless, of course, he has given it to her in payment for her services—but I don't expect he's quite that generous.) However, obviously she meant her dwelling place, so I gave my maid another admonitory glower. If Miss Concord noticed either Mary Jane's affront or my response, it didn't show on her face. Which was unexpectedly ladylike, but she is the daughter of a wealthy merchant, so she must have had *some* education. Not only that, my brother is far too high a stickler to choose a truly vulgar sort of woman to be his mistress.

"—snipping a few late roses, when someone came up behind me and put a sack over my head. I screamed and kicked, and he hit me so hard that my head spun. He dumped me in the coach, and immediately it started moving."

"How terrifying," I cried. The poor girl! Even Mary Jane's features showed a smidgin of sympathy now.

4

"I struggled to remove the sack, and a man said, 'Stay still, and I'll take it off you, but if you shriek, I'll put it right back on—but only over your head. I'm enjoying looking at the rest of you.'" She let out a shuddering breath. "I realized then that my skirt had ridden up past my knees, and I feared—well, I'm sure you can imagine."

I could, more or less. I'm innocent of the experience of sexual intercourse, but that doesn't mean I have no imagination.

"I promised not to shriek, and Lord Worsten—for it was he—removed the sack. I straightened my dress the instant I could, because I couldn't bear his—his eager eyes on my legs. He grinned *disgustingly*, and then noticed the swelling on my temple. He said, 'Did that oaf hit you? I do apologize. I'll punish him for that.'" She clenched her fists. "As far as I was concerned, Lord Worsten was the one who deserved punishment."

"Yes, indeed," I said. "But why did he abduct you?"

"I haven't the slightest notion. He looked me over in the most *revolting* way and said, 'You're not bad-looking, but I don't know what Derwent sees in you. There are much riper goods on the market.'"

"How horrid," I said faintly. I don't suppose any woman, lightskirt or not, likes to be told she's unattractive. Nevertheless, I could see what he meant. Miss Concord is pretty, but in an ordinary sort of way.

"He said—" She stopped. "No, it's too crude to repeat."

Mary Jane was beginning to look surprised. She, like my mother, assumes that a fallen woman gladly accepts the advances of any man who offers. I find this hard to believe. I have never wished to encourage any man's advances, but naturally, one finds some men less repulsive than others. Or even finds one of them somewhat attractive, as I had recently found to my dismay.

"How dare he?" Miss Concord clutched the shawl about herself. "He knows I belong to Lord Derwent and no one else." She gulped. "At least, that's what I thought. He said Lord Derwent is getting bored with me." Tears brimmed in her eyes.

"How awkward," I said weakly. By what I have heard, gentlemen do tend to change mistresses as often as waistcoats, although there are, of course, exceptions. My deceased husband was faithful to the same mistress for almost five years, but he was truly in love with her, poor man.

Miss Concord had been Julius' mistress for several months, as far as I knew. "I'm terribly sorry," I said, "but sadly, gentlemen seem to have very little natural constancy."

"I don't believe it," Miss Concord said. "It's not—it's not like that between Ju—between Lord Derwent and me."

Heavens, she had almost referred to my brother by his Christian name. Perhaps that is usual between a man and his mistress, but I was hard put not to feel revulsion. And surprise, for Julius is extremely protective of his dignity. Only family members use his Christian name, and that sparingly, for he has been Lord Derwent from the moment of his birth.

Valiantly, Miss Concord muffled a sob. "Lord Worsten said—he said he was doing Lord Derwent a favor by taking me off his hands."

"By abducting you? That's absurd."

"That's what I thought, but I was too frightened to say so. He kept looking at me and touching me, and I was terrified he might try to take me then and there—" Her voice caught. Heavens, one would think she was a frightened virgin.

"And then the coach tipped toward the ditch, and Lord Worsten was thrown against the side. He must have hit his head, for he lay there and didn't move."

"So, you got out and ran," I said. "Well done!"

"Yes, but if you hadn't come along, his coachman would have caught me. Or *shot* me!"

For a few minutes, we were silent. What a ghastly situation. "I see why you don't want to go home," I said, "for what if Lord Worsten has someone abduct you again?"

"But what if he was right, and Lord Derwent doesn't want me there anymore?" She dabbed at her eyes. "He was perfectly amiable when I saw him last."

My brother is seldom amiable, but that was beside the point. How dreadful to be cast off! "Derwent has many faults, but he is an honorable man. He would not dismiss you without providing for you." Unless, I supposed, she wanted to go to another man—but clearly, she did not. "Well! I shall bring you home with me, and I'll write to Derwent and ask him to clarify the situation."

Mary Jane stifled a protest. A lady does not invite her brother's mistress into her own home. It's unheard of!

On the other hand, my late husband's mistress was my dearest friend. And Corvus, the anonymous caricaturist, had made several scandalous drawings featuring me. In other words, I was already somewhat notorious. Not that I was likely to reveal this particular escapade to anyone, for if my mother found out, all Hades would break loose. Fortunately, Julius wasn't likely to tell her about it. A gentleman does not discuss his mistress with his mother.

I would have to ask John Coachman and the groom to keep silent on the matter as well; they might obey, as they are my father's servants and don't like my mother any more than I do. As for Mary Jane, she would go to her death rather than reveal that she had waited on a fallen woman.

"My lady, I mustn't go to your home," Miss Concord said. "It wouldn't be proper." My maid nodded her agreement.

I wasn't about to let stupid propriety get in the way of saving her life. "Yes, but you're perfectly ladylike, so we'll pretend you're someone else. Fortunately, my brother never parades you at the opera." The only reason I knew about their liaison was that Miss Tubbs, a gossipy friend of mine, happened to hear about it by way of her housekeeper, whose nephew is a footman in Miss Concord's father's household. Servants are a useful source of information that well-meaning relatives think unsuitable for a lady.

"We have never gone out in public together," she said. "He is most—most considerate of my feelings." *Or at least he was till now*, said her expression. Her lip wobbled again. I was beginning to wonder if she had fallen in love with Julius. It's hard to imagine—I find him intolerable—but to each her own.

"I'll say you're a friend from somewhere in the north who is stopping briefly in London," I said. "Hmm. We'll call you something prim and proper, like…oh, Edith. Or Millicent. Or…"

"My second name is Gwendolyn," she said. "Will that do?"

"Gwendolyn is perfect—such a sturdy, down-to-earth name. It sounds very Welsh, so we'll give you a Welsh surname, too—how about Evans?"

"I don't know the first thing about Wales," she said.

"Nor do most of my acquaintances. If anyone asks, we'll say your family is from the Lakes, near my father's estate there. That's not too terribly far from Wales, and I can guide the conversation so you won't seem ignorant. But I don't expect anyone will even see you at my house, for I'm sure Derwent will sort it out quickly."

I certainly hoped he would. I also hoped he wouldn't be furious with me for interfering in the abduction of his mistress. I found it impossible to believe he would be so lost to kindness and commonsense as to 1) abandon her, and then 2) prefer that I had left her to be assaulted or murdered, but he tends to think the worst of me regardless of what I do. He would almost certainly be mortified—and a mortified man is likely to lash out.

However, that problem would wait until later. First, we had to make Miss Concord appear respectable. Unfortunately, most of our clothing was in trunks lashed onto the rear of the coach. I dug in my travel bag for a brush. "Tidy your hair, and I'll lend you my bonnet." Hopefully, she didn't have vermin, but the only other time I had met her, she'd been clean and well-groomed. "There's a cloak under the seat. That will cover your muddy gown."

"Which hat will you wear?" she asked, after settling my bonnet on her soft, brown curls.

"None," I said, taking the hairbrush and tidying my own hair. "If anyone sees me walking hatless from the carriage to my front door, they are welcome to gossip about it."

She looked as if she wished to say something, but bit her lip and didn't. She, like everyone else, has surely seen the caricatures of me. Not that Julius would have shown her, or at least I don't think so; he finds scandal most upsetting. I wondered if she believed any of the nonsense about me, such as pushing a footman down the stairs, having a Sapphic relationship with my husband's mistress and/or a ménage à trois, et cetera.

The one occasion on which we had previously met, she'd seemed frightened of me, but perhaps it was because she feared Julius would be upset if he learned of it. Honestly, gentlemen are such a nuisance.

By now, we were through Islington and had passed the nursery where my cook buys herbs for my tiny kitchen garden. "Not long now," I said, and rapped on the little door in the roof to speak to John Coachman. "Please keep what happened today to yourselves. The lady with me is a friend who came with us all the way from the Lakes."

"Very good, my lady," he said, and soon we reached my street. A gentleman just rounding the corner started at the sight of my coach, grinned in his typically smug way, and wiggled his fingers at me.

I nodded politely as we passed, but said, "Drat." At Miss Concord's surprised gaze, I said, "Sir Pinkerton Jones-Worthy. Such a bore, and he's sure to call on me."

A minute later, we pulled up before my house. I stepped out of the coach and spied my near neighbor, Sir Devlin Curtis, just leaving his house to mount Fever, his black stallion. He is my mother's favorite cicisbeo and quite tolerable, despite the fact that he probably spies on me and reports to Mother. So do many of her other friends, alas.

He nodded and smiled at me, and then, as Miss Concord descended, he started in surprise. "A friend, Lady Rosamund?"

"Why, yes," I lied, "Miss Evans is from the north and has come to London for a visit." I turned to her. "My dear, this is Sir Devlin Curtis, a close friend of my mother's."

"And a longtime friend of Lady Rosamund's as well." He is a widower, an elegant, proud sort of man, tallish with a pleasant voice and impeccable manners. I understand why he appeals to my mother, although he is a little too perfect for my taste. "Charmed to meet you, Miss Evans."

"So very kind," Miss Concord said. Sir Devlin bowed, motioned to his man to hold the horse, and reentered his house just as Stevenson, my butler, emerged to welcome me home.

He introduced the new housekeeper, Mrs. Kelly, for I had dismissed the previous one before leaving for the north. I had specified that the new housekeeper must be tolerant and good-natured, and this rosy-cheeked woman seemed exactly that. Definitely better than Mrs. Cropp, who idolized my mother and had thwarted me to the best of her ability.

Onward with this tale. Mrs. Kelly hurried off to order a room prepared for 'Miss Evans,' and meanwhile, I took her up to my bedchamber for a quick wash and change of clothing. Fortunately, she and I were of a similar size, except that I am a bit taller. Since I was stuck wearing dismal mourning clothes, there were a number of colorful dresses for her to choose from, with only minor adjustments required.

While Mary Jane assisted her, I dashed off a short note to Julius and gave it to Morose Maurice, my gloomy footman, to deliver and wait for an answer. Medway House is only a few streets away from mine, so it wouldn't take long. "Now we'll have tea and some of Cook's delicious cakes, and Lord Derwent will be here in no time."

The tea was lovely—I insist on having the best Bohea—and the cakes were as marvelous as always, but Julius didn't come.

Chapter Two

"Perhaps he is out with friends," I suggested, when after two hours Maurice had still not returned. "Maurice must have gone to find him."

Another hour later—it was dark by now, and we had almost finished a light dinner—Maurice finally returned, pouting. "I waited like you told me, my lady, but Lord Derwent isn't home yet, and his servants wouldn't tell me where he went."

How annoying, and typical of the close-mouthed servants at Medway House. They have been trained by my mother—ah, except for Julius' valet. "I shall go speak to them myself," I said, and rang for Mary Jane. "Find Miss, ah, Evans something to read and tuck her up in bed."

I donned a pelisse, bonnet, and a pair of stout boots, and, refusing to order the carriage, walked the short distance to Medway House, with Maurice glumly accompanying me. He rapped on the door, and as soon as a wary-looking young footman peered out, I pushed my way across the threshold. "Where," I asked in my most imperious manner—learned at my mother's knee, so to speak, "is Lord Derwent?" The footman gaped at me without saying a word. "Has he returned?" I asked.

"No, my lady," said the footman, who is called Charles, like all the footmen in Medway House.

If I still lived in Medway House, I would mentally designate him as Blond Charles, based on the wisp of fair locks peeping from under his wig. Not that I wouldn't prefer to call him by his real name, if I knew what it was, but my mother would never permit it.

"Very well then," I said, "where has Lord Derwent gone?" Perhaps Charles had been eavesdropping and heard my brother say something pertinent. He might blurt to me what he'd keep from my footman.

No such luck. "Like I told Maurice, I mean James, I dunno where he went to, neither."

(He was referring to the fact that until recently, all the footmen in my house were called James—the standard name used by my deceased husband's family.)

"Then find someone who does." I stripped off my gloves. "I shall wait in the drawing room. No, don't stay to light the candles. Maurice will do it."

Blond Charles disappeared toward the rear of the house, and a few minutes later, Bates, the butler, sailed into the drawing room and bowed. "Good evening, Lady Rosamund."

"It would be a good evening," I retorted, "if I could but speak to my brother. Kindly tell me where he has gone."

"That's just it, my lady," he said. "As I—and several other members of my staff—told your footman, we don't know."

"Didn't he tell you where he was going?" I'm sure I sounded shocked. Julius plans his days. He doesn't dash out in a ramshackle way.

"He did not." Bates sounded offended, rightly so by his reckoning, and by my mother's if she knew of it. She believes a noble household must be orderly in the extreme—not that she considers that when she is overset and causing a great deal of chaos and disorder.

"When did he leave?"

"Late this afternoon, perhaps an hour before your footman came here."

"Did he leave in a vehicle or on foot?"

"I'm sure I don't know, my lady. He didn't call for his curricle to be brought round, but he may have hailed a hackney. No one actually saw him go." His expression gave me to understand that a gentleman was not obliged to inform his servants of his plans, much less his hysterical little sister.

I almost stamped my foot. I wasn't the least bit hysterical, but my mother and Julius believe I am unbalanced, and their concern trickles down to the servants. Therefore, I had to mask my annoyance with an assumption of regal calm. "Where is Jenkins, then? Perhaps he has some more useful information."

"He's gone to the Croaking Frog," Bates said. "For choir practice." (Not a church choir, you understand, but a group of men who sing old-fashioned songs popular with the common folk. My father, who is enamored of every aspect of British lore, encourages this.)

Much as I wished to, I couldn't go barging into a tavern to question my brother's valet. Not only was it *not* the sort of environment to which I—the daughter of an earl, granddaughter of a marquis, and cousin of a duke—am accustomed, it would cause talk, which would upset my brother. My goal was to avoid talk, although my arrival and air of urgency might well cause the Medway House servants to gossip. Drat.

For a brief moment, I wished Mr. Gilroy McBrae were close at hand. He can insinuate himself into any environment and gather information. His abilities are quite astonishing, as I had recently learned during a house party in the Lakes. (Yes, I shouldn't have attended such an event while in mourning, but my father approved, so who are you to object?)

"Did he receive a message from anyone shortly before he left?" I asked.

Bates visibly suppressed a sigh. "I believe he did, my lady, but I do not know from whom."

"Then let us look for it, and perhaps we shall have an inkling of where he's gone."

With great reluctance, Bates accompanied me to Julius' bedchamber, but no crumpled message was to be found in the wastebasket, nor in the empty fireplace. We proceeded to his study, which was deplorably tidy. I rifled through the documents on the desk whilst Bates tried to mask his disapproval, but it was all the usual sort of thing—correspondence with Members of Parliament, letters from petitioners, estate business (as he manages the Kent property for my father), and bills.

And a crossed and recrossed letter from my mother, which began with a plea to keep an eye on me when I returned to town. It was nosy of me (and highly improper) to read it, but I wished to know if she had any horrid stratagems planned. However, I couldn't do so with Bates breathing down

13

my neck, so to speak.

Fine, I would get rid of him. "What a nuisance this is." I opened the top drawer, pulled out a quarter sheet of foolscap (Julius has it nicely cut ahead of time into various sizes, as he would never waste paper) and a pen and penknife. "Kindly fetch me a pot of coffee. *Hot*, please." That might offend Bates further—the very idea that he would bring anything but scalding hot coffee!—but it would also keep him busy for several minutes.

I began to sharpen the quill, and reluctantly, he left. I slipped the letter out from the pile, but soon realized I would never get through it in time. I folded it and secreted it in my reticule, hoping Julius would think he had misplaced it, and opened a bottle of ink.

Heavens, what to say? Bates was sure to read my note unless I sealed it—and even then, he might attempt to peek. Very well, it would be urgent and imperative, whilst revealing nothing.

My dearest Julius,

Please come to see me at your earliest (heavily underscored) *convenience. I must consult you immediately* (again underscored) *on a most delicate matter. I fear a most unpleasant scandal will erupt unless you are here to scotch it.*

At this point, Bates returned with the coffee. I thanked him, read over what I had written so far, and pondered how to make Julius realize how urgent the matter was.

I fear Corvus will hear of it if we do not make haste. Who knows where he is lurking and listening?

I knew perfectly well where Corvus lurked—or at least dwelt, for he might at the moment be at a *ton* party as anything from a guest to a footman—and that he considered my brother fair game for his caricatures. He might take pity on Miss Concord, if I asked him to. However, our friendship, such as it was, was rather strained, and I didn't in the least wish to contact him.

Back to the letter. Ha! I knew what to add.

I dread the consequences if our dear mother is rendered prostrate once again. Yours worriedly, Rosamund.

Julius was obsessed with protecting Mother and would come hotfoot. Satisfied with my effort, I gulped down the coffee, pondering what to do next. He might not return until late, if he was at a card party or carousing with his cronies. I wondered what he was wearing when he left, but Bates wouldn't know (or admit to knowing), and Jenkins wasn't here.

There was one more place to ask—his stables. I folded the note, addressed it to Julius, and left it on the desk. "See to it that Lord Derwent receives this the instant he arrives home," I told Bates, "and in the meantime, where is the footman who answered the door? I want him to take me through to the mews."

"But, my lady—"

I was tempted to take pity on him. It's not easy dealing with a lady one must obey, but of whom one has also learned to be wary. It's absurd, because however peculiar I may or may not be, I have never actually harmed any servant…

Ah, but the first caricature, the one in which Corvus showed me pushing a footman down the stairs, was widely believed to be true, and servants are particularly credulous.

"Don't fuss, Bates. What harm can it do if I ask the grooms a few questions? None at all, and your footman will be perfectly safe as long as he doesn't pause at the head of a staircase with me right behind him."

He gawped, and I laughed. "Only a jest, Bates. Come, I'm in a hurry. I have a guest at home and must return to her."

I believe he would have insisted on accompanying me himself, but fortunately my jest had ruffled him. On the way to the mews, I asked Blond Charles if he had received the message that arrived shortly before my brother's departure.

"Yes, my lady." He shuffled his feet. Heavens, why was he so uneasy? There were no staircases nearby.

"Did you know the man who brought it?" I asked.

After a pause, he admitted, "'Tweren't a man, my lady, but a girl. A housemaid, I reckon."

Ah. He was young and easily embarrassed. "I see. A pretty one, was she, and you don't wish to be reprimanded for flirting. Well, I shan't tell."

"Thank you, my lady, but she was the one done the flirting." A pity it was dark, for I would wager he was blushing. "I'm finished with women, I am. They cozens you and then drops you like a brick." He cleared his throat. "Beg pardon, my lady."

Rightly so. Servants are not supposed to speak unless spoken to, and never to volunteer information about their tedious personal lives.

"Come now, you'll be fine in a few days," I said, as if to a child—for servants are often little better. "Do you know by whom the girl is employed?"

"No, my lady. I ain't never seen her before, and happy never to see her again, neither."

Another trail that led nowhere, but I tried one last question. "Was she dark or fair, buxom or slim?"

He cleared his throat, poor lad. "Fair, and—and plump as a ripe peach, and didn't she know it."

"Dear me," I said. "You're better off without that sort of girl, but I'm sure another one will be perfect for you."

The grooms were about to bed down for the night, but Hanson, the head groom, answered my questions readily—and truthfully, I think, for I noticed immediately that Thunder, Julius' favorite mount, was not in his stall.

"Aye, my lady, his lordship rode away in a right hurry and said he might not return tonight."

I was relieved to hear this, but also exasperated. If either Maurice or Bates had thought to question the grooms, I needn't have come here and made such a fuss. (On the other hand, I wouldn't have Mother's letter in my reticule.)

"He didn't say where he was going?" I asked.

"Not as such, my lady. He did ask if my nephew, Jacky, is still ostler at the Robin and Worm at Barnet, not liking to stable Thunder at the Red Lion or the Green Man, as those fools can't think of nothing but besting one another."

Why Barnet, of all places? "He didn't say whether he meant to stay at Barnet, or merely to change horses?"

"No, my lady, but he was in a tearing hurry. Didn't want to stop and chat like he does sometimes."

It was hard to imagine my brother hobnobbing with the grooms, but perhaps he lets down his guard with them. My brother is very high-strung, and the company of horses can be quite soothing.

"His lordship was frowning something fierce," said the other groom. Hanson's brows drew together, for I'd been addressing the head groom, not his underlings.

That didn't stop the stable boy, who had paused in his sweeping, from volunteering his opinion as well. "He were awful scary-like, if you ask me. Like he were ripe to strangle someone."

"Thank you," I said, before Hanson could remonstrate with him. "That was very helpful." I gave Hanson a shilling and sixpence to each of the others, and walked silently home with Maurice.

What a pickle we were in! Evidently, a maid from the Kensington house had come with the news of Miss Concord's abduction. Had the servants seen that it was Lord Worsten who had taken her? Surely someone would have tried to help her! Although to be fair, members of the lower classes are rightly hesitant to lay hands on a peer, as they could be hanged for doing so. Perhaps they had instead written to my brother, telling him what had happened.

Well! It hardly mattered how Julius had learned of the abduction. He seemed to know where Worsten was headed and had ridden *ventre à terre* to the rescue. Was Barnet his destination, or only on the way to it?

I arrived home to find that Miss Concord had refused to go to bed, but instead asked for some mending to do while she waited for my return. Mary Jane sat with her in the drawing room, the picture of martyrdom.

Miss Concord sprang up from her chair as I entered but had the sense to say nothing, for Maurice was right behind me. What a relief she knew how to be discreet.

"Bring us chamomile tea, Maurice," I said, for I sensed we needed to calm down. "You may go to bed," I told Mary Jane. "Miss Evans and I will help each other undress."

Stiffly, she rose and left the room without even taking my outerwear. I was in for a scold.

"Thank you for sending her away," Miss Concord said. "I think she feared

I would steal the silver if I weren't securely locked in my bedchamber."

I rolled my eyes, which is frightfully vulgar. Only a few months ago, I wouldn't have done so, but I had begun to realize what a useful gesture it can be. Without a single word, I conveyed my annoyance with Mary Jane and my trust in Miss Concord's honesty. Not that I really knew she was honest, but for the moment she was my responsibility, and well worth risking a few spoons.

"Have you any news, my lady?" She looked even more worried than I felt.

I shed my hat and gloves with a sigh. "Nothing particularly useful." I threw my pelisse over a chair, but I wasn't ready to sit. I paced back and forth, relating all that had happened, and then said, "I wish we knew what was in the message Derwent received. He set out for Barnet—if that was his destination—or perhaps to take either the Great North Road or the Holyhead Road, for the two diverge at Barnet." I had passed through Barnet that very day on the way home.

"Or another nearby road," she said. "It needn't have been a coaching road, if he was on horseback. Perhaps he chose to ride for a reason."

"That's true," I mused. "The coach carrying you headed north, so we must assume he followed it on his way to rescue you."

Her lip quivered, and she bit it to stop the trembling. "Do you really think so?"

"I don't know what to think," I answered truthfully, "but it makes sense. Otherwise, why would he ride out of London immediately after you were abducted?"

Of course, this didn't necessarily mean he wanted to keep her. He might simply be enraged that his so-called friend had made off with her without so much as a by-your-leave. The stable boy had said Derwent looked as though he would like to strangle someone—not that my brother would do any such thing. He would either get into a fistfight (likely a drunken one), or he would challenge Lord Worsten to a duel.

Good Lord, I hoped not. He's not a bad shot, but how stupid to set oneself up as a target. However, I didn't voice these thoughts, for it wouldn't help Miss Concord feel any better.

"We'd best get to bed," I said, "and if we haven't heard from Lord Derwent by morning, I'll go to Kensington tomorrow and question your servants. They may know more than we do."

With palpable reluctance, she agreed to this. We both went to bed—or at least, she did, after I unlaced her stays and wished her goodnight.

Mary Jane was waiting in my bedchamber. "She is the most stubborn female I have ever encountered. You said she was to go to bed, but would she oblige you by doing so? No! And then she told me I needn't wait up, that she would wait for you in the drawing room. As if I would permit her to run free in the house, taking anything she chose!"

"Don't be absurd," I said. "She's the daughter of a wealthy merchant, not a petty thief." (Not that many merchants aren't thieves, judging by the prices they charge, but that's a different matter.)

"She's a fallen woman about to be tossed into the street," Mary Jane said.

"Mary Jane, do you really believe Lord Derwent would do anything so dishonorable?"

That quieted her, as she thinks highly of Julius. "No, my lady." After a reluctant pause, she added, "She sets excellent stitches, I must say. And her manners leave nothing to be desired."

"She was brought up to be a lady," I said. "Perhaps her father hoped she would marry some doddering lord, and she felt being my brother's mistress was a better bargain." I found this hard to believe—but just barely. I know far too many ancient widowers who would gladly snap up a rich, nubile young woman. At least my brother is young and reasonably good-looking. "It seems Lord Derwent has always been kind and respectful to her, and so must we be."

Almost immediately, I regretted that last bit, for it implied that I felt obliged to treat her well only for Julius' sake. This wasn't true. I am trying to learn not to disapprove of what I don't understand. I pitied her for her own sake, and felt a pricking of shame at not saying so.

Fortunately, Gilroy McBrae wasn't there to hear me, for he would have known, and he would have given me a look that said he knew.

Morning came. We hadn't heard from Julius, but that wasn't too surprising, since he would likely sleep late if he arrived home after midnight. We breakfasted together on shirred eggs and muffins. Mary Jane had artfully arranged Miss Concord's hair to cover the bruise on her temple—a gesture that meant she would comply with the charade that my guest was a lady.

What a pity she was the daughter of a merchant, for I quite liked her. If she had been introduced to me as the daughter of a country squire, I would have had no difficulty believing it. I wondered if her ladylike diction had been drummed into her by a governess, or if she had attended an expensive school. (It would have been rudely inquisitive to ask, so I refrained.)

By the time we were finishing breakfast, I decided we had waited long enough for my inconsiderate brother to at least send a reply. I sent Maurice over to Medway House to see if he had returned during the night—although it seemed unlikely. If he'd ridden to Barnet or farther, he would likely have spent the night where he was.

Miss Concord thought the same. "I'll come with you to Kensington," she said. Judging by her wan face and the dark circles under her eyes, she hadn't slept much. Nor had I, but better than she, I assume, since I wasn't in danger of being dismissed by a bored protector. Not that I ever feel entirely safe, except with my father, for my mother frets almost constantly about my peculiarity.

Drat! I hadn't finished reading Mother's letter to Julius, which I'd started the night before. She began by complaining about her ill health (absurd; she's as stubbornly robust as a mule), then went on to plead with Julius to have me watched closely when I returned to London, for fear I would act in a manner unbefitting a respectable widow.

After trying to further decipher her crossed and recrossed writing by my bedroom candle, I gave up and concealed it in an old book on knot gardens, meaning to try again early in the morning—but I'd slept late, so it would have to wait for now.

Oh, very well, if you must know, the prospect of reading more of my mother's horrid thought and plans made me feel quite ill. I had enough to worry me at the moment.

"Are you sure it's wise to accompany me to Kensington?" I asked Miss

Concord. "Yesterday, you feared Lord Worsten might abduct you again."

"I still fear that, but my servants may be too much in awe of you to say anything useful. We'll be careful." She pondered. "They took me from the garden, which leads into a mostly empty lane. We'll go in by the front door. I can't imagine them grabbing me on the street." She sucked in a breath. "Actually, I *can* imagine it."

"Don't," I said. "It's highly unlikely. Lord Worsten isn't a criminal, just a stupid crony of my brother's. He won't want to cause a scandal."

"And be featured in one of Corvus' prints," she said with a twitch of the lip. "Corvus seems to know all the worst gossip."

(Yes, because he's a master eavesdropper, and I don't mean that as a compliment.)

"I hope he doesn't find out about me being abducted," she said, "although a scandal about that might make my father finally give up on me."

I blinked. "But surely…" Dear me, how was I to express it without sounding frightfully insulting?

"You needn't worry about hurting my feelings," she said. "I am inured to my loss of reputation. Everyone assumes my father has disowned me, but far from it. He has no one but me to leave his fortune to, so he hopes to find a suitable candidate to succeed him in the business who will also take me as I am." Poor girl, no wonder she sounded bitter. Doddering old men are bad enough, but a fortune hunter who automatically detests his wife would be even worse.

"That does sound horrid, but better, perhaps, than being left destitute?" I managed.

She shrugged. "You haven't seen the sort of man he chooses."

My heart bled for her. I don't approve of wanton behavior, but a single foolish mistake shouldn't ruin one's life forever. "Then we must ensure that Lord Derwent provides for you suitably."

Hopefully, I sounded confident (which I wasn't, not in the least), but if Julius proved intractable, I would find a way to help her myself. I wondered if such a charitable action would impress Gilroy McBrae—and stopped wondering immediately. The daughter of an earl, granddaughter of a marquis, and cousin of a duke has no need to impress anyone.

We were embarking on our second cups of coffee when Maurice hastened into the breakfast room and bowed. "Lord Derwent has not returned, his valet Mr. Jenkins does not know where he went, and are you at home to visitors, my lady? Mr. McBrae is here to see you."

Chapter Three

Speak (or in this case think) of the devil. I didn't want to see McBrae—I wasn't *ready*—and it was far too early for morning calls, so why was he here? I should say I wasn't receiving, but I couldn't—simply *couldn't* deny him. I owed him too much.

"Also, my lady..." Maurice shuffled his feet, which is not unusual in a very young fellow (such as Blond Charles yesterday), but absurd in a middle-aged man.

"Yes, Maurice?"

"Miss Tubbs just turned the corner, carrying a rolled-up sheet of paper."

Ominous news, and not the sort of warning a footman should relate to his mistress (although in a butler, it would be allowable). Maurice knows his place, but he has my best interests at heart, hence his awkwardness. He knows Miss Tubbs delights in bringing Corvus' latest efforts to me in the hope of detecting shock or horror and that I appreciate being forewarned.

"Thank you, Maurice. Show Mr. McBrae in here, and if Miss Tubbs does indeed call, put her in the drawing room." He left, and I said, "Drat!"

Miss Concord stood. "I'd best run up to my bedchamber and stay out of the way."

"Not at all," I said. "We don't want the servants to think there is a reason to hide you." Also, her presence would keep McBrae's call on a formal basis, or so I hoped.

Gilroy McBrae appeared promptly. He didn't look the least bit awkward, drat the man, bowing in a friendly manner and smiling inquiringly at my guest. I introduced her as my friend Miss Evans and offered him coffee, which he accepted with annoying alacrity.

"Thank you, my lady," he said. "I met your man Maurice at Medway House, where I had an appointment with Lord Derwent."

"You had?" I asked, astonished. Since when was he acquainted with my brother? In August, up in the north, McBrae had been masquerading as a footman, but it would take a particularly perceptive individual to realize that, which my brother is not. Perhaps they had London friends in common.

"Yes, we were to go to Jackson's Saloon for some sparring." He snipped sugar off the loaf and added it to his coffee.

Boxing is one of those violent sports to which gentlemen are addicted. However, that didn't concern me. His apparent friendship with my brother did.

"But he's not at home, and from Maurice I learned that he left in a rush yesterday and did not return last night."

"Maurice should have known better than to tell you that," I grumbled. "I suppose you induced him to confide in you."

He grinned. "No need to use my vaunted charm of manner, as the servants at Medway House were in a bit of a pother. The butler tried to say that Lord Derwent wasn't receiving visitors, but I had already heard Maurice asking the Medway footman whether his lordship had returned home last night."

You see what I mean about eavesdropping? He's positively shameless. Vaunted charm, indeed!

Ah, perhaps I have confused you. I should have mentioned that Corvus and Gilroy McBrae are one and the same. I had sworn to keep his secret, and he had agreed to refrain from producing scandalous prints featuring my mother.

"Does no one know where Lord Derwent has gone?" he asked.

"No," I said, wishing I could say more, but I was obliged to conceal Miss Concord's identity and her plight. "However, it need not concern you. I daresay he will return soon." I cast about for a subject of conversation and found none. McBrae, who is never at a loss, asked politely after my father, and then about the journey from the north.

Fortunately, Maurice soon came in and said glumly, "Miss Tubbs is here, with Sir Pinkerton Jones-Worthy. I showed them into the drawing room."

I groaned. Miss Tubbs is a gossip, but also a friend of sorts, so I would never rebuff her. Sir Pinkerton had doubtless informed her of my return. I would never consider *him* a friend. He delights in spreading lascivious rumors with the worst possible interpretation attached.

McBrae downed his coffee. "I'll go out the back and return by the front," he said. "No point in giving that fellow food for speculation."

I shuddered at the thought of what gossip might arise that McBrae and I were more than acquaintances. "Particularly when there is absolutely no truth behind it," I said, and immediately wished I hadn't. McBrae has a *tendre* for me, and although I have come to like him very much (when I'm not at odds with him), it is simply impossible for me to return his affection in the way he would like.

Or maybe I am being cowardly. I still haven't worked that out—but sometimes I wonder if it is because I'm afraid to do so…which brings me directly back to feeling like a coward. So much for not giving way to fear.

He didn't show by even the twitch of a muscle that my remark had wounded him, but I knew it had. I have wounded him too often not to know. On the other hand, maybe my unfortunate remark would deter him from returning by the front door.

Unlikely. Along with his nosiness comes a great deal of tenacity.

On with this tale. He duly left in the direction of the service stairs, and Miss Concord and I made our way to the drawing room, where Miss Tubbs and Sir Pinkerton awaited us.

Miss Tubbs is a thin, untidy busybody, but a sufficiently pleasant companion for a visit to a museum or a display of artwork (although she tends to linger at any display of nakedness). Sir Pinkerton is tall and lanky, with a tendency to dandyism and an irritating titter, but it pays to stay on his good side.

After the customary greetings, including an embrace from Miss Tubbs, a smirk from Sir Pinkerton, and the briefest of nods from both of them to 'Miss Evans'—whom they saw as a provincial nobody—Miss Tubbs got straight to business.

"I beg your pardon, my dear, for arriving so well in advance of the usual hour for morning calls," she said, "but I have brought the latest print from Corvus. It appeared several days ago, but I knew you wouldn't have seen it yet in the north. You're in it, so you can tell me if it's true."

Why must Corvus continue to put me in his prints? "If what's true?"

"That Cynthia Benson married Sir Roderick Frockmartin!"

Was that all? "Yes, my dear Cynthia is now Lady Frockmartin." Cynthia is my best friend and was my husband's mistress until his death some months earlier. "It was frightfully romantic." This was something of a lie, for I have always disliked Sir Roderick, but I suppose it was romantic from Cynthia's point of view. "She accepted his proposal at last, and he dashed up north to wed her before she had a chance to change her mind."

I hoped this was much the same as the story Cynthia would tell—not that she expected to meet many people in the immediate future, as she was shortly to give birth. (But this was a secret, as she became *enceinte* whilst my husband's mistress, and if it became known, everyone would snigger at Sir Roderick for taking on another man's child.)

"He is portrayed as a knight in shining armor," Sir Pinkerton said, helping Miss Tubbs spread the print open on the table. "Some knight! He only won the lady after his rival died—in an accident! Where's the accomplishment in that?"

How typical of Sir Pinkerton. He doesn't know the true story, so he takes what facts are available to make up his own. (Admittedly, Corvus does much the same, but in a more amusing way.)

"Have you no tact?" Miss Tubbs asked. "Lady Rosamund is in mourning for that very rival."

Sir Pinkerton ignored her. "Unless, of course, Sir Roderick caused the accident by devious means...."

How appalling, and how too close, in another way, to the truth. My dismay must have shown, for he said, "*Surely*, he didn't!" meaning, of course, that he hoped he had hit on some titillating gossip to spread about.

I wished I could roll my eyes, but that was far too vulgar for either of my callers. "No, I don't believe Sir Roderick has even an iota of deviousness in his character. He is certainly direct about his hatred of me." I sighed. "Poor, dear Albert! No one could cause an accident like that."

At this very moment, McBrae was announced. How much had he heard? *It doesn't matter*, I told myself, and then he bowed and smiled with such warmth and appreciation that I was shaken. "A pleasure to find you in town once again, Lady Rosamund," he said.

Good Lord, I feared I was blushing. How ghastly, and judging by the narrowing of Sir Pinkerton's eyes, he now suspected an illicit liaison in the making—for it was only slightly less scandalous (in Sir Pinkerton's conniving mind, that is) for McBrae to appear on my doorstep the instant I arrived in town, well before the hour for morning callers, than to be found at my breakfast table.

Drat again!

McBrae was already acquainted with both Miss Tubbs and Sir Pinkerton, so I introduced him to 'Miss Evans' again, and turned to inspect the caricature.

Sir Roderick and Cynthia were off in one corner. She was draped across his saddle bow as they rode away. True to his promise to me, Corvus had drawn no indication of her pregnancy, merely emphasizing her voluptuous bosom even more than usual.

The real subject of the caricature was my brother. It was a lovely, cheerful drawing. Julius sailed on a lake, looking windblown and happy. My father chatted on a dock with Sir Alphonse Lewis...and there I was, perched at the end of the dock, dangling my bare feet in the water.

Curse the man, he couldn't resist a little titillation. Meaning Corvus, I hope you understand. I am inured to sly innuendo from Sir Pinkerton, but Corvus had promised not to portray me in an unflattering way. Which he hadn't, I suppose. It was a little improper to bare my feet in the company of a gentleman unrelated to me, but my father's presence made it acceptable.

Sir Alphonse was saying, *I've never seen Derwent so happy*, and Papa's response was, *There are no henpecking females up here.*

Oh, dear. If that meant what I thought it did... It took all my resolution not to turn on McBrae with a snarl. He was supposed to leave my mother *be*.

Sir Pinkerton tittered. "It led to quite an uproar in White's the other night."

"In what possible way?" I asked, but at that very moment, Stevenson appeared with tea and drop cakes. How inconvenient, for Sir Pinkerton had finally said something that might prove relevant. However, it gave me an opportunity to glance at McBrae, who to my surprise had moved to sit by the window with Miss Concord and was showing her a book.

Stevenson withdrew, and I said, "Very well, you have piqued my curiosity. I can't fathom how either Cynthia Benson's marriage or a drawing of Lord Derwent in a sailboat would cause an uproar."

Sir Pinkerton chuckled. "Perhaps it was your dainty little feet." He tends to flirt with me, which is annoying, but I would get better results if I responded appropriately.

I huffed. "I'll wager nothing happened at all, and you are making it up to tease me."

"I would certainly do so if the opportunity arose," he said, "but no, it was the implication that Derwent had tired of his nagging mistress. Worsten offered to take her off his hands, at which Derwent took umbrage, like a child who has lost interest in his plaything until someone else wants it." He laughed again. "Most entertaining. They came to blows, but a few of us stepped in before he murdered poor Worsten. Derwent becomes belligerent in his cups."

"So I have heard," I sighed, unhappily digesting this news. This interpretation of the caricature seemed wrong to me, but what if it were correct? And if it were, how did Corvus know? And why would he publish something so unkind to Miss Concord? If she'd fawned all over Julius at the opera, flashing jewels, he might have felt justified in doing so, but she'd remained quietly out of sight of the polite world.

I hoped poor Miss Concord wasn't too overset, but I dared not look over to gauge her reaction. For the next twenty minutes my mind churned with suppositions, while Miss Tubbs and Sir Pinkerton regaled me with all the latest gossip, and McBrae conversed quietly with Miss Concord.

At last, Sir Pinkerton and Miss Tubbs rose to leave, and so did McBrae. I wondered if this was to fend off gossip about us or because he feared my wrath about the caricature.

"My dear Lady Rosamund," Sir Pinkerton said, "I hope we shall see a great deal of one another now that you are back in town." He gave me a flourishing bow, followed by an old-fashioned kiss on the hand.

Heavens, *why*? I believe it made me blush, for he smirked even more than usual as he ushered Miss Tubbs through the door and departed. McBrae followed the others out, then paused in the doorway. "Ah!" he said, "I had almost forgotten. Lady Rosamund, I brought a novel you might enjoy." He pulled a slim volume—the same one he'd shown to Miss Concord—from his coat pocket. "Have you finished with my copy of Donne's poetry?"

By now, the front door had closed behind the others. He put up a hand as I moved to pull the bell. "No, no, I don't want the Donne. It's yours to keep." He closed the drawing room door.

Evidently, he feared neither gossip nor my wrath, drat the man. He took a seat and helped himself to the last remaining drop cake. (It is not customary to serve refreshments during morning calls, but now and then, I do so because 1) my mother would disapprove, and 2) food and drink alleviate my boredom with chit-chat.)

Miss Concord let out a long, sobbing breath and covered her face with her hands.

"Then why didn't you leave?" I snapped at McBrae, partly in sympathy for Miss Concord, and partly because I was in a fever to go to Kensington. I wasn't sure what we would discover there. It seemed likely that Derwent had gone in pursuit of Worsten—but if so, wouldn't he have soon learned that Miss Concord had escaped and been picked up by my coach?

"You'd better tell me what's going on," McBrae said.

"Nothing is going on," I said, "and as for that horrid caricature...." I ground my teeth, longing to lash out at him, but I couldn't, for we were not alone, and a promise is a promise—at least to me, it is. Apparently, his scruples are more elastic than mine.

Miss Concord raised her head. "I have never, *ever* henpecked Lord Derwent."

I'm sure my mouth fell open, but only for a second. Evidently, McBrae had recognized her as my brother's mistress. I shouldn't have been surprised. He makes it his business to know everything.

"I'm sure you have not, Miss Concord," McBrae said, "but people know very little about you, so they came to a mistaken assumption."

"Then whom did Corvus mean?" she asked, and suddenly clapped her hand over her mouth. "I'm so sorry, I shouldn't have asked." She flushed, mortified. "It's not my business, and I wouldn't dare to—to…" She floundered to a halt without finishing her sentence.

It was inappropriate of me to explain the print to her—I scarcely knew her, and she was in no way my social equal—but it would be cruel not to. Besides, if I didn't explain it, McBrae would.

I flapped a hand. "Corvus meant my mother, the Countess of Medway. He seems to get a great deal of pleasure from insulting her, although this particular dig went astray. It would never occur to Mother, or to most of society, that she could be accused of henpecking."

Miss Concord nodded in understanding…which meant that my brother had complained to his mistress about our mother! Can you imagine anything more improper? And here I thought Julius was the epitome of propriety.

I also thought he idolized Mother. He certainly did his best to obey her ghastly commands with regards to me.

"Perhaps the dig was meant for Lord Derwent," McBrae suggested. "Since he of all people knows that you didn't henpeck him—knows how patient and considerate you are—perhaps he will now realize how much better life would be out from under Lady Medway's thumb."

I found that hard to believe. Julius is deaf to anything he doesn't want to hear. It sounded to me like 1) flattery – for how could McBrae know whether Miss Concord was patient and considerate? and 2) a flimsy excuse for his unforgivable blunder in this latest caricature, and so I would tell him when I got the chance.

Miss Concord sniffled, and dabbed at her nose with one of my lace-edged handkerchiefs. The more I saw of her, the more I realized she was every inch a lady. "You're very kind, Mr. McBrae, but how did you know who I am?"

"I have friends in Kensington. Someone pointed you out to me," he said vaguely. There was more to it than that, I was sure. I understood now that he had taken her aside and pretended to discuss a book in order to keep her from revealing her distress. Which was indeed kind of him, but her distress was his fault in the first place.

"I believe we should confide in Mr. McBrae," Miss Concord said. "With Lord Derwent missing, I would feel much safer going to Kensington if a gentleman, rather than a footman, were to accompany us."

There was a great deal of sense in what she said, so I made an effort to appear agreeable.

Not enough, apparently, for she went on in a gentle, persuasive tone, "As a friend of both yourself and Lord Derwent, he is surely to be trusted. Derwent only spars with gentlemen he esteems."

Julius wouldn't esteem him if he knew who had drawn that caricature, as well as others that had mocked both him and my mother.

In fact, the more I thought about it, the more it became clear that this whole mix-up was *McBrae's fault.*

Chapter Four

Fifteen minutes later, we were ready to leave.

McBrae had gone to fetch a hackney, as we didn't wish anyone to know with whom Miss Concord had taken refuge. Since I am a bit notorious, people might recognize me, so I was obliged to wear a veil. It went well with my mourning costume, but again, my dubious fame was *McBrae's fault.*

I do beg your pardon. It's frightfully ill-mannered of me to go on and on about McBrae, but I couldn't vent my spleen to Miss Concord, nor to McBrae until I got him alone. However, I had good reason not to wish to be alone with him, so all I could do was bottle up my annoyance and act as if nothing was wrong.

Fortunately, presenting a serene front is one of the accomplishments of an aristocratic lady. She must never give way to strong emotions, and she should placidly ignore those of others, so as to avoid causing further awkwardness.

Not that Mother obeys this dictum, and McBrae knew no such consideration, either. Before leaving to get the hackney, he explained my too-obvious annoyance to Miss Concord. "I believe Lady Rosamund is overset at the thought of Lady Medway's reaction, should she happen to learn the real import of the caricature."

"I can only hope she won't," I said, although that was perhaps the smallest factor in my uneasiness. I was far more worried that she would learn that Miss Concord was staying in my house. "Very well, Mr. McBrae. There is indeed something going on, which we fervently hope will not end up in the scandal sheets, nor in one of Corvus' caricatures."

He took that without a blink. "Naturally." Behind the bland face, I knew his mind already worked busily at how to shock and amuse the *ton* without harming poor Miss Concord. Yes, that was considerate of him, but I was too incensed to admit it. However, in keeping with Mother's dictum, and not wishing to upset Miss Concord further, I put on a cheerful front, and we went upstairs to don our outerwear.

I was in quite a state of nerves, which meant my peculiarity raised its unpleasant head. After Mary Jane helped me on with my bonnet and pelisse, I chased her out of the room to take care of Miss Concord. Not that any such assistance was required—Miss Concord, I had begun to realize, was perfectly able to take care of herself—but I needed a few moments alone to check my reticule.

Spare handkerchief (the other was up my sleeve; I checked that too). Hairpins. Paper and pencil. A few coins for hackney fare and incidentals. Several more coins. I counted them all, firmly shut the reticule, then tipped them out and counted them again. And again.

I am sure you realize how foolish this was, but when I am uneasy, my urge to check things over and over seizes hold of me and won't let go. I only stopped because of Mary Jane's footsteps outside my door.

I pulled the strings tight, and immediately wished I'd thought of something more useful to bring—my pistol. My father had finally given me one of my own, saying that as a widow, I might often be traveling alone. I didn't anticipate the sort of trouble where one needs a weapon, but after yesterday I felt it was better to be safe than sorry.

However, I dared not get it out now, for Mary Jane would have hysterics if she saw me slipping it into my reticule. It had been there for the last leg of our ride down from the north, but only Papa knew; he had loaded it for me before we left him with his friends. (I couldn't imagine actually using it, even if highwaymen had stopped us.)

My maid bustled in. "Mr. McBrae is here with a hackney, and 'Miss Evans'"—she sniffed—"is ready. I do trust you are taking her home."

"I don't think that would be wise," I said frostily. Such impertinence on her part, but she has been my maid forever and therefore feels she has the right to take liberties. "We may be gone a while. I'd best use the chamber pot again before we leave." (If that seems too vulgar to put in print, I beg your pardon, but I had to think of an excuse not to leave my room just yet.) "Tell them I'll be right down."

Glowering, she left again. I fetched the pistol from its hiding place behind my books and stuffed it into my reticule. As for the chamber pot...drat! She might take the fact that it was empty as a sign that I was merely suffering from nerves. With great difficulty, I resisted the urge to check my reticule once more and hurried out the door. I do my best to conceal my peculiarity, but she knows about it, as does everyone in my family, and she fears it will suddenly develop into something far worse.

Madness, to put it bluntly.

But I'm not mad, nor do I intend to become so. I made my way downstairs, and soon we were squeezed into a hackney coach headed for Kensington. Like many hackneys, there was really only room for two. I couldn't help wondering if McBrae had chosen this one on purpose to tease me. Or just because he liked being squashed up next to me.

I sighed internally. I shouldn't enjoy being so close to him, but despite the inevitable awkwardness, I did. Perhaps this was only because it made me feel safe—or perhaps I was lying to myself again.

"Very well," he said in a businesslike manner (nothing loverlike about it), "tell me what's amiss."

"Miss Concord was abducted yesterday by Lord Worsten," I said briskly. "Fortunately, she escaped."

His brows drew together. "Fortunate indeed! Tell me what happened, Miss Concord. Where, when, and everything you recall."

She proceeded to recount her horrid adventure, but naturally with much more composure than the day before. She made a great deal of my rescue of her, which I waved away, although McBrae's appreciative gaze made me blush. Fortunately, my veil hid my flushed cheeks. I then made a point of informing him that Miss Concord was to stay with me until my brother returned, and wondered immediately if I had said that to win even more of his approval.

He nodded abstractedly—seemingly unimpressed, which was precisely what I deserved—and said, "Let's go back to the beginning, Miss Concord. You were alone in the garden? No one knew you were there?"

"The cook and scullery maid may have noticed as I went through the kitchen to get the shears, but it's not unusual for me to gather herbs or flowers." She paused. "I don't think anyone saw what happened. The garden walls are high, and it can't have been more than a minute between the time the man put the sack over my head and when we drove away."

"A skillfully-managed abduction," he said. "More efficient than one would expect from Lord Worsten. I wonder whom he hired."

"Does it matter?" I asked.

He shrugged. "Maybe, maybe not. Miss Concord, did you see any of your captors apart from Lord Worsten? The coachman and groom, perhaps?"

"Only the one who pursued me, and he was quite far behind."

"I saw them clearly, but only for a moment," I said. "One was a big, bear-like man with a broken nose who blasphemed at the sight of my coach, at which John Coachman took offense and kept going."

I resisted the urge to tell McBrae that John Coachman's name really was John, not a family habit like calling all footmen James or Charles. It wasn't relevant to our conversation, and I had already sought enough of his approval for one day. "The other was smaller and wirier," I added, "but he was half hidden by the horse he was trying to calm."

"The big one sounds like a bruiser," McBrae said. "Not the sort one would expect Worsten to be acquainted with, but one never knows."

"It was he who fired at Miss Concord," I said, "although I can't imagine what he thought to accomplish by harming her."

"Perhaps he hoped to frighten you into abandoning her," McBrae said. "I assume we are going to Kensington to question the servants—to see if anyone saw the ruffians, and to find out what was in the message to Lord Derwent, in the hope that it will give us more information about where he may have gone."

We ladies nodded our agreement. (You notice, I hope, that by now I thought of Miss Concord as a lady—which just goes to show that another of the tenets of my upbringing had been shattered, first by the mistress of Sir Alphonse Lewis in Westmoreland, an actress whom I liked very much, and now by my brother's mistress, a merchant's daughter).

A few minutes later, we turned the corner into Miss Concord's street, and she yelped, "Stop!"

"Why? What's wrong?" I cried whilst McBrae rapped on the roof, and the hackney drew to a halt.

I craned across her to look out the window. In front of Miss Concord's house was a red coach with the wheels picked out in an ugly, mustardy yellow. A middle-aged man in knee breeches and a nankeen coat stood before it, gesticulating agitatedly. Three people, servants by the look of them, clustered in the doorway, and a number of men and boys lounged about, watching the goings-on.

"We can't go there now," she said, sliding down against the squabs to keep out of sight. "Please, just tell him to drive on."

"Who is that man?" I asked, lifting my veil to see better.

"Mr. Thomson, one of my suitors," she said bitterly. "The one my father favors at the moment. The servants must have informed Papa of my disappearance, as well as Lord Derwent." Under her breath, she muttered, "Traitors."

"I'm sure they meant well," I said, lowering the veil again. "They must be frantic, wondering where you are. One of the women is wailing."

"That will be Doris. She wants all the attention to be centered on her. If the others are upset, it's only because it will mean losing the bribes from my father."

Heavens! "But surely they were hired by my brother...weren't they?"

"Yes, but he only gives them ordinary wages, whilst my father pays them well for spying on me."

I know what it feels like to be spied on. "But surely Derwent wouldn't keep such servants."

"I didn't tell him they were spying. He has enough to worry him, and what would be the point? Other servants would be the same, sooner or later—except perhaps Hedley, the butler, who is devoted to Lord

Derwent—but that may be because he has been promised a pension."

How frightfully cynical she was. I knew Hedley, a kindly individual who'd been a footman in Kent during my childhood. It was good to know she had one reliable servant, but really, how horrid that she couldn't trust any of the others.

"Money overcomes almost any obstacle, if there's enough of it," Miss Concord said. "My father is keeping an eye on me, waiting for the day when Lord Derwent tires of me, so he can foist me onto someone else." She paused, nervously peering out. "Please, let's *go*. Someone may become curious about a coach just standing here."

"Go back home," McBrae said, opening the door. "I'll join the crowd and let you know what I learn." He jumped down, shut the door, and directed the jarvey to return to Mayfair.

Slowly, we drove past Miss Concord's house. McBrae was already amongst the crowd, looking like any other fellow who had nothing better to do than gawk.

"How convenient to be a man," I said enviously, and watched until he was out of sight.

"I rather like being a woman," Miss Concord said, "or I would if I could marry a man I cared for and have children." She bit her lip. "I beg your pardon. Perhaps I shouldn't have… I'm sorry if not having children is a source of sorrow for you, my lady."

She was referring to the commonly-held assumption that I am barren, since I hadn't conceived in over four years with Albert Phipps. It is a logical assumption with no basis in fact.

"It's not," I said. "I've never cared much for children." This isn't precisely true. If it were possible for me to do as she said—to marry a man I cared for, submit to marital congress with him, and have children as a result, I expect I should be pleased…but it wasn't possible, for even if I could tolerate the required intimacy, my husband would have to be told about the charade that was my previous marriage. Even if I wanted to keep it a secret, my utter innocence of the marriage bed would give me away.

Worse than all that, what if he learned about my peculiarity? I would do

37

my best to hide it, but Derwent had betrayed me once by telling my first husband about it immediately after the wedding ceremony. I couldn't trust him not to do the same again.

"I don't want to go home," I said grumpily. "If others know of my return to London, there will be more morning callers, and more discussion of that annoying caricature, and more speculation about Derwent's dispute with Lord Worsten."

"Do Corvus' drawings really annoy you?" she asked, a hint of mischief in her eyes. "Even when making dreadful suggestions, he emphasizes your prettiness. I think he's in love with you."

"Lust," I retorted, sure I was blushing. "The effrontery of the man knows no bounds."

"True, but his drawings are beautiful." She sighed. "I hope Mr. McBrae is correct in that people misunderstood the latest one."

"He's usually right," I muttered. I don't understand why McBrae irritates me so. The more I get to know him, the more I value his friendship, so he should therefore annoy me less.

"Why not tell the butler to say you're not seeing callers?" she asked. "That you're too tired after the long journey."

"Because the callers may include friends whom I don't wish to offend—and who are likely to know traveling doesn't tire me."

She sighed again. "I am so *very* worried about Derwent. I wish there was something you and I could *do* to find him."

"I agree, but since we are stuck being useless females, we may as well amuse ourselves." I rapped on the roof and told the jarvey, "Take us to Hatchard's bookshop."

Usually, I adore shopping at Hatchard's, but today I couldn't find anything appealing. Both Miss Concord and I enjoy the nonsense published by the Minerva Press, but adventure and romance are not quite so appealing when one fears for the health and safety of a loved one.

Fortunately, Hatchard's has a good selection of serious works, and Miss Concord soon appeared engrossed in a volume about the care and cultivation of roses. I say 'appeared' because she did such a good job of hiding her worry and distress. For a merchant's daughter, she was startlingly ladylike in many ways.

Suddenly, I had a brilliant notion: to learn more about Scotland, the better to understand McBrae. The assistant brought me a dozen books and hovered respectfully, eager to please the daughter of an earl, granddaughter of...et cetera, et cetera. I waved him away as kindly as I could, as I was a little embarrassed at my choice of subject matter.

One title caught my eye: *The Romance of Scotland*. Dear me! Can there be anything romantic about that barbaric country to the north?

Thank heavens McBrae wasn't here to divine that thought. Far too often, he knows what I'm thinking, particularly if it is to his disparagement or that of his country.

A soft 'ahem' came from behind me. I turned to find a gentleman with whom I'm scarcely acquainted—and happy to keep it that way.

He bowed over my hand. "Your servant, Lady Rosamund. How delightful that you have returned to town."

"Good day, Mr. Brill," I drawled. "How *do* you do?" He is the son of my mother's greatest enemy and has her cold, heavy-lidded eyes. He had never professed himself delighted to see me before. He is addicted to games of chance and spends very little time doing the pretty to the fair sex—a blessing for us ladies, believe me.

"I'm doing excellently well, now that you once more grace our fair metropolis." How strange of him to make me such a compliment. Judging by his uneasy stance, he felt awkward doing it. Perhaps he doesn't do the pretty because he doesn't know how. Why, then, must he choose to practice on me?

"Ambrose, darling—" Mrs. Brill came up, feigned a start at the sight of me, darted her tongue from between her lips, and finally summoned her version of a smile. "Lady Rosamund, what a charming surprise!"

How unexpected. She usually ignores me, reserving her unpleasant smiles for my mother's visits, when she makes snide remarks about my inability to 1) keep my husband in my own bed and 2) conceive a child.

"Good day, Mrs. Brill. I trust you enjoy your customary good health." I wondered what she would find to disparage about me now that Albert was dead. Not that I care what she thinks of me, but veiled insults are so tedious. I began to wish I had returned home to face morning callers instead.

"What *are* you reading, dear child? *The Romance of Scotland!*" She tittered and said in a gently chiding voice, eerily reminiscent of my mother, "How absurd. There's nothing romantic about that backward place."

I'd had precisely the same thought a few moments ago. How utterly mortifying to have even a thought in common with Mrs. Brill.

"Evidently, the author of this book believes there is." Ambrose Brill removed it from my hand and began to flip through it. "Do you seek high romance and adventure, Lady Rosamund?"

"Not at all," I retorted. "My father has invited me to accompany him on a visit to Scotland next summer, and I thought to learn a little about the place."

"Ah, dear Lord Medway." His tongue flicked out from between his lips and as swiftly retreated. I almost choked, for I had wondered in the past whether he had inherited this trait from his mother. Do you wonder that I compare them to lizards? Those cold eyes, those darting tongues.

"I trust he's doing well," Mr. Brill said and cleared his throat. "Dare I hope that his lordship accompanied you to town? I wish to pay him a call." How strange. Was he even acquainted with my father?

I glanced at his mother; she watched her son with narrowed eyes.

"He's visiting friends a few hours north of here," I said. "He may come for the opening of Parliament." Papa never comes to London if he can avoid it, but he might intend to sign his proxy over to one of his friends.

I spied Miss Concord hovering a few yards away, retrieved my book from Mr. Brill, and said briskly, "Ah, there you are, Miss Evans. Have you chosen something?" Hurriedly, I conjured an excuse. "We really must fly, or we'll keep the dressmaker waiting, which would be *frightfully* impolite of us."

Not that I have ever concerned myself about keeping such a person waiting—a dressmaker must surely await the pleasure of an earl's daughter—but McBrae would doubtless disagree with such an inconsiderate attitude, and as usual, he was probably right. On the other hand, the dressmaker was doubtless equally inconsiderate of her inferiors. It is the way of the world.

Drat, why must McBrae intrude into every thought? It was particularly irritating this time, since the impatiently waiting, hard-done-by, cruel-to-her-underlings dressmaker didn't even exist.

I introduced 'Miss Evans' and tried to make a hasty adieu, but Mrs. Brill went on and on about quiet dinners and exclusive musicales which a lady in mourning might attend, and her son bowed cumbrously over my hand and swore to call on me at the earliest opportunity. At last, we escaped to complete our purchases, while one of the attendants found us a hackney.

Unfortunately, our departure was not to be quite so easy. We were accosted next by Henry Charting, an abrupt sort of man with a long nose and an even longer chin. "Lady Rosamund," he cried, "well met!" He flushed. "London was a—a veritable desert without you."

Good Lord. He had never waxed poetic before, and certainly not about me. Hastily, I introduced my companion. Mr. Charting gave her no more than a nod, then grabbed my hand and kissed it. "Dear lady, my heart beats only for you."

A firm voice beside me said, "Don't be an ass, Henry."

Mr. Charting muttered something crude under his breath.

I withdrew my hand in relief as Sir Devlin Curtis bowed. You may recall him—my mother's cicisbeo who lives a few doors down from me. He is Mr. Charting's maternal uncle; they are both tall, with the same long nose and pleasant voice, but there the resemblance ends. Sir Devlin is all elegance and propriety, whilst Mr. Charting considers himself a great sportsman and cares little for anything else. Poor Sir Devlin tries unsuccessfully to give him a little town bronze.

"My dear boy," he said, "Lady Rosamund is in mourning and does not welcome such gallantries."

Mr. Charting reddened, a spasm of annoyance crossing his face, but Sir Devlin ignored him and turned with a smile to my companion, asking how she was enjoying London so far. He helped us into the waiting hackney, and we escaped.

"Whatever has got into everyone?" I asked as we drove slowly along Piccadilly. "Mr. Charting usually tries to remember his manners in the presence of ladies, but he has never been quite so—so....”

“Lover-like?” Miss Concord offered, her lip quivering.

“Ugh,” I said, which is a vulgar little word used by my sister's children, but perfectly appropriate under the circumstances. “He *cannot* think I would welcome such a notion. Apart from such absurd flattery, imagine having to listen to the details of disgusting prizefights at all hours of the day and night.”

She made a sympathetic face.

“As for the Brills,” I said, “she is my mother's sworn enemy, and I'm scarcely acquainted with her son. Did you notice how he sticks his tongue out like a lizard, just as she does? Horrors! I wonder why they were so determined to be friendly today.”

Beside me, Miss Concord choked on a laugh.

“Yes, it would make me laugh, too, if I didn't find their lizard-ness so off-putting.”

Miss Concord bit her lip, hesitated, then came to a decision. “That's not why I laughed. It's because—please don't take this amiss—but I believe Mr. Brill means to court you.”

I gaped at her. “Surely not.” What a ghastly notion. “But why? He's never shown the slightest interest in me before.”

“You were married before. Now you're a wealthy widow.”

I had to acknowledge the truth of this. “But I'm not quite six months into my year of mourning.”

“I believe that is what Sir Devlin meant when he said you didn't welcome such gallantries.”

“Yes, it's far too soon.” Actually, anytime would be too soon. The thought of being courted and pushed into remarrying made my stomach twist and churn.

“That gives your suitors six months to persuade you. The first men into the lists have the greatest advantage—although come to think of it, Sir Pinkerton Jones-Worthy beat those two by a couple of hours.” She chuckled. “He's not much better.”

Aghast, I blurted, “Sir Pinkerton? Surely not. Imagine that titter every day for the rest of one's life."

"Does he need money? Does Mr. Brill? Or Mr. Charting?"

"I have never interested myself in financial matters, so I don't know." Would I now be pursued by fortune hunters? I slumped in my seat, sorely tempted to flee back to Papa and the safe, rustic, lonely north. "What am I going to do?"

"You don't find it at all amusing?" She paused. "I'm sorry; evidently not. I'm sure you're capable of fending them off. There will be others, but eventually they will give up, or you'll find someone you wish to wed."

(Impossible, as you are already aware, so I shan't explain it again.)

"At least no one will try to force you to choose someone you abhor," she said.

"I never know what my mother will try to force me to do," I said and regretted it immediately. Miss Concord was proving frightfully easy to talk to, but I shouldn't be so indiscreet—although considering her intimacy with my brother, she might have learned too much about me already. Did she know about my supposed instability?

Surely not, for Julius was indiscreet only when foxed, and he would never allow himself to be intoxicated in the presence of a lady.

"If I were you, I would choose that lovely Mr. McBrae," she said.

"I *beg* your pardon?"

"He's head over ears for you," she said. "Surely you're aware of *that!*"

I managed a shrug. "I know he finds me attractive, but he doesn't intend marriage." Thank heavens, for that would make our situation even more awkward. It's bad enough that he disapproves of me and lets me know, and worse that he wants to make me his mistress. Not that he has asked me in so many words, but his actions have made it clear.

"No? Why not?"

"Because—because, well, it's preposterous. He's an impecunious Scotsman, and I'm the daughter of the Earl of Medway."

"So what? He's a gentleman, and you are a lady." She stuck out her chin. "If you're in love with each other, why shouldn't you marry?"

"We aren't in love," I retorted, stopping myself just in time from spouting some nonsense about love matches being only for the underbred. Despite my best efforts, my mother's dictums tend to surge to my lips, especially in moments of disquiet.

The thought of intimacy with McBrae made me uneasy. Actually, the thought of intimacy with any man did—but admittedly, far less so with McBrae than with any other gentleman of my acquaintance.

I liked him, and he lusted after me. And to be fair, he seemed to have a certain amount of respect for my intelligence. To be fair again, he had taught me a certain amount about matters of which I had no previous experience, and he had also saved my life.

But none of this had anything to do with love.

"Perhaps not yet," she began, then quailed slightly at my frown. "I apologize if I offended you, my lady. I shouldn't have presumed." She paused. "In any event, love, or at least mutual respect and affection, are what one should hope for in a marriage."

I'd had something akin to mutual respect with Albert Phipps, and most of the time, we'd managed remarkably well because of it. "True, but I don't plan to marry again."

She looked as if she wanted to ask why, but stopped herself, no doubt for fear of offending me further. Good, for I had no intention of explaining myself.

I wondered once again if Miss Concord was in love with my brother, but couldn't wed him because of 1) her lost reputation and 2) her inferior social status.

On the other hand, she was a substantial heiress, which made her an eligible, if not precisely a desirable choice. She was also an amiable young woman—a lady in every way except her birth—who would make my brother a far more comfortable wife than any of the well-bred girls our mother tried to foist onto him.

I suppressed a sigh. Evidently, my brother didn't wish to marry her, or he would already have done so. They were both of age, so no one could do anything to stop him. What a pity.

Fortunately, McBrae didn't want to wed me, either. I couldn't possibly marry anyone, even if I wanted to. I would carry the reason for that to my grave.

Chapter Five

By the time we arrived home, the hour for morning callers had passed, so Miss Concord and I were free to stew about Julius' disappearance without maintaining a façade. I sent Maurice back to Medway House to see if there was any news. (There wasn't.) I glanced through what little correspondence I had received: 1) a note from Miss Tubbs suggesting a visit to the British Museum the following week, 2) a kindly letter from Lady Danby, welcoming me back to town, and 3) an invitation from Lady Baffleton for that very evening to a small gathering of music lovers.

Which likely meant something by Bach or perhaps Purcell, which would be elegant and unexceptionable for a widow in mourning. Unfortunately, Mrs. Brill had mentioned the selfsame musical evening. If I attended, she might think I wished to encourage her son's suit. (If he seriously meant to court me, which I still found hard to believe.) Not only that, I didn't wish to abandon Miss Concord to herself.

We sat about drinking tea, reading about Scotland (me) and mending sheets (Miss Concord), until Stevenson entered and said in a pinched tone that a message had arrived from Mr. McBrae, and that the fellow insisted on delivering it into my hand.

"Show him in," I said. Poor Stevenson; no butler likes to be ordered about by an unknown servant, but I had warned him to expect either McBrae or an urgent message from him.

I greeted McBrae's servant with a relieved smile. "Thank you, Hamish." I turned the sealed message over. "Will you wait for a response?"

"Master Gil says no need, my lady." His gentle Scots accent somehow comforted me, although I haven't the slightest notion why. Hamish was devoted to McBrae and had been kind to me in the past, but I had to admit (at least to myself) that I'd rather hoped for McBrae himself.

Hamish bowed and withdrew, and I tore open the seal.

> *My Lady,*
>
> *The irate Mr. Thomson intended to abduct Miss C this morning, with the consent of her father, who hoped to force a speedy wedding. When Miss C was found to be missing yesterday, the servants assumed they had mistaken the date for the abduction, and therefore raised no outcry. The devoted butler is away for a week visiting a sick relative—hence, we must suppose, the choice of today for the abduction—so perhaps one of the maids has a conscience, or fears Lord D's wrath and therefore wrote to inform him of Miss C's disappearance.*
>
> *But if this is the case, how did Lord D know that Lord W, not Mr. T, had taken her? Perhaps the conscientious maid saw her being taken and knew it wasn't Mr. T's coach.*
>
> *Meanwhile, Lord W has not returned to Town. Has he gone to nurse his chagrin elsewhere? Where might he have intended to take Miss C? To a love nest in the country, perhaps?*

(At this, I bristled. He should not use such a vulgar term when addressing a respectable lady.)

(But clearly, he doesn't consider me respectable, at least not in the usual sense.)

> *Advise keeping Miss C close for now, to minimize the possibility of scandal. Corvus may not have intended her in his recent caricature, but one cannot predict what he might do, were he to learn of her current predicament.*
>
> *Yours ever,*
> *Gil*

Well! What effrontery, to sign the note as if we were on a first name basis! Even worse, a *nickname* basis, which indicates a degree of intimacy that simply did not exist. As for that reference to Corvus…! I knew an urge to crumple the letter and toss it onto the hearth.

But it was too warm for a fire, and meanwhile, Miss Concord waited in suspense. Irritably, I passed the letter to her.

"Oh, how dare he!" she cried after a swift perusal, and I am ashamed to admit that I was so fixed on my own annoyance that for a moment I assumed she was objecting to McBrae's familiarity.

She trembled with fury or shock, or both. I could hardly blame her. Two planned abductions in as many days are far more than any woman, respectable or not, should be obliged to contemplate.

"I wonder where Lord Worsten is," I said, trying to infuse a little calm into the situation. "I would have expected him to return to town once you escaped—although if a number of his friends knew about his plan, McBrae's suggestion that he is nursing his chagrin elsewhere makes sense. Or he may be unwell after being knocked senseless when the coach went into the ditch."

"I don't care what happened to him," she raged. "Love nest, indeed! How *disgusting*."

"Yes, Mr. McBrae should not have expressed it in such indelicate terms, but I expect he meant a hunting box or some such place."

"I don't care about indelicate terms. It's what Lord Worsten would have *done* to me there." Tears sprang to her eyes. "I hope he's miserable, for he deserves to suffer, and so does Mr. Thomson. But where is Lord Derwent?" She wailed. "I don't know what to *do*."

How selfish of me to fret about matters of propriety and protocol, when she was so upset. "Unfortunately, there's not much we *can* do, but I think he's right—that you should stay out of sight."

"Can your servants be trusted?" she asked after a moment.

"Not to betray you?" Goodness, she feared yet another abduction attempt. "I believe so. Mary Jane would not so demean herself, and I hope none of the others realize who you are—but even if they do, they have far more reason to oblige me than Mr. Thomson."

"My father may offer a reward," she said. "If word gets out that I was abducted, and your coachman or groom sees an opportunity...."

I didn't think Papa's coachman and groom would do anything so stupid. "I shouldn't worry about it. In any event, by tomorrow, Julius will most likely have returned."

"I hope so." She returned to her stitchery, and I picked up the invitation card, pondering. It seemed to me that there was one thing I could do—keep my ears open for relevant gossip.

I told her so, adding, "You had best go to bed early. If anyone asks after you, I shall say you are fatigued from the long journey." But most likely they wouldn't; she wasn't a particularly noticeable person, and those few who had met her considered her a nobody.

Which is horrid but the way of the world, and in this instance, it was useful. Since the series of unpleasant events of the spring, when I attempted twice to appear to be a nobody, I have often wondered how it would feel to be an ordinary person. To move about unnoticed, much as McBrae did this morning in Kensington. I expect I should miss my consequence, but what freedom might I experience in return?

Enough philosophizing. After dinner, I had my town coach brought round, and I didn't keep the horses waiting too terribly long by checking and rechecking my reticule. Why would I? I enjoy Lady Baffleton's gatherings, and a member of the House of Medway would never be deterred by the likely presence of an undesirable suitor.

The instant Lady Baffleton's porter opened the door, I knew something was amiss. The babble of conversation from above broke over my ears like a wave. Usually, such gatherings are rather quiet.

Lady Danby's forceful tones reached me over the hubbub. "You will say nothing about it. Nothing at all!" After a short pause: "Yes, obviously. Don't play the fool, Sir Pinkerton. You all know what I mean."

As the porter took my cloak, a familiar voice reached my ears, and I glanced up to see Mr. Charting at the head of the stairs. "Lady Rosamund, what a pleasure to see you again—twice in one day!"

The babble stopped dead, but after a tense moment, it rose again, more subdued now. Mr. Charting blew a kiss at me—can you imagine the gall? Thank heavens, Lady Baffleton moved swiftly past him and came partway down the staircase to greet me. "The most dreadful news, Lady Rosamund. Lord Worsten is dead!"

I reeled with the shock—literally, for I had to grasp the banister rail. "Oh no," I gasped, "whatever happened?"

"No one seems to know for sure. He is—was, I mean—a healthy young man."

"Indeed, yes." By now we had reached the drawing room, where four musicians had set up at one end. Lady Danby bustled up, encased in violet satin. Usually, I find her taste in clothing to be atrocious, but at least it is colorful. I was so *sick* of wearing black.

She clasped my hands. "Welcome home, dear child." Lady Danby is the same age as my mother and persists in thinking of me as scarcely out of the schoolroom. "But what distressing news to hear upon your arrival." She smiled at me kindly—rather more than usual, as she tends to be somewhat astringent. Was there something of uneasiness in that smile? Or worry?

"Distressing indeed," I managed, despite the whirling sensation in my head.

"Lucky she *did* arrive," Sir Pinkerton said with a grin. Mrs. Brill and her son, I noted with dismay, were in the room as well. So was Sir Devlin Curtis, looking grim.

Sir Pinkerton's gaze combined lustful appreciation—slightly sickening—and his usual guile. "For only yesterday you passed down the Great North Road, did you not, my lady?"

I gathered my wits about me. "What does the Great North Road have to do with anything?"

"Only that Worsten was found dead by the side of it," Sir Pinkerton said.

"Not only on the roadside, but in a *ditch*," Mr. Charting said, not to be outdone.

"Left to welter in his own blood!" A young lady whose name I had forgotten—a cousin of Lady Baffleton's—said this with a shudder worthy of the stage.

"By highwaymen?" I said, because I had to say *something*. "But highwaymen don't usually kill their victims."

"No, they don't, do they?" Sir Pinkerton's smirk was unpleasantly pronounced.

"How terrifying," I said, because once I'd said something, I had to say something *else*. My voice quavered a little, so I clapped a hand to my palpitating heart. (It really was beating rather quickly, so I had no need to feign my distress.) "I was fortunate indeed."

Lady Danby turned a frown on my two supposed suitors. "You should know better than to mention such a dreadful sight in the presence of a delicate lady."

"It was a delicate lady who embroidered it to the point of dreadfulness." Sir Pinkerton motioned toward the dramatic young woman, whose name, I now recalled, was Miss Trent. "Pure fabrication, I expect. Ladies are prone to exaggeration, as we gentlemen all know—and love you for it, of course."

"It's *not* fabrication," Miss Trent sniffed. "Someone *said* so."

He snorted. "Did anyone here see the corpse?" Sir Pinkerton's voice is penetrating, and there weren't more than twenty-five or so guests, but no one answered in the affirmative. "For all we know, it wasn't highwaymen after all, and he simply overturned his curricle and landed in the ditch." He cast a mocking glance at Mr. Charting. "Unless the ditch was fabrication, too."

"It was not!" Charting retorted. "The news is all over my club."

"In this instance, I feel obliged to support my nephew's assertion," Sir Devlin said. "The news is indeed in his club, and apparently, Worsten *was* found in a ditch. As for the dramatic mention of blood, I daresay that came from the imagination of a club servant, from whence it spread by the usual means." (Which was a bit of a dig at Miss Trent for believing the gossip of the lower orders—unfair, as often it's the only way one gets to the truth.)

"Quite likely," Lady Danby said. "My son got it from his valet, whose cousin is employed by a gentlemen's club."

"But—" I stopped myself just in time from protesting that Lord Worsten wasn't driving a curricle—although perhaps he had been when the accident happened. If it was an accident. "Surely someone would have gone to his assistance if he had overturned his curricle."

"Perhaps he was beyond help," Lady Danby said. "Or perhaps thieves finished the job the mishap had started, so to speak."

"How absolutely *awful*," I said, needing to know more. "Did he have no servants with him? A groom, perhaps? I can't imagine such a dreadful deed going unnoticed on a busy road. Isn't it patrolled by men from Bow Street? I'm sure my poor, dear Albert told me so." I was babbling and knew it, but my tongue was running away with me. "Maybe they only do so at night, and they can't be expected to catch everyone. When did it happen?"

"No one seems to know," Mr. Charting said.

Lord Baffleton, our host, said, "We're not certain. Apparently, he left town yesterday, and we didn't learn about it until an hour or so ago." He beckoned to Mr. Brill, who hovered nearby. "You heard something at White's—isn't that right?"

Mr. Brill flicked his tongue. "That's correct, sir. By what I understand, his body was found by a farmer this morning, and remains in Highgate pending the inquest tomorrow."

Sir Pinkerton's calculating expression meant he sensed some worthwhile gossip. "One can't help but wonder what Corvus will make of it."

I was about to ask why Corvus would make anything of it, when our host spoke. "Well, well," Lord Baffleton said with forced heartiness, "nothing we can do about poor Worsten, but fortunately, our music tonight is somber and thus befits the unhappy occasion. Please take your seats, everyone."

I latched onto Lady Danby. "May I sit with you? I shan't be able to bear it if I must sit next to Sir Pinkerton. Or Mr. Charting. Or Mr. Brill. His mother actually smiled at me today."

She chuckled. "You have become a very desirable catch."

"I am not a *catch*," I hissed, "like a fish pulled out of a pond. What a hideous expression that is." Not, I must admit, that I had ever objected to it until it was applied to me.

She steered me to a seat she had already marked as her own and settled me between herself and Mrs. Phipps, the ancient great-aunt of my deceased husband. "We'll have to find a better *parti* for you."

"I don't want any *parti*, thank you very much," I retorted.

"You will, dear," Mrs. Phipps said. "Once you've done mourning Albert, you'll welcome a new husband." She cackled. "I imagine Albert was quite exciting in bed. So very virile! You'll begin to miss that, if you don't already." She lowered one eyelid in a slow, ghastly wink.

Sometimes I wonder if my mother will ever stoop to such vulgarity in her old age. Believe it or not, Mrs. Phipps was once a prim and proper high stickler (or so I've heard), so why not my mother, too?

"How about that one?" She motioned with her chin at a handsome man a few seats on the other side of Lady Danby. It was Lord Cyril Telfrey, one of the younger sons of a marquis. "I have seldom seen a more beautiful young man. Definitely worth a good, long ogle."

What an annoying old lady she was.

"Spare my blushes, Mrs. Phipps," Lord Cyril said, flashing his charming grin at me, but of course I was the one doing the blushing.

When I was sixteen years old, my mother suggested him as a potential suitor for my hand. I wasn't out yet, but my mother plans ahead. She intended to introduce us at an alfresco picnic in Kent, in the hope that I might captivate him into waiting a year or two for me. I was paralyzed with dread at 1) the thought of captivating anyone and 2) the prospect of carnal intimacy. The emphasis on his extraordinary good looks made it even worse. Fortunately, he didn't attend the picnic.

Now I am well acquainted with him and not the least in awe of his male beauty, and I rather like him. He's kind, easygoing, and a graceful dancer, and is confident without being cocky.

And, thank goodness, he's not the least bit captivated by me.

"If I were to embarrass Lord Cyril with an ogle, whether long, short, or in-between," I said, "Lady Danby would tell my mother, and I would never hear the end of it."

"Your mother's a bore," Mrs. Phipps said. Fortunately (because for obvious reasons, I could neither agree nor disagree with that remark), she went on to ask if it was true that Lady Benson had snapped up Sir Roderick Frockmartin.

By the time I finished regaling her with my tidy version of their romance, the musicians had done their last-minute tuning up and the performance began.

The cessation of conversation gave me the opportunity to think, and to wish McBrae were there. I was a little surprised not to see him, as he is a close friend of Lord Baffleton. I'd hoped he might have reason to speak to me, although we wouldn't be able to exchange more than a few words—if that—with any degree of privacy.

Very well, I admit it. What I really wanted was the simple comfort of his presence. I feel safe when I'm with McBrae—except for two reasons: 1) the lust he feels for me, and 2) the fact that he doesn't know the truth about me and never will. It's actually one reason, I suppose—for if I could tell him my deep dark secrets, he would stop lusting after me.

But he wasn't there, and meanwhile, uneasy thoughts tumbled and churned in my mind. Something strange was going on; something wasn't being said, something that would upset me. My reasons for this suspicion were as follows:

First, the sudden silence when Mr. Charting announced that I had arrived. I have a very fair notion of my social status, and while it's quite high, it's not the sort that creates a hush, particularly amongst a group of people who are already acquainted with me.

Next, the worry in Lady Danby's smile. Worry about what?

Also, the lack of definite information about the manner of Lord Worsten's death, as well as Sir Pinkerton's remark about what Corvus would make of it. Make of what, exactly?

Added to all that, the abduction of Miss Concord and Julius' disappearance, and I couldn't help but fret.

Instead, I had to close my eyes or gaze dreamily at nothing, as if I were absorbed in the music. Bach often makes me drowsy, but not this time.

On second thought, it was lucky McBrae wasn't there, for the more I thought of this tangle, the more enraged with him I became. If he hadn't published that caricature, Lord Worsten wouldn't have thought to relieve Julius of his mistress—a stupid, childish prank—and Julius wouldn't have pursued him. (If that was what he had done.) Julius was in no way connected with his death, but we all know what people are like, particularly the *ton*, who have nothing better to do than gossip about one another.

Yes, I know I was at Lady Baffleton's specifically for gossip, but now my mission had become complicated. I must gather what information I could, whilst at the same time refute possible slander of my brother without seeming to believe it or even care.

By the time the musicians took a bow, I had armed myself with the languid hauteur which Mother taught me from the cradle. There are many degrees of hauteur, and this one has served me well. It is comprised of faint surprise underlaid with languid indifference.

I didn't expect the first probing question to come from Lady Danby.

First, she asked after my father, so I told her a little about my stay in Westmoreland with Papa. We meandered toward the dining room, where refreshments were set out. Wine and tea, drop cakes, parkin (a favorite in the autumn), cream puffs…aah.

I took a cup of tea, a cream puff, and a little square of parkin. Lady Danby led me toward an empty corner, but the room was full of busybodies, and soon one of them might accost me. I nibbled on the parkin, savoring the ginger flavor. It's best eaten with a bit of custard outdoors on bonfire night, but I love it anytime.

"How is your mother?" Lady Danby asked. "She hasn't been in town lately. Derwent comes and goes, though. Have you seen him since you arrived?"

I frowned at her. So much for languid hauteur. "No, why should I?"

"No reason, my dear." Judging by her vague expression, this almost certainly meant the opposite. "Did he appear to enjoy himself up north?"

I huffed. "I suppose you're referring to that stupid caricature. Derwent loves sailing, so naturally, he enjoyed himself. I don't know where Corvus got that notion of henpecking females, but he should be ashamed. It's complete nonsense."

(Note that I didn't betray my mother, despite knowing perfectly well which nagging female Corvus referred to.)

"Corvus doesn't know the meaning of shame," Mr. Brill said. He had sneaked up behind us with Miss Trent on one arm and Mrs. Phipps tottering on the other.

Mrs. Phipps cackled. "He needs to have it birched into him."

"That won't do it." Sir Pinkerton joined our little circle. "He longs to be birched—but only by our dear Lady Rosamund."

"In that case, he will have to long forever," I said, recovering my hauteur.

"And keep on doing it to himself." Mrs. Phipps reveled in the license afforded the aged to say exactly what they wish, no matter how vulgar or lewd. (If you're wondering, this conversation referred to two earlier caricatures, one in which I birched Corvus—which never happened and never will—and one in which he, with great difficulty, birched himself.)

Poor Miss Trent seemed frightfully uneasy with this conversation, and no wonder. When one is an "innocent", either one does not understand lewd jests, and therefore feels awkward, or on the other hand, one does understand but must pretend not to. Miss Trent was doubtless in the first category. She glanced about, as if wishing she could leave the conversation—in which case, why didn't she? No one obliged her to hang on Mr. Brill's arm.

I ate the rest of the parkin and contemplated the cream puff with misgiving. I adore them, but I prefer not to look a fool thanks to a cream mustache. Perhaps tiny bites would make it manageable.

"Mistresses do tend to nag, though," Mr. Charting said. "Grasping females, every one of them."

Sir Devlin frowned exasperatedly at his nephew. If Mr. Charting hoped to win my affection, he was going about it the wrong way.

"You would be grasping, too, if your livelihood depended on the whims of a lecherous man," I retorted.

"Or a bloody unfair man," he said, and stomped away.

"What was that about?" I asked, picking up the cream puff and taking a bite. Delicious!

"I stopped his allowance," Sir Devlin said. "I regretted the necessity, but I have given him long enough to learn to behave in a gentlemanly manner. Until he does so, he is on his own."

"Poor Mr. Charting," I said. Now I saw why he might wish to wed me. Unfortunately, he would have to find another way out of his financial difficulties. "However, it's nothing compared to what happened to Lord Worsten."

There were several murmurs of assent.

"I wonder what Corvus will make of it," Sir Pinkerton said. "The lecherous Lord Derwent, tossing his mistress to the equally lecherous Lord Worsten, now unfortunately deceased. Maybe she landed on his head, kerplop!"

I wiped cream from my lip and looked down my nose at him. "Corvus' caricatures always have a grain of truth in them, but he perverts it. Your suggestion has none at all." I took a couple of delectable little bites.

"Oh, but one can't help but fear that it *does*," Miss Trent began, but Lady Danby intervened.

"Hush, Miss Trent. This nonsense about Lord Derwent is exactly that—just nonsense. Don't let it worry you, Lady Rosamund."

What nonsense? I couldn't ask with all these people watching. "I have never let Corvus worry me. I certainly shan't begin now." I took the last creamy bite.

"Brava, Lady Rosamund!" McBrae stood in the doorway, clapping. "One of these days, Corvus will get his comeuppance."

I swallowed the mouthful in a hurry, wondering if his next caricature would show me stuffing cream puffs into my mouth. Well, I didn't care. I wiped my face with my napkin and said, "That is a matter of indifference to me, Mr. McBrae."

Chapter Six

By the time I finally escaped, I was in a dreadful stew—but I believe I managed to convince everyone (except McBrae) of my complete unconcern. He knew perfectly well I was vexed with him, so he avoided me.

Not that I attempted to approach him—it would only cause more gossip—but usually he comes up to me. In any event, I couldn't ask any of my pressing questions with all the gossips listening in, but my enforced silence only increased my agitation.

Meanwhile, he was his usual friendly, cheerful self. "So sorry," he'd said to our hostess, "I was unavoidably detained." *Doing what?* I wanted to know, whether or not it was my business.

"You missed the music," Lady Baffleton said with a bit of a pout, "and arrived in time for the refreshments. A typical male."

"My abject apologies," he said with a grin, and she forgave him instantly. I think she has a soft spot for McBrae. She took in a destitute maid-of-all-work and her little sister at his request.

Kindly do not understand this to mean that I was jealous of Lady Baffleton—naturally not—but that I do realize McBrae has some excellent qualities. However, I was simply not in the mood to appreciate them.

Lord Cyril came up to me with two more cream puffs and asked about my time in the north, but to my worried mind, his kindness felt like pity—how horrid! However, he is so well-mannered and easy to speak to that he actually made me chuckle a few times whilst I waited for an appropriate moment to leave. McBrae spoke briefly with Lord Baffleton and left again, thank goodness, and as soon as a few others had departed, I made my adieux and left as well.

Alone at last, I leaned against the squabs of my carriage and tried to relax.

Impossible. What were they saying about my brother? I thought I knew, but how was I to find out for sure without revealing my fears?

I descended from the carriage and swept into my house before I realized that the footman holding the door open was McBrae.

"What the—what the *devil* are you doing here?" I demanded, giving in to my urge to swear at him. "How did you get in?"

He closed the door and removed the wig he had donned as a disguise. "I asked Maurice to let me take his place."

"You bribed him!" I didn't want to dismiss my footman, but he should know better.

"Not at all. I explained the situation to him. I had to get in to talk to you privately without being observed."

I stormed upstairs, and he followed. Maurice hovered anxiously on the landing.

"Bring us tea," I snapped. "And brandy." I led McBrae into the drawing room and said, "Close the door." Yes, that was completely improper, but I didn't care.

I threw off my pelisse, tossed my hat onto a chair, and turned to McBrae. "This is all your fault."

He shrugged. "Maybe."

"*Maybe?*" I shrieked and then lowered my voice, for Maurice or another servant might be listening. "If it weren't for that stupid caricature, none of this would have happened."

He grimaced. "You may be right, but—"

"How dare you shrug it off as if it's nothing? Lord Worsten is dead, my brother is missing, and people are saying—" I paced across the room. "I don't know exactly what they're saying, because no one would put it in so many words."

"Surely you guessed."

I turned and paced back. "I suppose Lady Danby and the Baffletons meant to be kind, but I *hate* being treated like a—a fragile flower."

"They can't be expected to know how capable you are."

I ground my teeth. This was *not* the moment for absurd compliments. "The implication that my brother had something to do with Lord Worsten's death is absurd, and where *were* you this evening when I needed someone to tell me the *truth*?"

I gave an unladylike snarl and plopped onto the sofa with a complete lack of proper poise.

He sat next to me. I didn't have the energy to give him the sort of look that said he should go to the opposite end of the sofa. Or across the room.

"I was in Highgate," he said, "viewing the corpse."

That rendered me speechless for a second or two until curiosity raised its head. "How does one arrange to view a corpse?"

"A friend who studied medicine in Edinburgh now has a practice in Highgate—but even if I didn't know him, I expect I would have found a way."

Yes, McBrae is expert at digging up information that is none of his business, and whilst this is usually to be deprecated, at times it is useful, even life-saving.

"But...why did you want to see it?"

"To learn the truth about how Lord Worsten died. I rode up there the instant I heard about it this afternoon. He was beaten and stabbed, then left in a ditch by the side of the Great North Road some way north of Highgate. He was found early this morning, but judging by the state of his corpse, he died last evening. Some carrion-eating birds—perhaps kites—had found him first."

"So he *was* left to—to welter in his own blood." I swallowed, grateful to McBrae for giving me not only the truth, but an unvarnished version, even if it did make me feel rather ill. "That's how it was described by someone tonight."

"By whom?" he asked sharply.

"I believe..." I collected my fragmented thoughts. "It was Miss Trent, a cousin of Lady Baffleton."

He nodded. "I know the lady."

"She said she'd heard it from someone else, but she didn't seem to remember whom. Sir Devlin said it was most likely a servant, and Lady Danby agreed, for her son learned the news from his valet, who heard of it from a relative employed at a club." My mind was less scattered now, but my stomach still protested. I wished I hadn't eaten those cream puffs. "Who identified him? Or what—" I almost gagged. "Or what was left of him."

"The birds hadn't done much damage yet, and his card case was in his pocket. Also, the local magistrate was acquainted with Lord Worsten and knew him immediately."

"It doesn't sound like the work of highwaymen," I said, in control of myself now. "Which is exactly what I said at Lady Baffleton's, and Sir Pinkerton gave the ghastliest smirk. I should know better than to blurt my thoughts aloud. One never knows how he will twist them into something *completely* untrue."

McBrae cocked his head to one side with the calculating look that means he's drawing a picture in his mind.

I huffed. Not that I would object if he caricatured Sir Pinkerton, but I didn't wish to deviate from the subject at hand. "The thing is, highwaymen—or footpads—would have taken his card case. It was certainly worth something."

"True."

An unpleasant thought occurred. "Beaten...how? He bumped his head when the coach tipped toward the ditch. There must have been a bruise. You don't think—you don't suppose Miss Concord stabbed him before she ran?"

"Did she have blood on her hands? Her gown?"

I shook my head. "Not at all."

"He was bruised as if in a fistfight, and also stabbed several times. Once from behind, which was unlikely a killing blow, and several times from the front. Viciously, I should say, and it would have been messy."

I let out a breath. "Oh, how dreadful." But much as I liked Miss Concord and didn't want to see her as a murderer, I couldn't let myself even *think* that my brother might have done it. "Maybe his coachman and groom killed him, if they feared punishment for letting her escape."

I expected McBrae to stand up for the servants immediately, but he only said, "It's possible, but why risk their lives by committing murder? The worst he could do was dismiss them—and they would likely get back at him by selling the story to the broadsheets."

"Is that where you get your information?" I asked bitterly, and immediately regretted my outburst. I knew perfectly well that McBrae didn't need to bribe anyone. He used his eyes, his ears, and his ability to play a part. "I'm sorry. That was unfair, but I'm still furious with you."

"I know, lass. I know." He spoke to me so kindly, with a hint of his Scottish accent—or rather, one of his Scottish accents, for I have heard at least two—that I almost burst into tears. Which is completely absurd! I'm not the watering-pot sort, and besides, why would kindness make me weepy? I simply *cannot* understand the strange effect he has on me.

"With good reason, I admit," he said.

"Aha." That helped me regain my composure. "What happened to *maybe*?"

"A number of things that don't make sense. I may have been a catalyst, though—similarly to when I drew you pushing the footman down the stairs."

"A catalyst...?" I said, astonished. "For the poison pen?" I thought about the unpleasant events of that spring. What he said made a sort of sense. "Perhaps, but not in such an obvious manner as this time."

"True, but think of it this way. If Derwent followed Worsten to rescue Miss Concord and found that she had escaped, would he waste his time murdering him? I don't think so. He might come to blows with him, but his first thought would be to find Miss Concord. He would have headed back towards London. Instead, he simply vanished." He spread his hands. "Why?"

I wished I knew.

"Not only that, Worsten's servants, as well as the coach and horses, are missing as well."

"The coach wasn't found near his body?"

"No—if it had been, he would have been discovered much sooner."

That prodded my memory. "Maybe...maybe they weren't really his servants and coach. There was no crest on the panel. Most likely, they were hired only to perform the abduction, as you suggested this morning. In fact, a hired coach would make sense, for if Lord Worsten feared Derwent would follow him, he wouldn't want his vehicle to be easily recognizable."

"All good points—but again, why would they murder him? Think about it. What would Worsten have done when he regained consciousness and found Miss Concord gone? He would berate them for incompetent fools and refuse to pay them. Any self-respecting criminals would simply leave him there and drive away."

Self-respecting criminal—surely a contradiction in terms! But if I objected, McBrae would try to convince me of the contrary, and once again, I had more important matters to think about.

"Perhaps they abandoned him alive but semi-conscious, because of the accident, and—and someone else came by and killed him." Such as my irate brother, but I didn't say it, because it was simply impossible. "It doesn't seem likely, though. There is quite a bit of traffic on that road. Surely someone would have come upon them."

"Perhaps not, if it was already dark," he said. "No, I think something rather more unusual than highway robbery is going on. The fact that servants in London already knew he'd died covered in blood means to me that someone—likely the murderer—slipped up when discussing the news, inadvertently revealing something he shouldn't have known."

"You think a London servant killed him?"

"Possibly, but more likely a gentleman did."

What an appalling notion, and impossible to believe—although not quite as impossible as that Derwent was the culprit.

"A gentleman would more likely have the time and the means to follow Worsten and then return to town with no one the wiser." McBrae shrugged. "We'll find out what happened to the men and their vehicle, which may lead us to the murderer's identity, but in the meantime, we must protect your brother's good name. Unfortunately, when he had the altercation with Lord Worsten at his club, he threatened to kill him if he so much as touched Miss Concord."

I groaned. That explained the unspoken gossip tonight. "Derwent wouldn't stab his—his *friend*, or even an acquaintance. He would hit him or challenge him to a duel." Which is stupid, but it's honorable according to the gentlemen's code of behavior.

"You and I know that, but now Derwent is missing and Lord Worsten is dead. The obvious conclusion is that Derwent killed him and fled."

"Surely no one really *believes* that," I said. "It's absurd."

Maurice arrived with the tea tray and brandy. McBrae prepared the tea himself as if he were the host—how very strange—and poured me a cupful with a dollop of brandy. "Here you go, lass."

He shouldn't address me in such a way, but after spending a week with him at Lewis Grange, trying to unmask a murderer, I had become accustomed to it, as well as to one version of his Scots brogue. Usually, he speaks with the Eton-and-Oxford accent he learned at school (I assume), but I rather like the Scots. It has a kinder, gentler sound to it.

"I'm *sure* no one will accuse Derwent," I said. "He didn't do it. And he's the heir of the Earl of Medway, not a—a common man." McBrae would probably think less of me for expecting my brother's status to save him, but it was the truth. Aristocrats are treated with wary respect, whereas common men are most often not.

He poured himself a brandy. "I'll do my best to find out what really happened. For now, let's concoct a story."

"A story?"

"An alternative to the gossip. Your friends and acquaintances will besiege you for information, and offer unwelcome commiseration. What will you tell them?"

Oh, God. I didn't want to tell them anything. I was sorely tempted to flee London myself. I took a gulp of tea.

"You like making up stories," he said. "Did you ever finish the one you started at Lewis Grange?"

"That was nonsense." So much so that I burned it. "This is real!"

"We must think of a different explanation for Derwent's sudden departure from town. Something that doesn't involve chasing after Worsten to rescue Miss Concord."

Inspiration struck. "That—that he took Miss Concord *with* him," I said.

"It's perfect, since she's missing, too."

He grinned. "Perfect indeed."

"But I can't tell my friends that he left town with his mistress." I felt myself blushing. "I wouldn't *know* something like that."

"No, but you might suspect it, based on whisperings amongst the servants—yours and those at Medway House. After all, where else would she have gone? I recognized a newsman in the crowd outside her house today, so all London will soon know she disappeared. We may as well make use of that."

Trust Corvus to be well acquainted with newsmen—vulgar sorts who seek out scandals to sell to the broadsheets. By now, though, I had myself under control and held my tongue.

If not for the dreadful situation, I might have enjoyed making up a packet of lies. "I'll spread it about that…that one of the maids is enamored of a footman at Medway House, who eavesdropped on Derwent talking to his valet, who had learned—by way of the butler in Kensington, who overheard the traitorous servants there—that Mr. Thomson was planning to abduct her. Derwent spirited her away to a safe place and ordered his valet to claim ignorance of their whereabouts."

McBrae chuckled. "That's a sufficiently convincing tale for those who want to believe it, and we can't do much about those who don't."

I took another gulp of tea. "Or maybe I'll say he didn't even tell his valet where he'd gone. As far as I know, that's the case. It's good to have a speck or two of truth amongst the lies." As Corvus often had in his caricatures.

"Aye, and in the meantime, I'll find out where he really *has* gone."

The ghastly thought which had been lurking in the back of my mind now came full force to the fore. Horror crashed over me. "What if—what if he and Worsten fought, and—and Julius was injured, too, and—" I could no longer speak. Tears rolled down my cheeks.

What if my brother was dead in a ditch as well?

McBrae put an arm around me and pulled me close. "There, there, lass. Dinna greet."

Obviously, he was telling me not to cry—but I couldn't help it. Nor did his closeness bring me any comfort this time. "What if Julius is dead, too?" I imagined my brother's eyes pecked out by kites, and sobbed.

"That would be sad indeed, but let's not jump ahead." He produced a handkerchief. "How likely is it that both he and Worsten were carrying knives?"

I sobbed into the sizeable square of linen—much more useful than the scrap of fabric in my reticule. "Not at all," I gulped. So much for not bursting into tears.

"Nor is it likely either of them knew much about how to use one. It's quite a different skill from fencing. Even if Derwent had a knife...." He shook his head. "No, he's good with his fists, but I can't see him stabbing his friend over and over."

That got me out from behind the handkerchief. "Absolutely not!" I wiped my eyes, blew my nose, and moved out of his grasp. This wasn't the first time I'd sobbed my heart out in his arms. It was *not* a good habit to fall into.

"In any event," McBrae went on, "he'd be in too much of a lather wanting to know where Miss Concord had gone—and since Worsten was unconscious when she ran off, he didn't know either, unless his hirelings told him—but likely they wouldn't know whose coach she rode away in, either."

A memory rose before me. "Maybe they did. My father's coach has a crest on it, and when my coachman pulled up beside them to ask if they needed help, the big one said something I wouldn't repeat even if I were familiar with such language, but I believe he meant they were in deep trouble now."

"This was *before* you rescued Miss Concord?"

"Yes, so maybe they thought it was Derwent's coach, and when they realized Miss Concord had escaped, they tried to recapture her. Then when that failed, they murdered Worsten and fled." I paused, pondering. "But it wasn't dark yet, so if they'd killed him right then, he would have been found much sooner."

"Not only that, if Derwent was in pursuit, he would have been coming *from* town—from behind them—not going toward it, as you were."

"Perhaps they feared it was my father." A horrid thought assailed me. "Or my mother. Oh, God, what if she comes to town?"

"For my sake, I hope she doesn't," he said softly. "I won't know how *not* to caricature her."

It was a jest—perhaps—but I couldn't laugh, or even snap at him. "She'll get letters from her busybody friends, and she *will* come to town. And if I know my mother, she'll blame it all on me. She'll say it's my fault Corvus caricatured me in the first place. My fault he dares to caricature her and Derwent. She'll insist on staying at my house, and she'll try to control my every move. And if she finds out that I rescued Miss Concord...."

I couldn't finish the sentence. I was shaking. She would do all in her power to have me locked up as insane.

"You did what was right, lass." He squeezed my hand to stop the trembling. "She can only control you if you let her do so."

The prospect of standing up to her made me ill, but I gritted my teeth in determination. "If she invades my house, I'll—I'll—"

"You'll bar the door to her. You're a strong woman—far stronger than your mother could ever hope to be."

My father had said much the same not long ago, but I didn't believe it from him, either. "I'm terrified of her. Did you know that one of her dictums is *A member of the House of Medway does not know fear?*"

"Damnation," he murmured. "What better caption for a caricature? This scandal will destroy her, poor woman, even without my help."

"Please don't '*help*,'" I retorted, withdrawing my hand.

He gave a gusty sigh. "Very well, my lovely darling. Your wish is my command."

"How dare you address me in such a way?" I demanded.

His eyes twinkled. "Indignation suits you, lass. Brings color to your cheeks and fire to your eyes."

He didn't need to tell me I was blushing. "And how dare you sign a letter to me with your Christian name?"

"That's my way of giving you permission to use it."

I almost blurted out something utterly stupid and insulting, but stopped myself in time. He didn't care about rank or the proper protocol, according to which I must give permission first. He would look at me with that expression that says he expects better of me.

How dare he? And yet he does, and when I'm not furious with him, I long for his approval. It's absurd. A member of the House of Medway should never so demean herself.

"You needn't use it if you don't wish to," he said, "but I can't promise I won't call you Rosie in an unguarded moment."

"What rubbish," I retorted. "You'll do it to see how I react."

"Aye, to see those flashing eyes."

"Red, puffy eyes, you mean," I said. "This is not a proper time for flirtation, Mr. McBrae. My brother is missing and—and—"

"I stand abashed—but it did get your mind off your mother."

Anguish rolled over me. "It did *not*," I wailed. "*Nothing* can."

"Och, come now, lass," he huffed. "You're not really afraid of her." He rolled his eyes as if my terror was folly. Sheer nonsense. Nothing at all.

I clenched my fists. "You don't *know* what I'm afraid of. You don't under*stand*."

"I'd be happy to try, if only you'd explain." He sighed in exasperation. "Which you won't. We've had this conversation before. Whatever it is, stop fussing about it. If she ever does something intolerable, I'll rescue you."

As simple as that, was it? If I were at all like my mother, I would have dumped the contents of the teapot over his head. As it was, I sprang up and splashed only the contents of my cup in his face. "Rescue me, will you? At what *cost*?"

Chapter Seven

He stood as well, radiating such fury that I quailed. "What *cost*? No cost. *Never*." He retrieved the handkerchief I had sobbed into and wiped his face. "I have put up with your many insults because you can't help being ignorant and proud, but this is too much."

I put my nose in the air, retreating behind the very pride about which he'd berated me.

"Yes, I want to share a bed with you," he said, "but nothing I do for you—*nothing*—in any way puts you under an obligation to me." He turned away, touching the handkerchief to his lips.

I had never before seen him lose his composure. "I beg your pardon, Mr. McBrae. I am overset and spoke without thinking."

"Aye, but if you said it now, you've thought it before. Gah! Do you really find me so disgusting?"

I didn't know whether he meant physically or morally, and I wasn't about to ask. "Not at all, but—"

The door burst open, and Mary Jane plunged through with Miss Concord right behind.

"How dare you upset my lady?" Mary Jane cried.

Miss Concord tried to push past her, and my maid whirled. "Get away from here. You're not wanted."

"I've as much right to eavesdrop as you do," Miss Concord panted. "I need to know what has happened to Lord Derwent."

"You're a ruined woman. A strumpet. You have no rights whatsoever!"

"I am *not* ruined, and I shall never be a trollop, a strumpet, a harlot, or any of those disgusting terms used to deride unfortunate women."

"Unfortunate? Ha! You're no better than you should be, and—"

"Enough." I put up a hand, and they both quieted. "Mary Jane, I appreciate your concern for my welfare, but any discussion between me and Mr. McBrae is our business and ours alone. Go to my bedchamber and await me there. Miss Concord, I will come to your chamber shortly and explain the situation. Please leave, both of you."

"Thank you, Lady Rosamund." Miss Concord promptly withdrew.

"Good riddance," Mary Jane muttered. "Now, listen to me, my lady—"

"Mary Jane, if you would prefer to be reprimanded in front of Mr. McBrae and anyone who happens to be eavesdropping, that's perfectly fine with me."

"Unnecessary," McBrae said. "I'd best be leaving." He bowed, went quickly down the stairs, and let himself out the front door.

By the time I got to bed, my head pounded fiercely. I went first to Miss Concord and briefly explained the situation. She mastered her shock and horror far better than I had, and apologized for eavesdropping. I apologized in return for my maid's insulting remarks. I suggested that we try to sleep for now and make further plans in the morning.

Mary Jane got the scold of her life. "If I ever find you eavesdropping on a private conversation again, I shall dismiss you forthwith."

"But, my lady, I was only trying to protect you, innocent as you are, from that Scottish rake."

"He's not a rake. He is a gentleman of impeccable morals." That was stretching the truth, but all I could think of was how kind he had been and how stupidly I had behaved in return.

Suddenly, I had one of my brilliant notions—a bit of a surprise, seeing as I was overwrought and miserably unhappy. All I wanted was to be alone and indulge in a good cry.

"In any event," I said, "I'm not the untouched innocent you clearly believe me to be." This was untrue, but she couldn't know that for sure.

She gaped. "But, my lady...."

"You have not been with me all night, every night of my life, and frankly, what I have done in the past or may do in future is quite simply none of your business. Please unlace my corset. I shan't need you for anything else tonight."

She did as she was bid. I don't know whether she worked slowly on purpose or because she was thinking about what I had said. Either way, I wasn't about to put up with it. Once she'd finished with the corset, I took up my hairbrush. I was about to order her to leave immediately when she spoke.

"Oh, my lady! Don't tell me you caroused with that dreadful Mr. Lewis!" (Lancelot Lewis is the handsome, flirtatious son of Sir Alphonse Lewis, whose house party in Westmoreland my father and I attended that summer.)

I was about to deny it when I realized doing so would invite further questions. I feared that if she fussed and fretted and tutted and bemoaned, I would lose my temper and shout at her. I had given the servants enough to whisper about this evening. A proper lady rebukes her servants in a calm, aloof manner. (Also, she doesn't throw tea in a gentleman's face, no matter how stupidly dismissive of her concerns he may be.)

"I don't *carouse*," I said, "and if I had, I certainly wouldn't tell you when and with whom."

"Oh, my *dear* lady. That uppity Scotsman is bad enough—a nobody and not even good-looking—and now Mr. Lewis. Never did I think you would fall for the lure of a handsome face. I don't know what your poor mother would say."

Did she realize she had hit my greatest sore spot? I don't think she meant to threaten me with my mother, but in effect, that's what she did. I had trusted Mary Jane for years, and suddenly I could not.

"My mother may go to the devil, and you may go with her for all I care." I put up a hand, because she was about to scold me again. "I mean it, Mary Jane. I am sorely tempted to rid myself of you immediately. However, in consideration of the kindness and dedication you have shown me in the past, I'm willing to give you another chance."

That silenced her. Her lower lip trembled. She folded her hands in front of her and lowered her gaze.

"In future, you will stick to the work you are paid for. You will not meddle in my affairs."

"Yes, my lady. No, my lady."

"You are not obliged to approve of Miss Concord—that is entirely your business—but whilst she is my guest, you will treat her with the courtesy due to a fellow human being. Calling her names is beneath you."

She said nothing, but clasped her hands together so tightly that her knuckles whitened. She was as enraged with me as I was with her, so I took pity on her. I would have no choice but to dismiss her if she lost control and yelled at me. She had already lost much of my respect, along with the privileges a longtime, trusted servant enjoys—and she knew it. It was a sad moment for both of us.

"You may go now," I said, and she left.

I didn't precisely cry myself to sleep, but I shed quite a few tears before drying my eyes and slipping down to the kitchen to warm myself some milk. It didn't help much. I had made everything worse. I had lost McBrae, and I might have to get rid of my dear maid as well.

Please try to understand. I hadn't behaved much better than her tonight—in a moment of panic, I had mortally offended McBrae—but one cannot treat a servant as an equal. It simply will not do. I had no choice but to give her a stern rebuke.

How much had she overheard? She knows about my peculiarity. I try my best to hide it from her, but I think she agrees with my mother that I am unbalanced—and therefore, she feels she has an obligation to tell me what to do. To keep me safe, perhaps. I don't know. But if she were sufficiently upset with me—or about me—what might she do?

I slept at last and woke feeling utterly bereft. How strange that only a day or two earlier, I had pondered my mixed emotions about McBrae, had allowed myself to believe that I didn't know how I felt about him. Now that I no longer had his regard, I wondered how I would go on.

However! There was no use in repining—I had done what I had done, and I would just have to get out of bed and put one foot in front of the other, so to speak—which meant: 1) spreading the story McBrae and I had agreed upon

72

last night, 2) writing to my father to inform him of the ghastly situation, and 3) leaving London immediately after doing so.

If number three seems to you to smack of cowardice, you are probably correct, or at least partly so. I could not face the prospect of dealing with my mother. I feared what she might do if she learned I was housing my brother's mistress—a social solecism that put me beyond the pale.

(Please understand this to mean an imaginary, largely arbitrary line of conduct beyond which a lady never steps. The real Pale is a horrid term to do with the wild Irish, who are probably just ordinary people who prefer not being trodden on. Or so I assume; I began to think about such matters after getting to know McBrae.)

Drat the man, must he dominate every waking thought? Yes, you are probably sniggering at me. We had parted less than twelve hours ago, and I had only been awake a few of those hours. It would likely take me a day or two to become accustomed to his permanent absence from my life.

As for his promise to rescue me from whatever I feared…it didn't count anymore. He didn't know or understand what I dreaded, and after our horrid parting last night, I doubted he cared.

Maybe you think I'm exaggerating my mother's ability to harm me. Perhaps I am—I am a wealthy widow and therefore in control of my life—but my fear of her outweighs my common sense. Look at it this way: what if Julius returned, waxed irate with me, and supported her? Any woman is vulnerable if a male family member wants badly enough to control her, and my father can't protect me forever.

Well! If there is one thing that helps me out of the doldrums, it's a bath. I lounged in the warm water and let Mary Jane wash my hair. I believe it made her feel a little better, too. I had her dress me in the least dreary of my mourning gowns and went down to breakfast.

Miss Concord was sitting at the table, a half-eaten slice of toast before her, drinking coffee and pretending to read a novel. I served myself and motioned to Maurice to leave us alone. I had outlined McBrae's plan to her last night. This morning, I must put it into action.

"I expect to be besieged by morning callers today," I said. "I shall spout a great deal of nonsense about Derwent spiriting you away to a safe place, but I don't think we should just sit here, day after day, in suspense and doing nothing. Besides, it will be frightfully tedious for you, obliged to stay indoors and out of sight. One can only do so much stitchery without going mad."

She gave a twisted smile. "Stitchery calms me, but you're right. The servants will guess who I am, if they haven't already."

"Has anyone treated you with disrespect?" I demanded. "Apart from Mary Jane, who received a severe scold last night."

"No obvious disrespect," she said, "and Mrs. Kelly, the housekeeper, is particularly kind, but I fear someone will reveal that I'm here. If my father finds out, he will try to take me away."

"We shall leave town before he has a chance to do so," I said, but before we could formulate a plan, Maurice came in. For the second day in a row, a caller had arrived well before the usual time. "Lady Danby is here, my lady. I showed her into the drawing room." He paused in his gloomy way, weighing whether to add something.

"What is it, Maurice?"

"Lady Danby seems anxious. She went straightaway to the drawing room window and peeked out, and then she told me to keep an eye open."

"An eye open for what?"

"Men watching the house, she said."

Oh, heavens, were some pesky men who write for the broadsheets already here? How and what had they heard so quickly? "Tell her I'll be there directly." He left, and to Miss Concord, I said, "Mr. McBrae said there was a newsman in the crowd at the Kensington house." I fear my voice trembled a little at the mention of his name. How annoying. He was a thing of the past. "You had best go to your bedchamber until I know what's going on."

Lady Danby's call had nothing to do with newsmen, alas.

This morning, she wore a scarlet pelisse with a green bonnet and gloves—a dreadful combination, but at least it was bright and cheerful. Her expression was in complete contrast to her attire. She had drawn the curtains closed, rendering the room positively gloomy. Furtively, she hurried up and whispered in my ear, "Is Lord Derwent here?"

"Heavens, no—why would he be? As a matter of fact, he's out of town."

"Oh, *dear*," she moaned. "I wish I had told you everything last night. I fear this will come as a shock."

"That the gossips are suggesting my brother had something to do with Lord Worsten's death?" I huffed. "It's utterly absurd."

"I'm afraid not," Lady Danby said. "I understand your natural partiality for your brother, but only a few days ago, he threatened to kill Lord Worsten if he so much as touched his, er, mistress."

"I assume you mean Esme Concord," I said dryly, partly because this was no time for her to decide to protect me from such an improper subject and partly because I needed a few more seconds in which to summon enough bravado for the upcoming lies. "You may speak frankly. I'm not a child."

"You are to me, dearest Rosamund. You had best sit down. I have the most frightening news." She remained by the window, peering between the curtains.

I marched over and opened the curtains again. "If there really are pesky men from the broadsheets watching my house, surely it's best if everything appears as usual."

She shook her head. "The Bow Street Runners are after Lord Derwent!"

She was right—this sort of news was best taken sitting down. I subsided onto the sofa. Fortunately, Maurice appeared with coffee, which gave me a little time to recover a measure of composure. I had to clutch one of the cushions to hide the trembling of my hands.

"This is too much!" I cried the instant he left. "Who had the infernal gall to accuse my brother?"

The Bow Street Runners don't go chasing after peers without an excellent reason. Not that my brother is a peer, but he would be eventually—if he weren't hanged for murder first.

I was too infuriated to let this ghastly thought disturb me. "Please pour the coffee, Lady Danby. I am positively *shaking* with rage."

"I can see that, my dear. I don't know who accused him, only what my son told me not a half hour ago. He had business at Bow Street early this morning and happened to hear that a letter was delivered there late last evening, written by someone who claimed to be an eyewitness to the murder."

"An eyewitness! Impossible. Derwent didn't murder Lord Worsten. He would never do anything so dastardly. Who is this so-called eyewitness?"

"Apparently, the accuser was afraid to identify himself, for fear he would be found and killed by Lord Derwent."

"Oh!" I cried indignantly, rising and storming across the room. "My brother is not a common criminal, murdering inconvenient persons left and right!"

"Of course not, dear, but you must understand that even without an eyewitness, it does look bad for poor Derwent. He had publicly threatened to kill Worsten only a few days earlier, so Bow Street would be obliged to seek him in any event. We can only hope he has fled the country."

"He hasn't fled anywhere," I retorted, realizing it was time to embark on my story. "If you must know, he left town shortly before I arrived, taking Miss Concord with him."

"On his way to kill Lord Worsten?" she asked, aghast.

"No! Lady Danby, how can you think such a thing? I suppose I must tell you the truth."

"Yes, you'd better," she said dubiously. "Do sit down again, my dear."

I complied. "Miss Concord's father, a City merchant, found someone willing to marry her. A man named...Thomas? Thomson? Yes, I believe Thomson is what Derwent's valet said. In any event, a Cit like her father, someone of no distinction whatsoever. Miss Concord refused."

"Come now, why would she refuse? Far better to be legally wed than any man's mistress, even your brother's."

I shrugged. "Maybe Derwent pays her well. Or maybe this Thomson person is utterly repulsive. I should think he must be, for he had decided to abduct her, would you believe?"

"*Abduct* Miss Concord?"

"Yes, but fortunately, the butler at Miss Concord's house learned of the plan and warned Derwent, who spirited her away to a safe place."

"Which safe place?"

"I haven't the faintest notion. Jenkins—that's Derwent's valet—doesn't even know."

"Or *says* he doesn't," Lady Danby said. "Are you sure about all this?"

"As sure as I can be, given the fact that Miss Concord disappeared from her house the same day my brother left town and what gossip has trickled in from the servants at Medway House. Good gracious, Lady Danby. A bit of an altercation between my brother and a friend wouldn't lead to murder!"

I took a bracing swallow of coffee. I had run out of lies, but if I didn't keep talking, I might give in to despair. What was I to do? It was plain to me that whoever had written that letter was the murderer himself, for my foolhardy, bad-tempered brother was the perfect scapegoat. I needed time to think. To plan.

In the meantime, I did what little I could, asking Lady Danby to counter the prevalent gossip with what I had told her.

"Very well, dear, I shall, and if the Bow Street Runners come knocking, you must tell Stevenson to send them about their business." She picked up her reticule, went to the window again, and gasped. "You see! Someone is watching already. They have no doubt tried Medway House, and now they suspect Derwent is hiding here."

I looked to where she pointed, and my heart lifted. The sandy-haired man leaning against the railing, talking to Lady Danby's groom, was McBrae's servant, Hamish. "I know that man, and he's not a Bow Street Runner."

"Humph," she said. "Whoever he is, he shouldn't be lounging about, and so I shall tell him." She headed for the door.

"Please don't. He often does—does odd jobs for me," I improvised. "I expect that's why he's here."

"Then why didn't he knock on the area door like an honest man?" She was already at the stairs.

"I—I think he's shy." Another lie, but a strange desperation had come over me. I don't know why I didn't just tell her the truth—that he'd come from McBrae. I could easily come up with a lie to explain that—for example, that he was bringing a message from McBrae for my father. Be that as it may, I simply *couldn't*.

"Then he had best learn proper manners."

"No, you had better leave him be," I cried. *"Please!"*

Lady Danby gaped at me. "My dear child, what has come over you?"

"Nothing, Lady Danby, except that I would prefer that you not rebuke a man who has done nothing wrong." A few months earlier, she'd tried to do the same with a hapless footman, who turned out to be McBrae in disguise (and not hapless at all), but the principle was the same.

"I shall be the judge of that." She made her way down.

"No, you must not!" I followed her, hastily correcting my tone. "Please don't scold him, Lady Danby. He serves me, not you, and I'd really rather not upset him."

"Rosamund, don't be foolish. Servants must be admonished frequently, or they become lax and slovenly." She kept on going.

"If I am satisfied with his behavior, you have no right to interfere." Immediately the words were out, I regretted them.

Maurice moved swiftly to open the door, but instead of storming out, Lady Danby turned. "Rosamund, have you gone quite mad?"

I felt myself sway. I gripped the banister and closed my eyes to regain control of myself. I opened them again to find her peering at me.

"That was extremely rude of you, child. I don't know what your dear mother would say."

"I beg your pardon, but as I am no longer a child, my mother's opinion is irrelevant." I shouldn't have said that, either. I tried to amend my rash statement. "I take full responsibility for my many social solecisms. Kindly do not lay them at my mother's door."

"Dear God in heaven," she said, shaking her head. "You must go upstairs to rest, my dear, and your footman will tell Mary Jane to give you a tisane. I understand what it is. You're worried about your brother, so you are not yourself today—not at all."

That was about the only thing she got right. Or maybe I *had* gone a little mad. I had mortally offended McBrae last night. I couldn't bear to be responsible, even by association, for offending his servant, too.

"Your mother asked me to look about myself for a companion for you, deeming it an urgent matter, and I see she is perfectly correct," Lady Danby said. "Someone quite a bit older, known for propriety but with a kind heart. I shall see what I can find."

I almost shrieked that I neither needed nor wanted a companion, but that would only further convince her that she was right. In society's opinion, a lady should never live alone—not that one is ever really alone, what with servants constantly getting in one's way—and for a widow as young as I, the alternative to remarriage is a chaperone. Especially if said young widow is verging on mad....

I had anticipated this struggle, but not so very soon.

She marched out, and I beckoned to Hamish—a little too imperiously, perhaps, because I feared Lady Danby might still give him a scold. Perhaps that would have been preferable, but I fear she was too shocked and concerned about me to care. Without a glance at Hamish, she climbed into her barouche and drove away.

"I don't need a tisane," I told Maurice.

"Very good, my lady," he said, looking worried.

"Ask Mr. Jenkins—Lord Derwent's valet—to come here. He may be obliged to wait if I have a great many morning callers, but whatever you do, don't allow him to leave again. It is most urgent that I speak with him." I paused. "If the Bow Street Runners do happen to come, send them up to the drawing room."

"Very good, my lady," he said again, clearly appalled. I had a feeling he would retreat to the kitchen, explain the situation to the butler, and ask to be given some work far from the door. Thus, Stevenson would deter any unwelcome callers, and Maurice would not be taken to task for disobeying me.

Hamish approached, doffing his hat, and my heart filled with desperate hope. "Do you have a message for me?"

"Nay, my lady. Master Gil asked me to keep an eye on you."

Chapter Eight

n eye on me.

First my mother, then my brother, now Lady Danby aiding and abetting them... Surely McBrae didn't consider me mad, too! Dizziness assailed me. Blindly, I gripped the door.

"Is aught amiss?" That was Hamish's voice, and now Maurice was getting in the way, and next he would call for help, and...

Valiantly (if I may say so myself—for it was exceedingly difficult), I got myself under control. Perhaps it is improper to think of oneself as valiant, but I had begun to feel besieged.

"No, I'm perfectly well," I said snappishly. "Merely tired, having slept little last night. Bring more coffee, Maurice." To Hamish, I said, "You'd better come in. We can't speak on the doorstep."

Maurice hovered, ostensibly to close the door, concern still written on his somber countenance. I waved him off. "Coffee. *Now.*" Reluctantly, he retreated.

I led Hamish up to the drawing room. Why, you ask, would I bring a servant there? It's hardly the correct place to interview such a person, but I needed privacy to do so, and from what I knew of Hamish, he was trustworthy and devoted to McBrae.

With whom I was now furious! Or maybe I was desperately afraid. Or both. I closed the drawing room door and turned. "How dare he send you to keep any eye on me?"

A trace of a smile touched Hamish's eyes. "There's not much Young Gil won't dare, if it matters enough to him."

Yes. Indeed. I already knew that.

"Very well then, *why* did he ask you to do so?"

"He didna say, my lady. He was up all the night, working on an etching, and he wasna in the best of moods the morn."

A new caricature? Dread poked at me. "One of his own drawings?" I whispered, for Maurice might return quickly, thinking to protect me or some such nonsense. I couldn't risk him overhearing.

Hamish shook his head. "I canna say, as I didna see it." Either he was lying, or he really didn't know why McBrae had sent him, or what he had so urgently etched last night.

"When he's fashed, he isna one to talk," Hamish said. "But likely he fears you'll run into danger, trying to find out where your brother may be."

There was a hint of reproof in his voice, and the small part of me that wasn't well-nigh paralyzed by terrifying emotions reproached me as well. I knew McBrae didn't wish me harm, but neither did my mother and brother, as they saw it. I know it seems foolish, but whenever my fear of being shut away rears its ghastly head, I find it almost impossible to think clearly.

I took a deep breath and addressed myself to the current business. "I don't know what danger I could conceivably find myself facing, even with officers of the law making a nuisance of themselves. Has he told you everything that's going on? That my brother's mistress was abducted and has now taken refuge with me?"

"Aye, poor lass." He showed no sign of disapproval—but again, one never knows what to expect from the Scots. So far in my acquaintance with McBrae, I had been (mostly) pleasantly surprised.

Just then, Maurice reappeared with fresh coffee—and one cup, because it would never occur to him that I meant to offer coffee to Hamish. To tell the truth, I hadn't really thought of it myself until now. McBrae would be pleased with me (if we were still on speaking terms, which I was sure we were not).

Heavens! Such a thought shows you clearly the chaos of my mind, one moment suspecting him of watching me for signs of madness and the next seeking his approval, which I have sworn over and over not to do.

Perhaps, I justified to myself, I simply wanted to make amends for my earlier unkindness. Perhaps by showing respect for his servant, I was also showing it for McBrae himself.

Be that as it may (for I fear it was a little far-fetched), I snatched my cup before Maurice could whisk the previous tray away. He would no doubt report this further sign of incipient hysteria to Stevenson, but at least my mother wasn't in town. He left, leaving the door open, and Hamish shut it without being asked.

I thanked him and poured for both of us. "Help yourself to cream and sugar."

He did so without a blink. How strange. No English servant—or at least none I'm acquainted with—would readily, even comfortably share a drink with a lady so far above him socially. Perhaps the customs in Scotland are different.

I dithered over whether to ask him to take a seat, but fortunately, an idea (but not as brilliant as is often the case) descended upon me before I had to embarrass one or the other (or both) of us. Probably only myself, as he seemed quite at ease.

I stood. "Come over here by the window. I want to keep watch in case some Bow Street Runners do arrive. I must speak to them, and my butler and footman will do their best to prevent it."

He grinned, joining me at the window. "Aye, they will that. I'll answer the door for you, shall I?"

"What an excellent notion." I couldn't help but smile in return. "Mr. McBrae and I concocted a story to tell them. To throw them off the scent, so to speak. I expect I shall have to repeat it to all my friends and acquaintances, too. I only hope I can remember the details well enough to tell the same story each time."

He grunted. "Nobody will mind exactly what you said. They'll be too busy adding their own havers."

This was true—and useful for once. I wondered what 'havers' Corvus would add to his next caricature.

We watched silently, and at last, I got up the courage to speak. To apologize in an oblique sort of way.

"I fear I offended Mr. McBrae last night," I said. "I certainly didn't intend to. I spoke without thinking, and he took it badly."

"Och, is that what's eating at him? It's no wonder you misspoke, what with his lordship your brother missing. Dinna fash yourself, my lady. Young Gil's a good lad. He'll come around."

Come around to what? He was definitely fed up with me. Apart from his misplaced lust, he didn't even like me much, as far as I could tell. However, I reminded myself sternly, I had far more important matters to think about now. I could luxuriate in self-pity later.

At the window, Hamish tensed. "Who might that be coming up to your door, and sending his friend to watch the area stairs? I'll wager there's a third at the back."

"Bow Street Runners?"

He shrugged. "Well, it's no' any newsman I've seen, nor likely a bailiff..." He was out the door and down the stairs before the visitor had a chance to knock. I followed him to the head of the stairs in case Stevenson interfered. Hamish opened the door, and before the individual on the doorstep could get a word out, he asked, "Might you be from Bow Street, sir? Aye? Her ladyship wishes to have a wee word with you. Come right in!"

In any other circumstance, I would have burst out laughing. I imagine Bow Street Runners don't usually receive a warm welcome.

I took a seat on the sofa, poured myself some more coffee, and desperately tried to decide which role to play. Imitating my mother usually gets me out of a fix, but she would never deign to speak with a Bow Street Runner. Nor would Lady Danby. Nor Lady Baffleton. Not even Mrs. Brill. In fact, none of my acquaintances would stoop so low.

(However, my father might. He doesn't exactly stoop, though; he is a wonderful combination of confident superiority and genuine cordiality. Perhaps it has to do with the greater freedom of being male. McBrae has some of the same qualities.)

"Here he is, my lady: Mr. Linehorn from Bow Street." Hamish ushered a barrel-chested man inside, closed the door, and stood against it, arms crossed.

Since I couldn't think of anything better, I resorted to a pose of languid boredom, as I might with a social inferior whom I wished to discourage without giving the cut direct.

I set down my cup. "How kind of you to call, Mr. Linehorn. You have saved me the inconvenience of paying a visit to Bow Street. Do take a seat. Would you like some coffee? I'd be happy to ring for another cup."

The Runner looked in bewilderment from the chair to the coffee to my face, and remained standing. He cleared his throat and stood erect, hands behind his back. "My lady, this is not a social call. I have come in the execution of my duty. Lord Derwent stands accused of murder, and if he is hiding here, you must immediately deliver him into my custody."

I believe I managed a convincing laugh. "My dear man, surely you don't believe that absurd story. My brother Derwent is not the murderous sort."

Mr. Linehorn was the picture of expressionless stolidity. "It's not my place to believe or disbelieve, my lady, but merely to do my duty as required."

"Tsk," I said. "Not only is my brother not here, he is not even in town." I had another brilliant notion. "I was told someone wrote to Bow Street, claiming to have witnessed the murder. Such nonsense! The letter was sent by some young fellows playing a prank."

The Runner appeared taken aback, but he stuck to his duty. "It's not my place to judge that, either, ma'am. I have my orders. Where might I find his lordship?"

I gave a heavy sigh. "I suppose I shall have to tell you the truth." I did my best to feign embarrassment. "It's rather sordid, and not what a lady chooses to speak of." I sighed again. "My brother will be justifiably annoyed with me for discussing his personal business, but it's his own fault. Men are such fools."

"No doubt about that, ma'am. Where is he?"

I embarked once again on my story. "Off with his mistress at a love nest." I wrinkled my nose as if at a noxious odor. "He left in a dreadful hurry the day before yesterday, not long before I arrived in town. I've been up in the north of England, you see, visiting my father, the Earl of Medway. Ordinarily,

I would be happily ignorant of my brother's improper behavior, but it so happens that one of my maids is in love with a footman at Medway House, who overheard Derwent speaking to his valet, who had learned by way of the servants in Kensington—where he houses his mistress—that there was a plot to abduct her."

"A what?"

"It sounds frightfully medieval, doesn't it? Imagine, a forced marriage by way of abduction! I'm sure it's against the law in these modern times."

"Beg pardon, my lady, but it sounds like a farrago of nonsense to me."

"I quite understand, Mr., ah, Linehorn." I flapped a languid hand and sighed again. "It doesn't make sense to me either. My brother's mistress is the daughter of a wealthy City merchant, who naturally wants her to marry a respectable man. He even chose a husband for her, but she refused him. I find it incomprehensible, too." I added a line contributed by Lady Danby. "Far, far better to be respectably wed to a Cit than the mistress of a nobleman."

"Indeed, ma'am, but I didn't hear nothing about this when I visited Medway House this morning. Matter of fact, they wouldn't even speak to me."

"No, they're trained to refuse anyone who isn't invited, and to reveal no information whatsoever about their employers. My butler is just as bad—a true tyrant—which is why I sent Hamish down to open the door before Stevenson got in the way. Whilst I do not ordinarily deal with officers of the law—my mother would be aghast, and in fact, she might go into a decline if she knew—but I felt it my duty to set the record straight. Why should you waste your time on nonsense when there are real criminals out there needing to be apprehended?"

"We shouldn't, ma'am, but orders is orders." Glumly, he added, "They don't let me choose who to arrest."

"I *quite* understand, and I *wish* I could help you out, but I can't deliver my brother up to you, since he's not here—although to tell the truth, I don't suppose I would give him up even if he were. One doesn't, you know. Family loyalty comes first. But in any event, the instant Derwent heard of the abduction plot, he rode to Kensington to rescue Miss Concord. I'm surprised it's not all over the broadsheets yet. Or in one of Corvus' drawings, with Derwent as a knight in shining armor, Miss Concord draped becomingly over his saddle bow."

Over by the door, Hamish snorted. Meanwhile, the Runner was becoming impatient. "Where did Lord Derwent take her?"

I widened my eyes and blinked rapidly. It is supposed to seem appealingly feminine, but in truth, it makes one look idiotic. "But I *told* you—to a *love* nest."

"And where might this love nest be?"

"My dear man, I haven't the *slightest* notion. It's not the sort of thing a man tells his sister, is it? I asked Jenkins, his valet, but he says he doesn't know either, and he's an honest sort, so I believe him. Perhaps Lord Derwent took her to one of the Medway properties, which are dotted all over England. Perhaps to a cottage someplace that we don't know about. He could be anywhere by now."

"Including out of the country," the Bow Street Runner muttered. "Begging your pardon, but you're not bamming me, are you, my lady? You truly don't know where he is?"

"No, Mr. Linehorn, I don't." I was worried and afraid, and my distress must have shown. I'm sure my voice wobbled a little. "Please tell the magistrates all that I have just told you."

I nodded dismissal, and Hamish showed the man out. I pinched the bridge of my nose, wondering how many times I would have to tell the same story to a pack of nosy morning callers.

Hamish came back into the room, gasping with laughter. Can you imagine? A mere servant, laughing aloud whilst performing his duties—and at his mistress, too! (Not that I was his employer, but he *was* serving me at the time.)

"You could be on the stage, my lady," he said. Heavens, what an insult, but seemingly he had no idea until my appalled stare stopped him in mid-chortle. "Och, I was ever one for letting the wrong words slip out. Beg pardon, my lady."

"I'm not offended," I said hastily, which was a bit of a lie, but only for the few seconds it took to shake off the pernicious effects of my upbringing. Without my mother's strictures getting in the way, I realized he was complimenting me on my performance.

I summoned a more appropriate response. "I rather enjoy playing a role, in an amateur sense, of course. But I fear I didn't do well this time. I don't think he believed me."

"Likely not, but you sowed some doubt." He drained his coffee cup. "I'd best be on my way."

Oh, dear. I rather wanted him to stay. "What happened to keeping an eye on me?"

"Och," he said again. "You dinna want a minder, my lady, and I've plenty to do at home."

I struggled not to show my dismay, which only goes to show how overset I was. I wanted him there because he was my link with McBrae, but to what purpose? Think about it, I told myself sternly. 1) Hamish was not my servant, and 2) even if he were, I had no work for him to do, and 3) I didn't need McBrae in any way, shape, or form. He had more or less washed his hands of me yesterday, and I must do the same to him.

A sharp rapping from below recalled me to the fact that Hamish was still standing there watching me, cap in hand. "And there is *my* work, knocking at the door," I said. "I must repeat that performance to I don't know how many horrid, gossipy so-called friends. I don't know why I associate with them."

"You'd best think on that, hadn't you, my lady?" He popped his cap on his head and left me gaping. How dare he admonish the daughter of an earl, granddaughter of a marquis, and cousin of a duke?

I put it down to being a heedless Scot, whilst sadly admitting to myself that he was right. Except for Cynthia, away in the country with Sir Roderick, I didn't have any real friends. Certainly no one who understood my struggles, who shared my thoughts, who truly cared.

Except McBrae. Not that he really knew much about me, but...

But because I couldn't become his mistress, he was gone, too.

Well. My spirits have seldom fallen so low, but circumstances required me to conceal all signs of distress, and I fancy I did so. I shan't bore you with the rest of that ghastly day. I couldn't even drink more coffee to bolster my spirits, for then I would have been obliged to serve it to my dozens of callers. (Just over three dozen, to be precise.) These consisted of many of those I'd seen at Lady Baffleton's the previous evening, including my supposed suitors and Lord Cyril Telfrey (who, I believe, had come solely from concern for me; he's not the gossipy sort).

What's more, far too many people had now heard precisely how Lord Worsten was killed, and were eager to discuss it with bloodthirsty relish. Sir Pinkerton Jones-Worthy was by far the worst. He cannot help being his slimy self, but he tried to combine vile insinuations with fawning adulation. I couldn't help but wonder what a glorious caricature Corvus might make of it.

Having decided to stop thinking about McBrae, I shut down that thought immediately. I hope you will do so as well, in sympathy with me.

Ordinarily, there is a limit to the period during which one accepts morning calls, but if I told Stevenson to start refusing them, it would cause offense, or they would make up their own havers, as Hamish put it. I was obliged to spread my own version as widely as possible. I was wearily repeating the same nonsense when the final caller was ushered into the room—Sir Devlin Curtis.

He bowed over my hand. "I told Stevenson to say you are no longer accepting callers, Lady Rosamund. You've been subjected to more than enough ghoulish gossip-seekers for one day." He swept a steely glance around the room.

I muffled a giggle. Murmurs of protest, scowls of indignation, and embarrassed blushes ensued, but within a few minutes, all my remaining guests had gone—except for Sir Pinkerton, who paused in the doorway.

"I assume you're here to promote your boorish nephew's suit, Sir Devlin." He tittered. "A waste of effort. I don't suppose the sweet words Lady Rosamund hopes to have whispered in her bedchamber at midnight are the gory details of fox hunts."

Definitely not. I have no experience of bedchamber intimacies, but McBrae had whispered in my ear on one memorable occasion. It was unexpectedly stimulating, and I couldn't help but wonder what he would have whispered to me at midnight, if he had ever become my lover.

Fortunately, Sir Devlin's response swept away that foolishly saddening thought.

"Thus says the strutting cock who has an equally poor chance," Sir Devlin said. "Lady Rosamund can do much better than either of you."

"It's far too soon for any such thing," I sighed. "My poor dear Albert is scarcely cold in his grave, or so it feels to me."

What a bouncer that was, but Sir Pinkerton immediately apologized for upsetting me, cast a darkling glance at my neighbor, and took his leave.

I smiled tiredly at Sir Devlin and waved him to a chair. "Thank you. I was *so* fed up with repeating the same story to each group of callers—particularly since no one wants to believe it."

"What else are good neighbors for?" he asked. "I asked Stevenson to bring tea, unless you prefer a tisane, but I suspect that's what your mother would prescribe."

I chuckled at that. As her cicisbeo, he is well acquainted with my mother's megrims. "Tea will be much more welcome."

"With what, ah, unbelievable story have you regaled the *ton*?" he asked, with what in a less stern, proud sort of man would be described as a twinkle.

"It's not unbelievable," I said. "It's the truth, but they would much rather believe Derwent is capable of murder. Of stabbing his friend several times."

"It is indeed difficult to believe," he said. "Even in his cups, I can't imagine he would be so lost to a sense of honor."

"Certainly not." I proceeded to tell him the same lies, in the hope that he would help to spread them about. Stevenson appeared with the tea and a decanter of brandy—how thoughtful of him. He left, and I poured for both of us, putting a tiny dollop of brandy in mine and a larger one in Sir Devlin's.

"Miss Concord is definitely missing?" he asked. "I don't mean to disbelieve you, my dear, but servants' tales are notorious for misinformation."

"Yes, she is indeed missing. I sent a man to Kensington to confirm it. She disappeared the same afternoon my brother left town."

"Have we no idea where Derwent took her? Surely his stable hands know where his coach was headed."

"He didn't take a coach," I said. "He left on horseback."

"Tsk," Sir Devlin said. "My dear child, that lends far more credence to the assumption that he went chasing after Worsten."

"Not necessarily." I was ready for this, as one of my morning callers had made the same objection. "He received a message and left in a hurry, fearing she would be abducted before he arrived in Kensington."

"But surely he didn't ride off with her on his saddle bow," Sir Devlin said. "That's the stuff of romance, not real life. He must have hired a carriage."

"I expect so," I said. "He asked his head groom about stabling in Barnet, so perhaps he meant to hire a carriage there." At his raised brows, I flapped a hand. "Yes, I know it seems suspicious, because Lord Worsten's body was found on the way to Barnet—but if Worsten did indeed abduct Miss Concord, and Derwent went in pursuit, why would he ask his groom about stabling? How could he even know where Worsten was taking her?"

"That's a good point," Sir Devlin said contemplatively, "but I don't think your story will convince the Runners. In the meantime, you needn't remain here to endure the gossip. No doubt Corvus will gleefully latch onto this latest scandal."

"I have never let Corvus' drawings bother me," I retorted.

"Yes, you're a courageous girl, but think of your poor mother. I believe you should go to Kent. When she hears the news, she will need your support."

"No, she'll find a way to say it's all my fault," I muttered. Mother confides in him, so if anyone knows how she thinks of me, it's Sir Devlin. "Perhaps *you* should go there and be supportive, if you can stand the odor of burning pastilles."

He gave a mirthless laugh. "I understand that it will be unpleasant, my dear, but it would be improper for me to visit your mother when neither Lord Medway nor Derwent is there."

This was true, but it was also a convenient way for him to avoid my mother in one of her fits. "I mean to go to my father instead. He will be far more useful."

"All the way to Westmoreland? Surely an express letter would make more sense."

"It would, but I don't know where he is. I left him with a friend in Hertfordshire, but he intended to travel with him to interview some elderly laborers about magical black dogs or something of the sort. I'll go to Hertfordshire and follow him from there." (I confess to purposely misleading Sir Devlin. Papa wasn't likely to travel more than an hour from Lord Elderwood's house, but I needed an excuse to leave London.)

He pondered this, then shrugged. "It can't do any harm, although I doubt even the Earl of Medway will be able to prevent the Runners from seeking Derwent. Our best hope is to bundle your brother out of the country before they catch him—but we'll have to find him first."

Sir Devlin left, telling me not to worry. He promised to do what he could to locate Derwent, which was kind but not particularly comforting. If anyone could help me, it was McBrae—but I couldn't count on him anymore.

Chapter Nine

My head ached, and I longed for my bed, but I went straight to Miss Concord's chamber. She deserved to hear the latest ghastly news.

It seemed she already had. Joan, the downstairs maid, was sitting with her, a stocking with a hole in the heel on her lap and the tracks of tears on her flushed face.

Joan weeps over the merest trifles, but she works reliably and well, so everyone puts up with it, merely teasing her with the nickname Weeping Joan. However, she shouldn't be upstairs at all, nor should she be mending her stockings at this time of day when there is housework to be done.

"What in heaven's name is going on?" I demanded. "Yes, the Runners are seeking Lord Derwent, but weeping won't help, nor will abandoning your duties."

Joan leapt up at sight of me, curtseying. "I'm sorry, my lady, I'm sorry, but—"

But what? She had no excuse, and she knew it. I turned to Miss Concord, who, despite the dread written all over her face, spoke calmly. "That's not what she's weeping about, although everyone in the house knows about the Runners by now. She's upset over a rather more personal problem." Miss Concord sent a meaningful glance in the direction of the maid.

In addition to all the other problems? It was one of those days that simply can't get worse, and yet they do. I followed her glance, and immediately I knew. "By God, you're increasing!"

Joan burst into a flood of tears. "I'm sorry, I'm so sorry, my lady. I'll pack my things and leave. I'll go straight away, I swear. I would throw myself in the river, but that would be murder, wouldn't it, killing my own dear babe? But it's no better than I deserve, and yet, if I don't starve to death before he's born, he will go on the parish and likely die anyway. Oh no, oh no, I don't know what to *do*." She swayed, racked by noisy sobs, and dropped the stocking onto the carpet.

I shut the door, went over to her, and eased her gently back into the chair. "Stop it, Joan. I'm not my mother. I shan't throw you into the street."

"I told her so," Miss Concord said, "but she seems convinced that she deserves a miserable fate."

"For giving in to her animal urges?" I was tempted to roll my eyes. Spending a week with a group of actors, poets, and playwrights in the North had sadly affected my manners. "Most people do, but surely we can call the man to account." I eyed the bulge beneath her apron and counted the months in my head. "Oh, dear. Surely not Harold, who fell down the stairs." He was dead, so couldn't be forced to wed her.

"No, my lady, no! Everyone thought I loved Harold, but no, all I done was tell him to stay away from Henny, for she would never be faithful to him or anyone else. But if I hadn't scolded him for a fool, he would have been down the stairs by the time the master came home, and he wouldn't have been caught, and he wouldn't have lost his temper, and the master wouldn't have pushed him, and I wouldn't have been hiding down the corridor and seen it all—"

"My husband pushed him?" Well, well. That solved a little mystery from last spring, but it hardly mattered now.

"Yes, my lady, but it was an accident. The master didn't mean no murder, but he couldn't just take Harold's impudence, could he?"

I could imagine the scene—Albert chastising Harold for dallying with the maids, and Harold losing his temper, and Albert losing his in return.

"Harold told the master he was worse, leaving you alone and lonely while he went to Lady Benson every night."

"How—how courageous of him," I said, feeling rather guilty myself. Harold had died defending me, when I actually *wanted* Albert to leave me alone.

How unfair, poor man. Perhaps I should give a sum of money to his parents in compensation—not that it would make up for his life, but what if they'd counted on him to support them in old age?

Drat. You may not believe me, but this was *not* another instance of seeking McBrae's approval. I would have compensated them in any event, if I'd known the truth. (Except that I would probably be dead as well if it weren't for McBrae, but that was beside the point.)

"Yes, my lady, he weren't a bad fella, just a fool. Everyone knows what goes for the nobs just won't do for the rest of us. All the same, I worried for you, my lady. When Corvus accused you in that there drawing, it was my duty to tell the truth, but I *couldn't*, for who would believe me? I would have been dismissed for sure, maybe even thrown into prison, and—"

"Calm down, Joan. You were quite right to say nothing. As you said, no one would have believed you, and thanks to being one of the, ah, nobs, I was never in any danger of arrest—and since my husband is also dead, what he did doesn't matter anymore." I waited, while her sobs slowly subsided. "Now, if it wasn't Harold, who is the father of your child?"

She swallowed hard, wringing her apron in her hands. "Oh, dearie me! I wish I hadn't said nothing, but I thought maybe you already guessed, my lady."

Miss Concord tutted. "While you're confessing, you'd best get it all out," she said with a touch of asperity. "If Lady Rosamund were to get rid of every servant who eavesdrops, she'd have none left."

You do recall what I said not long ago about servants getting in the way all the time? One must conduct one's life in whispers—or put up with no privacy at all. What had Joan overheard?

"I'll die in a ditch for sure, but it's no better than I deserve, for I threw myself at him," she said. "I'm a wanton and a coward, but he ain't, he's a good man. He don't deserve to be tossed out on his ear. He was only trying to comfort me."

"Foolish girl," I said, "he is as much to blame as you are, and I have had enough of your histrionics. You eavesdropped, and therefore thought I knew what?" I bent a reproving eye on her.

"I heard you say one of the maids was in love with a footman at Medway House," she whispered. She wiped her eyes on her sleeve. "Then Mr. Stevenson was coming, so I ran up the stairs."

Miss Concord took up the tale. "I found her weeping in the corridor and asked her to come help me with the mending."

At last, we were getting somewhere—thanks to a foolish story I had made up! "Which footman?" I asked.

"You won't dismiss him?" she asked. "Otherwise, I won't never tell on him. I'll die first!"

I had had enough. "Stupid girl!" I said, much as my mother would have done. (I have since come to the conclusion that calling servants stupid serves no useful purpose, so I try not to do so, but my head was throbbing like the devil.) "I am only trying to help. *Who is the father?*"

"He don't know about the baby," she wailed. "He'll be ever so cross with me. He already *is* cross, but I don't deserve him."

"Apparently, he calls here regularly, asking to speak to Joan, but she refuses him," Miss Concord said.

"He has the right to know," I said austerely, "and he *should* be cross." The maid subsided once again into weeping. "Joan, I shall find out with or without your cooperation, so you may as well tell me now. In any event, I have no authority to dismiss an employee of Medway House."

However, my mother would do so when she learned the news. She would dismiss Joan, too, the instant my back was turned.

One of my brilliant ideas descended upon me like a benediction from above. Naturally, my father must be informed of the situation, but only a few servants and I knew where he might be found. I had already decided to write to my father and then leave town—so why not combine the two, and bring the maid and footman with me?

What nonsense, you're thinking. I should just write to him, as he would likely come to town immediately. You're absolutely correct—but I'll wager you don't live in daily dread that your mother will descend upon you and do her best to have you committed. (Or if you do, you have my profound sympathy.) While she was at it, she would have both maid and footman thrown into the street. It was my duty to prevent that.

Not only that, leaving town would protect Miss Concord from her father and her unwanted suitor. The more I thought about it, the more I felt flight was the perfect solution for all concerned. Now, like a gift from the gods, I had the perfect excuse to leave town with Miss Concord but *without* Mary Jane, who might lose her temper and therefore her position as my maid. I didn't want to lose her forever.

I didn't particularly want Morose Maurice along, either, but I couldn't leave without any servants at all, as it would look far too odd. I can't afford to seem any odder than I already am.

Not only that, I was doing a good deed. Joan would serve as lady's maid, and her paramour could be my footman. She would thus have no choice but to talk to him, and not just for a few minutes. They would be thrown together and obliged to work out their differences. Not that I fancied myself a matchmaker, but this sort of strategy had been employed by my father recently. I would put the problem before him, and between us we would find a way for the footman to afford a wife.

If amongst all this plotting it occurred to me that McBrae would approve, I dismissed that thought at once. His opinion mattered not a whit.

Another notion struck me. "I suppose it's the young blond one." No wonder he'd complained about women. However, he was now stuck with this one.

Joan clasped her hands to her heaving bosom. "How did you know?"

"He seems a pleasant young man," I said and gave a vigorous tug on the bell.

Soon my plans were in motion. I told Jenkins, my brother's valet, about the fiction in which I had included him. "I wish he had told me where he was off to, my lady," he said, and left to tell Blond Charles—whose name, it transpired, was Ivan—to be packed and at my door by eight the next morning.

I informed Mary Jane that she was to have a fortnight's leave beginning tomorrow. She stumped off to pack for both me and Miss Concord, muttering that she hoped Joan wouldn't ruin every stitch of clothing and misplace my jewels as well.

Miss Concord was understandably reluctant to visit my father. "Surely not, my lady. It wouldn't be right or proper to bring me there. I'm not respectable anymore, and I'm not even your sort."

"My *sort* is people I like," I said, "not those society dictates. My father is the dearest, kindest man. You have nothing to fear from him."

She didn't look convinced. "But...all the way to Westmoreland?" In other words, so far from Julius.

"No, no, my father is in Hertfordshire, only a few hours away. He's visiting friends there, and you needn't worry about them, either. They're the strangest people, utterly unconcerned with propriety and even more obsessed with folk magic than my father. They spend the entire time with Papa discussing the Horned God of the Celts. They'll hardly notice we're there."

"But...shouldn't we be doing something, *anything*, to find Lord Derwent?" Her lip wobbled; we both feared finding only his remains.

"We shall, if we think of something," I said. "On our way, we'll go right past where Lord Worsten was found and into Barnet, where my brother seemed to be headed." I pondered. "Moving forward, I believe we must make a few assumptions." I put up a finger. "One, that Julius is alive—because if he isn't, I really don't care who killed Lord Worsten." Which may be callous of me (as well as contradicting my belief, recently argued with McBrae in the north, that justice matters), but I would be mourning my brother, while I'd been barely acquainted with Worsten.

I raised another finger. "And two, that Julius did not kill Lord Worsten, which leads us to an obvious conclusion: someone else killed him. In order to save Julius, we must identify the murderer."

This seemed a horrendous task, now that McBrae was no longer here to help. But I did not intend to allow his desertion (which was at least partly my fault) to stop me.

"How do you propose to do that?" Miss Concord asked.

"I believe we should start by making a list of people who had reason to want Lord Worsten dead." This method had worked well for me in the past. It hadn't actually helped me identify the culprit, but it served to organize my thoughts.

"Such as whom? He was one of Julius' close friends, and despite how horrid he was to me, I believe he was generally well-liked."

"Yes, but obviously, someone didn't agree. Disliked or feared him, or merely owed money and couldn't pay...aha! The betting book at White's!"

An hour later, I stood on the pavement whilst Maurice rapped on Lady Baffleton's door. It should have been half an hour, but my peculiarity had gripped me with a vengeance, and I checked the contents of my reticule several times and then the contents of each of the hiding places in my bedchamber. How exasperating, for I had promised myself that on returning to London, I would keep my peculiarity under control. Eventually, thoroughly annoyed with myself, I forced myself to stop checking and left home.

The only way for a lady to learn about recent wagers in that infamous book is to ask a gentleman who is a member for help—and the polite way to approach such a gentleman is via his wife.

Lady Baffleton is the same age as I, and although we are not close, we move in the same circles. I assume she likes either me or my status, as she invites me to most of her parties. Her butler conveyed me at once to a drawing room at the back of the house, where Lady Baffleton was spending a little time with her two children.

Drat! Miss Trent was there, too. I would have preferred not to mention my errand in her presence, as she is a feather-headed girl with a flapping tongue, but needs must. After exchanging pleasantries and complimenting Lady Baffleton on the children, I explained that I wished to see Lord Baffleton on an urgent matter of business. I didn't wish to specify precisely what business, because a lady should not interest herself in such an improper subject as murder. In any event, both Lady Baffleton and Miss Trent assumed that my brother had killed Worsten in a fit of rage and fled the country. (Not that they said as much, but their sighs of pity made it clear—although I suspected Miss Trent was more curious than sympathetic.) I trusted that Lord Baffleton, being somewhat acquainted with Derwent, would not make such a ridiculous assumption.

"I hesitate to disturb him," I said, "but I plan to leave town in the morning."

"I quite understand," Lady Baffleton said. "The gossip must be intolerable. Lady Danby came by earlier, fretting about your state of mind."

"My state of mind is fine," I retorted, and clamped my lips against an unkind remark about Lady Danby. Lady Baffleton might understand my indignation, but stupid Miss Trent would simply repeat it word for word into any willing ear. In fact, judging by the eagerness in her gaze, she was champing at the bit to do so. I hoped she hadn't been there when Lady Danby came by, but I could hardly ask.

"Anyone would be upset under the circumstances," Lady Baffleton said. "I'm sure my husband will be happy to see you. I believe Mr. McBrae is with him, though."

Drat and damn. The last person I wished to see! (This wasn't entirely true, for I longed to see him as he was before I insulted him and he gave up on me. But that would never happen, and therefore I preferred not to see him at all.)

"I hope you don't object," she said, for my face had doubtless betrayed me. "I believe his discretion may be relied upon."

"I'm sure it may." I couldn't very well draw back now. Not only would it reflect badly on McBrae, but I wouldn't get the information I needed otherwise.

Lady Baffleton left Miss Trent with the children and escorted me to the study. The room was filled with smoke, for the two gentlemen were indulging in what is known as 'blowing a cloud.' Disgusting, but one can't expect otherwise from males.

"Dearest, Lady Rosamund is here on a small matter of business," she said, ushering me in. The gentlemen sprang to their feet. Lady Baffleton coughed and waved helplessly at the smoke, and the gentlemen exchanged a glance of consternation, whether at exposing us to their filthy habit or at our intrusion into their male fastness, it was hard to say.

I managed a laugh. "My father indulges from time to time, so I'm used to it."

"I don't believe I shall ever become accustomed," Lady Baffleton said. "Isn't there enough smoke in the air already from hundreds of chimney pots, without adding even more? But men will be men." She threw up her hands, smiled, and left me there.

"Please have a seat, Lady Rosamund," Lord Baffleton said. I did so, nodding briefly at McBrae. Unfortunately, I couldn't quite avoid catching his eye. I don't know how I managed to retain my composure, for his expression was cold and utterly indifferent.

"I apologize for disturbing you," I said. After they had stubbed out their cigarillos and seated themselves again, murmuring the usual 'no such thing' and 'delighted to be of service,' I got straight to the point. "I am certain that my brother did not kill Lord Worsten."

"Absolutely not," Lord Baffleton said. "Mr. McBrae and I were just saying the same."

"I am relieved to hear that," I said. "Unfortunately, someone sent a letter to Bow Street saying he witnessed my brother murdering Worsten, and now the Runners are after him. They went to Medway House, and then came to mine, believing I might be hiding Derwent there."

"What effrontery, intruding upon the comfort of a well-bred lady! They shall be severely chastised, even if I have to speak to the magistrates myself." Lord Baffleton probably believed his patronizing smile was kindly and understanding. "You must be in need of refreshment. I have some excellent whisky, thanks to Mr. McBrae's father—but it's not really a lady's drink. Shall I ring for tea?"

I almost denied needing refreshment, but annoyance on my part wouldn't help. Meanwhile, McBrae hadn't moved a muscle, which wasn't surprising, but it hurt nonetheless, for in the past, he had encouraged me to use my logical mind. I reminded myself firmly that such support was over and done with.

"A small amount of whisky would be very welcome." I didn't particularly want any, but I expect I hoped to placate McBrae by approving of his father's no doubt illicit brew. If ever there was a sign of madness, it's my repeated efforts to secure his approval.

I shook off that perplexing fact and got back to business. "Actually, I'm glad the Runner visited me, for I was able to sow a few seeds of doubt in his mind. I told him the letter was a prank, thanks to some foolish young men."

If I hoped for a compliment from McBrae on my quick thinking, I was doomed to disappointment. Perhaps it was a silly idea, but it was better than nothing.

"I also told him Derwent had left town with his mistress to save her from being abducted."

"Which has the merit of being true," McBrae said—thus conveying to me that he hadn't told Lord Baffleton that it was a fabrication we'd concocted. "They may believe it if they've seen that." He indicated a news sheet on the table.

Really, he should have had the courtesy to pass it to me. Lord Baffleton politely did so, pointing out a piece which suggested disapprovingly that 'the disappearance two days ago of Miss C_____, the unfortunate daughter of a prominent City merchant, was due to the selfishness of Lord D_____, who prefers to keep her under his sinful protection rather than allow her to redeem herself in the eyes of God and the world by marrying a man of the merchant class.'

"It must have just come out, for no one mentioned it this morning," I said. "Unfortunately, it's not enough. The only way to clear my brother's name is to identify the real murderer."

"Or at the very least to prove that Lord Derwent couldn't have done it," McBrae said.

I hadn't thought of this, but I should have. McBrae is far more interested in saving the innocent than punishing the guilty. Much as I believe in seeing justice done, I couldn't help but agree with him where my brother was concerned.

"How do you suggest we do so?" It seemed obligatory to glance at him as I said this. Fortunately, he was gazing at the ceiling as if deep in thought. Deep in avoiding me, more like it, which was fine by me, or so I kept telling myself. "By finding someone who will swear they were with Derwent from the time he left town until the body was discovered?"

"Something of the sort, if necessary. First, I must locate Lord Derwent and see what he has to say."

You intend to look for him? I almost asked, but clamped my mouth shut just in time. Why wouldn't he search for my brother? They were friends. It had nothing to do with his disdain for me.

"How very kind, Mr. McBrae," I said, and immediately wished I hadn't, for his expression became even stonier, if that were possible.

To hell with him. I meant well. I'd been trying to express my gratitude, but he was welcome to take it as an insult if he wished.

"Naturally, he must be found and informed of the danger in which he stands," I said. "However, in the interest of finding the real murderer, I've been wondering who might have wanted Lord Worsten dead. Perhaps someone hated or feared him, or owed him a great deal of money which he couldn't afford to pay."

Lord Baffleton paused, decanter in hand, doubtless about to say something about not bothering my little head about such matters. I put up a hand to forestall him and said, "Or feared he would soon owe him, and decided to prevent it."

McBrae probably understood immediately, but I wasn't about to risk encountering that dead-and-petrified-fish stare again. Before Lord Baffleton could speak, I continued. "I imagine that after the fracas between Derwent and Lord Worsten, there were a number of bets placed about whether Derwent would lose Miss Concord to Lord Worsten, and how soon."

Lord Baffleton barked an astonished laugh. "Just what McBrae was saying not ten minutes ago. He wants to look at the betting book at White's." He passed me a few sips' worth of whisky. "As you can see, Mr. McBrae is doing what he can to help."

Yes, but I couldn't risk thanking him, for he would take that amiss, too. "Indeed," I said, trying for a tone between appreciative and coolly polite, which ended up flat.

"I'll write to let you know what I discover," McBrae said equally flatly.

"How very kind," I said again, "but I shall be leaving town in the morning."

"Ah yes," McBrae said sarcastically, "to avoid your mother." Lord Baffleton's brows drew together, and he glanced from McBrae to me and back again. I didn't blame him; McBrae had just insulted both me and my mother. Not only that, Lord Baffleton probably sees my mother as the perfect aristocrat. She would be devastated by the scandal surrounding my brother's disappearance. How could a dutiful daughter wish to avoid her? *Damn McBrae.*

"Yes, Mr. McBrae, to avoid both my mother and Lady Danby, who insists on finding me a genteel companion straight away," I retorted. "If I have to pander to Mother and her megrims while thinking of polite ways to fend off Lady Danby's poor relations, I shall not only go mad, but I'll make no headway whatsoever in identifying Lord Worsten's murderer."

Heavens! I'd just used the word *mad* in relation to myself without flinching. It only goes to show how furious I was. Lord Baffleton's next words made me even more so.

"Now, now, Lady Rosamund, you must leave the matter in our hands. We shall do our utmost—"

"While I sit at home, putting up with nosy morning callers and burning pastilles? I shall not!" I was sorely tempted to explain about the pregnant maid and her swain, but I clamped my mouth shut. I was done with attempting to gain approval from the irritating Scotsman. Instead, I merely said, "I intend to go to my father."

McBrae sat up at that. "All the way back to Westmoreland?"

"No, he's visiting friends in Hertfordshire, only a few hours from here. They're buried deep in the countryside, discussing hobgoblins and horned gods and such, so I doubt he has heard the ghastly news. He'll be outraged when he learns the Runners were sent after my brother without a shred of evidence except that he left town the same day Worsten was killed."

"And an anonymous letter, as well as a lot of gossip about their quarrel," Lord Baffleton said.

"True," McBrae said, "but one would expect Lord Derwent's reputation to stand for something. He's too starched up to go about stabbing people."

"Gets into fistfights when in his cups," Lord Baffleton said with an apologetic glance at me.

"So do many men, but can you imagine him riding all the way to Highgate whilst intoxicated, accosting Worsten at the side of the road, stabbing him multiple times, and vanishing?" I cried. "It's absurd. In any event, he left town with his mistress the same day, so he can't have done it."

"She won't be considered a reliable witness," McBrae said, "but there must be others who have seen him."

I had to tamp down my ire at this callous dismissal of Miss Concord, who was intelligent, educated, well-intentioned, and more reliable than many men, no matter what everyone would certainly assume. Unfortunately, she'd been seen in London when she was supposedly with Derwent. No one knew she and Miss Evans were one and the same, but it might come out if we weren't very, very careful. It was a good thing we were leaving town.

"In which case, we must find them, but it would be preferable to identify the real culprit as well," I said.

What a relief McBrae hadn't told Lord Baffleton the truth. His lordship is a good sort of man, but I don't think he is made for subterfuge. Judging by his pained expression, he was about to say once again that a delicate lady must not involve herself in such a distasteful matter.

I stood before he could do so. I was tired, and my temper was frayed and getting worse.

Lord Baffleton himself escorted me to the door. McBrae remained where he was.

Chapter Ten

I decided to take two coaches—my father's, which he would need in any event, and my own. A cavalcade has the advantage of looking impressive.

Not only that, Miss Concord and I, in Papa's coach, would have the privacy to discuss how to clear Derwent's name, while Weeping Joan and Ivan, in my coach with the baggage, would be obliged to speak to one another.

The next morning, as we were finishing a quick breakfast, Hamish arrived with a letter from McBrae. My hands trembled slightly as I took it.

Lady Rosamund:

We found a number of wagers of the sort we discussed yesterday. A few of the gentlemen involved were in danger of losing substantial sums if Worsten succeeded in stealing Miss Concord from Derwent. Lord Baffleton has undertaken to have his man of business make a discreet inquiry into the finances of those few.

Worsten was also named in other wagers. Again, Lord Baffleton's man of business will make relevant inquiries.

Kindly convey my regards to Lord Medway.

G. McBrae

What an absolutely useless letter! I don't know why he bothered to send it, unless 1) to show me we were back on an entirely formal basis—which I already knew—and 2) because he'd promised to let me know what he found.

Which he had *not*. He hadn't given me a single name to ponder! "What a waste of paper and ink!"

I began to crumple the letter, but Miss Concord snatched it away and quickly perused it. "It does inform you that he and Lord Baffleton are doing something."

"I learned that yesterday."

"Maybe he's concerned for your safety," she said in her mild way. "Perhaps he feared you would start asking awkward questions and put yourself in danger."

"I can't imagine why I would be in any danger, but surely I would be less so if I were in possession of all the relevant facts. Also, he knows I'm going to my father, where I shall be perfectly safe."

Miss Concord shrugged. "I expect he means well." Before I could grab the letter and tear it to pieces, she folded it neatly. "Shouldn't we be on our way in case some of your morning callers decide to come early?"

"Yes, you're right." I took the letter and stowed it my reticule. I could tear it up later. "Thank you, Hamish. You may go."

He didn't leave. "Och, my lady...."

What now? "Yes, Hamish?"

"Young Gil says I'm to go with you."

"What the *devil*?" I cried.

Miss Concord giggled. "Oh, dear. You *are* upset with him, aren't you?"

"Enraged," I replied with remarkable calm. "I don't usually resort to profanity, except silently to myself." I glowered at Hamish. "And if I refuse to take you?"

He shrugged. "I'll have to hire a horse and follow. Young Gil gave me a tongue-lashing yesterday for leaving here. I'm not obliged to obey him, ye ken, but if it matters that much to him, I'll do it."

Why, if McBrae was done with me, did it matter so bloody much? (This time, the profanity remained unsaid, as it should be.)

And why needn't Hamish obey McBrae? Generally, servants must follow orders. Perhaps it's different in Scotland. They're a rebellious bunch, known in the annals of history as 'that murderous rabble,' so I shouldn't be surprised.

"I'm sure he just wants to protect you," Miss Concord said.

Silently, I ran through more believable reasons, such as 1) he wants Hamish to spy on me, 2) he wants to make sure I really do go to my father, 3) he wants to make sure I don't get in his way, and 4) he simply doesn't want me anywhere near him. Which all amounted to about the same thing, but I wasn't thinking clearly.

As my father would put it (and as a lady shouldn't), I didn't give a hedgehog's arse for what McBrae wanted. On the other hand, Hamish was my only contact with McBrae, who was searching for my brother.

"Very well, you may come with us." I was tempted to relegate him to the second coach with the footman and maid, but he might balk and hire a horse—and besides that, I wanted Ivan and Joan to have some time alone. "You may pose as my courier—not that I've ever needed one, but I must have some excuse for your presence."

Maurice showed two callers into the breakfast room before I had a chance to dismiss Hamish—to do what, I hadn't the slightest notion, for everything was already arranged. Miss Tibbs bustled in, along with, of all people, Lady Baffleton's cousin, Miss Trent. What a pity Miss Concord was there, as she should really stay out of sight, but Maurice wasn't to know that.

Without being asked, Hamish poured coffee for my unwelcome guests, then stood by the sideboard like an attentive footman. Or rather, a spy pretending to be a footman. Like master, like man.

Miss Tibbs brandished another caricature by Corvus. "His latest!" she crowed, and a guilty flush crossed her face. In her fascination with all things scandalous, she'd probably forgotten that I might not relish discussing this particular scandal. "Have you heard from dear Derwent yet?"

I shrugged. "No, but why would I? He's gallivanting with his mistress—not the sort of thing a sister is supposed to know about."

She tittered. "True—although I don't know how you could help it, since the news sheets have it, and now Corvus is making the scandal worse."

I huffed, while wondering what horrid mischief McBrae had wreaked now. "Spare me."

"Oh, but Lady Rosamund, you're in this one!" Miss Trent cried.

"Hardly a surprise," I said languidly. "The man is obsessed."

Hamish helpfully moved dishes out of the way so Miss Tibbs could spread the caricature at the other end of the table.

A crowd of men—unsubtly portrayed as vultures—gazed down on the eyeless corpse of Lord Worsten. "Oh, how horrid!" I cried, appalled. Was this what he'd spent all night etching?

The crowd consisted of many well-known gentlemen, including all three of my so-called suitors. Sir Pinkerton was saying, "One rival the less, a dozen more to go," whilst another gentleman said, "She must be impressive in bed," and yet another tutted, "Not sporting of Derwent, not at all. So what if she's a shrew? He doesn't need her money, and we all do." Mr. Brill hovered with his tongue poking out, and Mr. Charting cringed at the rear, asking, "Who'll get snuffed next?" while Sir Devlin told him, "Don't fret, nephew. Everyone knows you don't stand a chance."

Sadly, this unkind remark attributed to Sir Devlin was entirely accurate. Mr. Charting had no chance with either Miss Concord (fictionally) or with me (in fact).

Meanwhile, Derwent and Miss Concord (not looking at all like the real Miss Concord; I had to give McBrae credit for that) were clutched scandalously together in an open carriage on its way out of town. I couldn't object to that either, for it led credence to our lie about my brother's whereabouts.

Worst of all was his portrait of me, unrealistically pretty as always, blushing and simpering at Lord Cyril Telfrey. How dare he! I *never* simper. And that wasn't all: I was hiding a switch behind my back!

"Dear me," I said. "Does Corvus see Lord Cyril as a rival?"

Miss Tubbs tittered. "For the privilege of being birched, it seems he does."

"One cannot deny that Lord Cyril is an excessively handsome man," Miss Trent said.

He's extremely well-bred," I said snappishly. "A consummate gentleman, and I don't believe he would relish being birched by me or anyone else."

Miss Trent giggled, and Miss Tubbs said wistfully, "Unlike Corvus, who repeatedly begs for it." I have a feeling she would rather like to be the one to do it. Perhaps I should suggest to old Mrs. Phipps to find an eligible *parti* for Miss Tibbs instead of bothering me. I don't mean that Miss Tibbs would necessarily want to birch her husband, but her obsession with scandal (and nakedness in particular) might be satisfied by marital congress.

Or so I assume. I had only begun recently to think of carnal pleasures as potentially...well, pleasant.

I thrust that thought away. For the moment, I couldn't completely oust McBrae from my life, but as soon as Derwent was safe and the real murderer identified, I intended to rid myself of all thoughts of him forever. I didn't *really* want to indulge in carnal activities. In fact, I was relieved at the thought of no longer being tempted, however mildly, to do so.

I glanced at Miss Concord, and all thoughts of my own difficulties flew from my mind. She appeared close to tears. "Oh, my dear Miss Evans," I said. "I'm so sorry if our loose talk offends you. We in London are accustomed to a great deal of impropriety, not to mention downright vulgarity. Corvus is particularly crude."

"Dreadful," Miss Tubbs said, "and the populace wallows in it."

"Yes, indeed," Miss Trent said eagerly. "Crowds gather at the stationers' windows to see his latest efforts."

"I do apologize," Miss Concord said in a suffocated voice, "but although I was warned that society in London is different from the countryside, I truly had no idea. So evil, and those ghastly eye-holes!" She dabbed her lips with a handkerchief. "Do forgive me." Quite a good act, considering she was overset by the horrid implications of the print. How callous of McBrae, for he must have known she would see it.

"There is nothing to forgive," I said and stood. "Well! Thank you for showing me the print, Miss Tubbs—I prefer to be warned when that dastardly artist has insulted me once again—but Miss Evans and I are leaving town this morning. We hope to escape before being obliged to endure a horde of nosy morning callers."

They blinked at me, mouths agape. I daresay they both took offense at my brusque dismissal, but I didn't care. I rang for Maurice to show them out.

As soon as they were gone, I ran over and took Miss Concord in my arms. "I'm so sorry you had to see that. Corvus really does deserve to be birched, and I do not mean that in a titillating way." I glared over her shoulder at Hamish, who had the grace to look abashed.

She sobbed once into the handkerchief, but quickly recovered herself. "It's just—just the thought of all those horrible men discussing me, speculating about my—my performance in bed, as if I really *were* a fallen woman—" She stopped abruptly, and now it was my turn to gape.

"But you are a fallen woman...aren't you?"

"No, I am *not*," she snapped. "I shouldn't have said anything, but that drawing makes me *sick*. What real mistresses must endure from their so-called protectors, being bartered with, bought and sold by lecherous men."

I was still a few sentences previous. "You're not a fallen woman?" I paused. "But...how?" I glanced toward Hamish and lowered my voice. "Perhaps it's best not to discuss it here and now."

"I don't care who knows," she said, and to Hamish, "Feel free to tell Mr. McBrae, if for some reason it seems necessary. He's a true gentleman."

I had ample reason to disagree, but I held my peace.

"Derwent rescued me," she said. "The son of one of my father's rivals tried to abduct me several months ago. He grabbed me on the street where I was shopping with my maid and dragged me towards his coach. I assume he wanted to force my father to permit him to marry me—but Derwent knocked him to the pavement, tossed me up before him on his horse, and galloped away."

"Heavens!" Good gracious—my stuffy brother really was a modern-day version of a knight in shining armor. "But surely... Why didn't he take you home?"

She shrugged. "I expect it was because I was hysterical, and he'd had too much to drink. He brought me to the Kensington house and promised to take care of me, that I would be safe with him. I thought he meant to make me his mistress, and what choice did I have? After such a public fracas, I was ruined anyway. But he never, ever defiled me. He was kind to me, and he apologized that people assumed I was his mistress, but he couldn't do anything to fix that. We became good friends, and—and I miss him so *much*." She hiccupped on a sob.

"You fell in love with him," I said.

"Yes, for how could I not? He is the kindest, best man I have ever known."

This was an entirely new side to my brother. I wondered about his sentiments toward Miss Concord. He was known to spend a great deal of time with her when in town. Once again, the thought occurred that she might be the very wife for him. Her expectations made such a match possible, if not ideal.

"Derwent has been a little distant lately," she said sadly. "I believe he regrets saving me, for what can he do with me now? He can't take a real mistress with me in the way."

"Nonsense. He could hire a house for her elsewhere."

Her lip trembled at that. I could hardly blame her, since she cared for my brother. "That's not the only problem," she said. "Lady Medway wants him to marry."

True. Mother nagged him constantly about the need to secure the succession by wedding one of the vapid ladies she prefers. What a pity he was so hidebound by society's expectations.

"He would have to get rid of me for the sake of his bride. He would not expect the poor girl to take her vows while knowing he still has a mistress." Miss Concord bit her lip. "Oh, I'm sorry! But I don't know how you bore it."

As usual, I couldn't tell the truth about my marriage. "It's commonplace amongst the aristocracy," I said with a nonchalant shrug, "and never concerned me in the least, particularly since my husband's mistress was my dear friend. Derwent's bride would consider his infidelities fair exchange for one day becoming a countess."

"Tsk," Hamish said. "It's gey immoral, that's what it is, and the lot of ye should be ashamed."

Miss Concord gaped at this effrontery, but it wasn't the first time I had encountered Hamish's rigid moral code. It wouldn't do to take it lying down. "Do you read homilies to Mr. McBrae, too?" I demanded.

"Dinna think to judge him, my lady," Hamish said.

"Because that's *your* purview?" I demanded. "You're as bad as my maid, passing judgment on what you do not understand. *She* considers Mr. McBrae to be a rake." I paused, wondering if I elaborated on this theme, it would annoy him enough that he would leave in a dudgeon.

No, most likely we were stuck with him, one way or another. He might prove useful. He might also remain in touch with McBrae and thus enable me to know what was going on.

Or he might stubbornly refuse to give me any information at all. Most likely, I would have to find out everything for myself.

We set out shortly afterward—not as soon as I would have liked, because my peculiarity did its best to delay me. After doing far too much checking, rechecking, and moving things from one hiding place to another and back again (including the letter from Mother to Derwent, which I at last put in my reticule, the logical place to keep it until I could finish reading it), I told myself firmly that such weakness was unbefitting a member of the House of Medway.

Although part of my anxiety was due to concern about Derwent, I knew perfectly well that I was even more upset by losing McBrae's regard. Well! I was *damned* if I would let my sadness affect my every waking moment. In the long run, I assured myself, getting rid of him would be for the best. (Not only that, there was *nothing* foolish about checking to make sure my pistol was still in my reticule.)

It was a typical, blustery autumn day, with alternating sunshine and clouds, but I hardly noticed the passing scenery. My thoughts absorbed me completely, and as had become a habit over the past twenty-four hours or more, I indulged in annoyance at McBrae.

How tedious of me! If you're not bored with it yet, I certainly am, and was then, too. I ordered myself to stop my internal whining and take a detached, objective look at the caricature.

Why would Corvus draw something so hurtful to Miss Concord? He'd been kind to her before, and never in the least disrespectful. He had portrayed her as a flaxen-haired beauty—although perhaps that was intended as a protective gesture; no one who'd seen that would imagine the quiet, ladylike Miss Evans and the hussy in the caricature to be one and the same. He'd mocked me, but he'd done that before. It was nothing but titillation, and irrelevant to the problem at hand.

Very well, then. If he didn't mean to be unkind to Miss Concord, what was he trying to accomplish with that print? 1) To further spread and give credence to our story that Derwent had left town with her, and 2) to suggest that various other men were rivals not for Miss C's favors, but for her hand in marriage.

How unlikely! If it were true, the gossips would have known, and someone—most likely Miss Tibbs—would have told me the instant I arrived in town. My notion of bets placed at White's made far more sense. There were other possibilities, such as 3) to suggest that the murderer might not stop at killing only one rival. How horrid—and rather frightening, except that I didn't believe it for a moment. Lastly, 4) to suggest that some of the men might be conspiring to rid themselves of other rivals.

Completely absurd! He should have stopped at 1). I opened my mouth to ask Hamish if he had any idea what McBrae meant by such nonsense, and stopped myself just in time. Maybe I was as unsuited to subterfuge as Lord Baffleton.

Instead, I asked Miss Concord if any gentlemen (as opposed to merchants) had asked her father for her hand.

"Not that I am aware, but it doesn't seem likely. He would have let me know straight away, as he would far prefer that I marry a gentleman than no one. He must have run out of patience. Ordinarily, he wouldn't encourage a suitor to abduct me."

"Perhaps he misses you and is concerned for your welfare."

"Maybe," she said dubiously. "I've always been a disappointment to him, for he wanted a son."

I know how it feels to be a disappointment. My mother would rather not have a budding madwoman in the family.

"Then what in heaven's name was Corvus thinking, to publish such an absurdity?" I asked. "Even the story about you and Derwent leaving town is a lie."

"Perhaps he heard it and believed it," she said, and again, I realized the precariousness of my position. What if I let something slip in an unguarded moment? Worse, what if Hamish heard me do it? He would never forgive me, and worse, nor would McBrae, believing I had broken my promise on purpose. Henceforth, I must avoid discussing Corvus' caricatures.

We passed the place where Miss Concord had escaped Lord Worsten's coach—an innocent patch of road in the autumn sunshine, with leaves swirling in the breeze. She noticed as well, judging by a tiny shudder.

Which reminded me... "Hamish, did Mr. McBrae tell you anything about where they found Lord Worsten's body?"

"Nay, my lady. North of Highgate is all I ken."

"We'll stop in Highgate to refresh ourselves," I said, "and perhaps you can ask in the inn. Someone is sure to know."

"Now, why would I want to do that?"

"Because I wish you to," I said. "It would appear odd if I were to do so."

"The body's long gone, my lady, and gawking at the site of a murder is a ghoulish thing to do—not proper for a lady."

"That's why I want you to ask. Do you argue like this with Mr. McBrae?"

"Nay, he's no' a lady, so why would I?"

"If you mean to be a hindrance rather than a help, you may get out and find your own transportation," I retorted.

Luckily, it didn't come to that. Just short of Highgate, we came upon a group of men clustered by the ditch at the side of the road.

A horrid fear assailed me. Several carts and a curricle were partially blocking the way. John Coachman would have insisted they move, but I rapped on the roof and called to him to stop.

"Open the door," I told Hamish, urgency suffusing my voice. "Let down the steps. I must see what they're looking at."

Miss Concord moaned. "Oh God, *oh God*, what if it's *Julius*...."

"Stay here, my lady." Hamish opened the door and jumped out, but didn't let down the steps for me—just hastened away.

Miss Concord was so pale I feared she might faint. I couldn't sit there in suspense. I had to get this over with as quickly as possible. I beckoned to my groom to let the steps down.

(If you're wondering why I didn't jump out, as I did when rescuing Miss

Concord, it's because 1) it's unladylike, and 2) I needed a moment or two to collect myself. I could not afford to break down before a crowd of people. Not that I was worried about Corvus caricaturing me—I wasn't—but some other artist might, and it would be in all the broadsheets, too. I must be prepared to maintain my dignity at all costs.)

I took a deep breath and went languidly down the steps, clutching my parasol.

Hamish had elbowed his way into the group of men, but now he hurried back out, hands up to fend me off. "You dinna want to see this, my lady."

Did he even know what my brother looks like? Probably not, which made it all the more imperative that I see for myself. "Why not? What is it?" A woman in a yellow bonnet was retching off to the side. I swept past Hamish and used the parasol to push my way between two men.

"Lady Rosamund!"

Heavens, it was Lord Cyril Telfrey, as calm and handsome as always. What was he doing here?

"You'd best stay back, m'dear," he said, "it's not a pretty sight," but I was already through.

In the ditch lay the body of a man—a large man in a sodden catskin waistcoat, with a familiar red neckerchief at his throat and a knife protruding from his chest.

Chapter Eleven

"Good heavens," I cried, "it's he!" Relief swept over me. I pressed a hand to my heart.

The gawkers turned as one to stare at me.

"He...who, Lady Rosamund?" Lord Cyril asked. "You know him?"

"Not as such, but I saw him only a few days ago, when—" There I was, almost blurting the truth again. "I was on my way down from the north, and a coach and pair were in difficulties at the side of the road. He and another man were trying to calm the horses. He was large and frightfully rude; I suppose that's why I remember him."

I turned to Hamish. "Go reassure Miss Evans that all is well." Surprisingly, he obeyed me.

By now, my coachman had lumbered over and said, "Aye, my lady, that's the man. Didn't want help, and used the sort of language no lady should hear."

"And this is a sight no lady should see," Lord Cyril said. "Come, let me return you to your coach."

"I'm not squeamish," I said, ignoring his proffered arm. I wasn't about to let this opportunity for information pass me by. I gazed innocently at the onlookers: A burly man, with a scrawny one hovering next to him. A severe-looking fellow in fustian. A farmer with a floppy hat and a pitchfork, and a man in a shabby beaver hat, with spectacles, a notebook, and a pinched expression. A few females hovered nearby—a blowsy wench, a crone, and the unfortunate woman who'd been sick to the side.

"Dear me, what a coincidence," I said. "Two murders on this road in only a few days. Is this by any chance the same ditch where they found Lord Worsten?"

Well! That certainly got things moving. A flood of commentary greeted me, from which I gathered that 1) they'd never seen such a thing in all their born days, 2) they weren't impressed by the Bow Street Patrol so far, 3) soon they would all be murdered in their beds, 4) Lord Worsten was found in the ditch near Farmer Hopkins' gate, and 5) it was the brother of that there Lady Rosamund in the printshop windows what killed him, and—

The babble ceased as they suddenly realized who I was. "You're her, the one in them prints!"

"I am indeed," I said, "but please don't believe anything that horrid Corvus fellow draws. He makes it up to torment me."

"Wants you to torment him, more like," said the burly man, and the scrawny one hooted.

"Tsk." Lord Cyril tucked my hand on his arm. "You shouldn't have to listen to such vulgarity." He tried to steer me away.

I frowned up at him. "I'm accustomed, Lord Cyril. The *ton* are just as vulgar, if rather more refined about it." I smiled sweetly at the rustics. "Surely, if he really wanted me to birch his buttocks, he would reveal himself to me, don't you think?"

That garnered assorted chuckles, snorts, and guffaws.

"Instead, he casts aspersions on my character—and by the way, my brother didn't do it."

"Run off with his fancy piece, I hear," the burly fellow said. My, that news had traveled fast...via the news sheets, even to these illiterates? Or via McBrae? I wished I knew what he was doing.

"Precisely," I said. "If you had the choice between bedding down with your fancy piece or stabbing your friend and finding a suitable ditch to drop him in, which would you prefer?"

That got everyone chuckling, except the woman in the yellow hat, who was sobbing into a violet fichu, and the bespectacled man, whose expression was even more pinched than before.

I let Lord Cyril escort me back to the coach. "My dear Lady Rosamund—"

he began.

"It's the best way to handle it," I said. "One must laugh it off. The lower classes enjoy making fun of us, so why deprive them of it?"

"I must say, it's extraordinarily brave of you," he said.

I expect I blushed. It was a rather sweet compliment, if completely undeserved.

"Where are you headed today? Two coaches?" he asked.

I had pondered our plans during the ride. Ostensibly, we were to go immediately to my father—but then I would be out of reach, unable to make any progress in discovering who had murdered Lord Worsten. The rabble might believe my jest (or might not), but the Bow Street Runners would still search for my brother.

In the north this summer, McBrae and I had collaborated to identify a murderer. We divided the labor, so to speak (for labor is a word that should never be applied to a lady, except during childbirth), but this time, I had no idea what McBrae was doing. It would be cowardly of me to retreat to the countryside and do nothing. (In fact, by remaining I would be obeying Mother's maxim about not giving way to fear—not that she would see it that way.) Clearly, I had no choice but to wade right in and try to solve this mystery myself.

"My friend Miss Evans and I are going to visit friends in Hertfordshire," I said, "but we mean to spend a day or two in Barnet first."

"Why Barnet?" he asked, and I had to think fast. Was I acquainted with anyone in Barnet?

Ah. "To visit the sister-in-law of my father's head groom in London and see how her son is doing—he's employed at the Robin and Worm and an excellent young fellow. I shall stay there as a kindly gesture. It's on our way, so why not?"

"It's a decent inn, if less than you are accustomed to. Your condescension will be much appreciated," he said, and I was glad McBrae wasn't there, for he would find this attitude insufferable—which was unfair, for how was Lord Cyril to know how the lower classes see us? Not only that, many of them are truly in awe of their betters and appreciate our small kindnesses (and our sixpences).

"They are good people and merit such gestures," I said. I felt as if I were trying to satisfy two opposing points of view, one of which wasn't even here—except that it was, for Hamish had returned and would no doubt report everything I said and did to his master. (Unless his master didn't care, but my conscience was having quite a wrestle with itself regardless. Apparently, some of McBrae's beliefs weren't going to leave me be, even if he did.)

I needed a reason to stay longer than what little time it took to make a polite call. "Also, to tour the area briefly, looking at properties. I wonder if it might be convenient to have a pied-à-terre a little way out of London, for those times when I have had enough of nosy morning callers."

Lord Cyril grimaced. "I was astonished at the vulgarity of their comments and questions yesterday. One expects better of well-bred individuals."

One should, I suppose, but I no longer did. "Despite his effrontery in seeking Derwent at my house, I preferred the Bow Street Runner, who was only doing his job, to all the acquaintances pretending to commiserate with me whilst reveling in the scandal." I sighed. "The worst are my suitors."

"They should be ashamed of themselves, clustering about you when it can't be six months since Mr. Phipps' unfortunate accident."

"A little less, and if and when I do remarry, I shan't choose any of them."

"A wise decision. You deserve someone who's not after your—" He cleared his throat. "—ah, fortune. I have my own pied-à-terre not far from here, for when I wish to escape the foolish ladies who sigh after me."

"That's the consequence of having a pretty face."

"They know nothing of me. Perhaps I'm a veritable bluebeard."

I laughed. "What a pity you can't ask Corvus to draw you in such a role. Everyone seems to believe his caricatures. That might drive them away."

Chuckling, he offered to show me around Barnet. He handed me back into the coach, bowed politely when I introduced 'Miss Evans,' and strolled to his curricle. All three of the female onlookers watched his every move, the blowsy wench doing her best to insert herself into his line of sight. What a pity McBrae was not there to see this! Poor Lord Cyril deserved a caricature.

The pinched man watched as well, looking more peevish than ever.

Ivan came up, said, "My lady," and flushed a deep red. "Begging your ladyship's pardon, but might we stop at the nearest inn? Joan is in dire need of the necessary."

"It's often so when women are with child," I said. My sisters complained of it, and my friend Cynthia and I had stopped frequently for that very reason on our journey north. "The inn at Highgate isn't far."

Soon we were on our way again. "Hamish says you identified the dead man as one of those who abducted me," Miss Concord said with a hint of reproach.

"Yes and no. I didn't mention you, only that we saw them stopped by the roadside and that he was very rude." Now that I had calmed down—thanks in part to Lord Cyril, whom no one could possibly see as a bluebeard—I told her we were going to spend a night or two in Barnet. "I haven't the faintest notion what Mr. McBrae is doing, but I can't sit idly by while my brother is in danger of arrest. I'll send Ivan and Joan ahead to my father in the morning, with a letter explaining the situation, and meanwhile, I'll pretend I'm looking for a property to purchase in Barnet."

She looked dubious, whilst Hamish was the picture of offense. "Young Gil is doing all he can, and it won't help him if you put yourself in danger."

"Why should I be in any danger?"

"Because now there are two—" He held up two fingers and poked them in my direction. "—dead men."

I wondered if he treated McBrae with such disrespect. "Yes, which I hope will convince the Runners that my brother had nothing to do with the deaths. I understand their reason for suspecting him of murdering Worsten, but why would he stab a coachman?"

"Because the coachman saw him kill Worsten." Hamish put up a hand. "I'm no' saying he did, my lady, but that's what they'll say."

I hadn't thought of that, but I refused to allow it to deter me. "Or the coachman saw someone *else* kill him. I wonder what happened to the groom we saw with Lord Worsten's coach. Perhaps he's the murderer. If the coach was hired, the coachman and groom likely came with it. Where do you suppose it is now?"

"I dinna know, and I dinna care."

"If he returned it to the stable it came from, he would likely be caught. If I were he, I would abandon the coach, take the better horse, and get as far away as possible. Or take both horses, sell one of them, and flee on the other."

"A lady shouldna think like a thief," Hamish said with a reproving frown.

"You're as starchy as my maid," I said. "I like making up stories, and if there's a thief in the story, I have to imagine what he would do."

"Tsk," Hamish said. "This is no' a tale for weans."

Another disrespectful remark for me to ignore. "However, much as I would like to believe the groom was the murderer, it's hard to imagine. He was a smallish man. Would he have been able to overpower that huge coachman? Even Lord Worsten was larger than he and no weakling. And why would he wish to kill either of them? If he'd done it for theft, he wouldn't have left his lordship's card case in his pocket."

"He would likely have taken his clothing, too," Miss Concord said. "It was of good quality and would fetch a worthwhile sum secondhand. Servants often supplement their income by selling their masters' castoffs."

"Exactly," I said. "It's just as Mr. McBrae surmised. Someone else must have killed Lord Worsten—someone who didn't need the card case or his clothing. Someone who perhaps has a substantial sum at stake." I made a decision—a painful one, but needs must. "I must speak with Mr. McBrae about what we saw today, even though it will be uncomfortable for both of us. We should share our information."

"Och, my lady, can ye no' leave it be? Young Gil already knows—" He stopped, guiltily by the look of him.

"Knows what?" I demanded, narrowing my eyes. "About the body we just saw?"

"I didna say that," he protested. "He knows it's likely one of the nobs killed his lordship, and I'll tell him about what we saw today." A pause. "Och." Seemingly he shouldn't have said that, either.

"When will you tell him? Is he staying nearby? In Highgate? Or Barnet, perhaps?" That was a more logical place to seek my brother, as he'd intended to stable Thunder there.

"I dinna know, but he'll find me—and you needna talk to him at all."

Hamish could say what he liked, but I did need to talk to McBrae. I sat back against the squabs and thought about Hamish's blunder. If McBrae already knew about the dead coachman—and Hamish knew he knew—then the only explanation was that McBrae had been there in disguise.

A month or two ago, when McBrae was pretending to be a servant in order to investigate some thefts, he'd disguised himself merely by shifting his facial muscles. I know that sounds odd, but I can't think of a better way to describe it. He told me that if he was properly disguised, even someone who knew him well wouldn't recognize him.

I closed my eyes and thought back to the group of gawkers by the ditch. First, I dismissed the females. McBrae is clever, but not clever enough to become a blowsy wench, and the other two women were far smaller than he.

The burly fellow was too large, and his friend too scrawny. Fustian-clad, too thin; floppy hat, too round-faced; pinched expression under a beaver hat… Hmm. His height certainly matched, and his hair was as dark as McBrae's and a similar length.

On the other hand, perhaps he hadn't been there at all, and Hamish just wished he hadn't revealed that McBrae was nearby—although where else would he be, if he was trying to learn where my brother had gone?

We duly arrived in Highgate, refreshed ourselves with ale and the necessary, and were about to leave again when who should come plodding into the innyard but the man with the pinched expression.

I subjected him to a good, long stare. He caught my eye, tipped his hat, and continued on. Meanwhile, after a covert glance at Mr. Pinched Expression, Hamish began to fiddle with the steps. Ha!

I called, "Fellow, come here!" and when he turned his head, I beckoned imperiously and said, "Yes, you. I wish to speak with you."

Pinched Expression shrugged but shambled toward my coach. His expression said plainly, *What does this madwoman want with me?*—and I hadn't even started talking. If he wasn't McBrae, I was about to supply more fodder for the gossips, or for a caricature indicating that I truly was mad.

For once, I didn't care. I put my chin in the air as he approached. What a pity I couldn't peer closely enough to analyze his face—but to tell the truth, I didn't really wish to. His altered features made me a little ill last time, and this was far worse. I looked down my nose at him and took a chance. "You—" I pointed rudely with my parasol "—are one of the gossip hounds from the news sheets." Would he deny it?

He didn't—but nor did he admit it. "And who might you be?" After a pause, he added "madam," which felt more like an insult than a sign of respect. The voice could be McBrae's, but the accent was that of a somewhat educated Londoner—rather like one would expect Miss Concord's father to be.

Drat—I'd forgotten Miss Concord's presence. She had already climbed into the coach, while I had not, but she would hear every word. I couldn't unmask McBrae here and now. Not that I'd made any promises about it, but I was sure his strange ability to disguise himself was privileged information.

"You know perfectly well that I am Lady Rosamund Phipps. You've been hovering outside my house, questioning the Bow Street Runners."

He looked me up and down with an insolently appraising eye, but I refused to let it disturb me. I couldn't care less what the vulgar think of me, and if this was McBrae, he was doing it on purpose to make me uneasy. We were fencing with one another, for McBrae knew I could unmask him—but in attempting to do so, I might just as easily look like a hysterical fool.

"Mayhap I have," he said at last, with a smirk that didn't sit well on his peevish face. "Bow Street Runners always have the latest news."

"Yes, but in this instance, the news is inaccurate. If I were to tell you the true story, you'd be ahead of everyone—even Corvus."

He spat—how unutterably vulgar. "*That* for Corvus."

I tittered. (I know, I know! You're wondering what came over me, and so did I. Tittering! I'm still appalled. But I was somewhat off balance—and he'd spat *in my presence*.)

By now, I was more or less convinced that he was McBrae—since I had, of course, never seen Pinched Expression outside my house—but I might be wrong. Perhaps he was just an opportunistic sort of man. I couldn't push it any further now.

"Oh, Corvus isn't so bad. He provides amusement, after all." I turned away and added over my shoulder, "If you choose to hear the truth, I'll be at the Robin and Worm in Barnet for a day or so."

"Robin and Worm? It's not suitable for the likes of you, my lady."

Heavens, he sounded almost polite. More important, why did he care where I lodged in Barnet? I climbed into the coach and seated myself next to Miss Concord.

"How kind of you to be concerned for me, but the Robin and Worm is perfectly adequate," I said, hoping this was so. "My coachman doesn't trust his horses to the Red Lion and Green Man." This at least was the truth.

"But the nobs stay at the Red Lion. Your sort." Oh, it was McBrae all right; he'd betrayed his annoyance with me by rolling his r in a very Scottish way before reverting to educated Londoner. "Sir Pink Summat-or-other is expected there by tonight."

Why was Sir Pinkerton coming to Barnet? "How inconvenient, since I left town to get away from my fellow nobs."

"Even the handsome gent you were speaking to? He takes his ale at the Green Man. Surely you'll want to flirt with him again." Pause. "My lady."

Good God. Was McBrae jealous? No, of course not—if he were, he wouldn't encourage me to go where I might find Lord Cyril. Why did he want me to stay with the other so-called nobs? (I loathe being called a nob. Is it an abbreviation for noble, or is there a crude meaning?)

"Perhaps I would enjoy a light flirtation," I said languidly, "but not if I also have to associate with Sir Pinkerton and God knows who else. I shall go to the Robin and Worm."

"And lodge with the Bow Street Runners? Enjoy yourself, my lady." With this parting shot, he marched toward the stables, muttering under his breath.

What an unpleasant choice—between Sir Pinkerton and the Runners. Meanwhile, where was McBrae lodging? Did he fear I would reveal something to the Runners if I stayed at the Robin and Worm? Obviously, I wouldn't do so on purpose, so…inadvertently?

"What a horrid man," Miss Concord said. "I can't believe he actually spat in front of you!"

"Frightfully vulgar," I said. "But what else does one expect from such a fellow?"

"I don't recall seeing him near your house," she said.

"He was extraordinarily furtive," I lied. "I've seen him before, lounging near the area door, hoping to speak to the servants. Well! He doesn't deserve to have an exclusive story from me. Perhaps if he approaches me in Barnet, I'll pretend I've never seen him in my life."

Miss Concord laughed. "That would serve him right."

Hamish glowered but said nothing.

"A pity," I said airily, "because I rather hoped he would serve to muddy the waters further with the Runners. Ah, well. One can only expect so much from that class of person."

Poor Hamish—I was insulting both him and his master, and he couldn't say a word.

A half-hour later, a large bay cantered past us—and who should be riding it but Mr. Pinched Expression! Miss Concord was dozing beside me, so I took a chance and rolled my eyes at Hamish.

He crossed his arms and glared at me in silence, while I continued to wonder what McBrae was trying to conceal from me.

We made it through Barnet to the Robin and Worm, despite ostlers from both the Red Lion and the Green Man emerging in hordes to try to change our horses. Fortunately, both my coachmen were ready with their whips, so we passed without incident.

The Robin and Worm was down a lane, a short distance from the main road, and proved to be a charming half-timbered building with various gables and a large yard. Gillyflowers, asters, and chrysanthemums still bloomed, adding to its rustic charm. It wasn't the sort of place I would ordinarily choose—Pinched Expression McBrae was right about that—but only because I am accustomed to staying at the more modish inns.

A spare man with an uneasy smile hurried out to greet my party. "You do us great honor, my lady." He bowed deeply. Heavens, had McBrae told the landlord to expect me? No—Lord Cyril sauntered out behind him.

"Welcome to Barnet," he said. "I thought to give Bostock here a little warning. He has the best rooms prepared; you may be sure of that."

"So kind," I said, rather surprised. He nodded politely to 'Miss Evans,' who curtsied and then went into the inn, discussing the arrangements with Mr. Bostock. Once again, it occurred to me what an admirable female she is—so helpful and down-to-earth. She will be wasted on my foolish brother.

"I have an unexpected guest of my own," Lord Cyril said. "Young Brill asked to come by for a spot of fishing."

Heavens, how strange. "I didn't know you were particularly friendly with Mr. Brill."

"I'm not, but I can't help but take pity on a fellow who wants a day or two away from his Mama's apron strings."

I made a face. "That's kind of you—but don't tell him I'm here."

"Another of your suitors?"

"So it seems—but I expect it's his mother's doing. She was quite terrifyingly polite to me the other day. I don't think Mr. Brill is short of money…is he?"

"Not that I'm aware, but he's often in the cardroom at his club. However, I believe he's reasonably well off, so perhaps he can afford some losses."

"Then I can't think why he would suddenly show an interest in me—and it's even more unlikely that Mrs. Brill would do so, unless it's to exact some ghastly revenge on my mother. They're sworn enemies."

"You're very well connected," he murmured. "The Brills are an old family, but not of the *haut ton*."

"True, but she is the daughter of a viscount and can boast connections with two dukes." Once again, I hoped McBrae wasn't anywhere about, listening with disgust to this discussion of pedigrees.

"Henry Charting is coming to stay with me as well," he said glumly. "And no, he's not really a friend, for we have little in common. He may already be at my cottage, for all I know. He wrote to me in haste."

"What a strange coincidence! Yet another of my suitors." For coincidence it must be, as they couldn't have known I would be in Barnet as well.

"Is he? He didn't give me any time to refuse, but I probably wouldn't have

126

done so, as it's most likely another attempt to escape supervision—in this case, that of Sir Devlin Curtis. Or perhaps to nurse his chagrin at being deprived of his allowance. I believe he has some money of his own, but not enough to support his sporting lifestyle."

I wrinkled my nose. "One can hardly blame Sir Devlin for trying to mold his nephew. Not that there is anything wrong with sporting pursuits, but Mr. Charting isn't as gentlemanly as one would wish."

"Indeed," Lord Cyril said with feeling.

"Well, it hardly matters," I said. "Perhaps I'll cut my stay short and look about me another time. I hear Sir Pinkerton is stopping tonight in Barnet as well."

"What the devil for?" He grimaced and was swift to apologize. "Beg pardon for my language, but I can't tolerate the man."

Hamish had suddenly decided to make himself useful, and by now, our bags were unloaded, and servants scurried about whilst grooms led the tired horses toward the stables. We were about to enter the inn when a horse galloped into the yard, and who should throw himself off but the Bow Street Runner.

"Aha!" he cried.

I looked about me, wondering what he was aha-ing about. He stalked stiffly up to me and was about to speak when he caught Lord Cyril's glare, halted, and bowed. "Your servant, Lady Rosamund." He nodded at my companion. "Sir."

"Lord Cyril," I said, "Mr. Linehorn is the Bow Street Runner in charge of exonerating my brother."

"Excellent," Lord Cyril said, catching on immediately. "It goes without saying that Lord Derwent is innocent."

"Begging your pardon, my lord, my lady, but there's them that disagrees. I've just come from seeing another murdered corpse."

"That horridly vulgar coachman? Yes, Lord Cyril and I saw his remains a short while ago." I put up my hands as if to fend off a ghastly memory. "He was sufficiently revolting in life; I cannot express how much more so he was in death."

"An entirely unsuitable sight for a delicate lady," Lord Cyril contributed.

"You were acquainted with the victim, my lady?" the Runner demanded.

"I wouldn't put it quite like that." I explained about our encounter with him a few days earlier. "I should know better than to succumb to curiosity, a human failing which I possess in ample measure. A crowd of people were gathered by the ditch, and I couldn't resist. Imagine my dismay when I recognized the corpse."

"Aye—when you realized that your brother had killed yet another innocent man!"

Well! Hamish's prediction had certainly come true.

"What an absurd conclusion you have reached, Mr. Linehorn," I said. "Lord Derwent had no reason to murder a mere coachman, a man who was unknown to him and—if my brief encounter with him is anything to judge by—not an innocent sort of person. If I've ever seen a villain, it was he. Not only that, Lord Derwent left town with his mistress a few days ago. Why in heaven's name would he come to Barnet, when he has various Medway holdings within a reasonable distance to choose from instead?"

"To get rid of the witnesses to his dastardly deeds," Mr. Linehorn said. "If that murder wasn't enough to prove he's here, we've received information that Lord Derwent is holed up in Barnet."

I gasped. "Information from whom?"

"I am not authorized to disclose the source," he said stiffly.

"I daresay it's another anonymous letter," I scoffed, while my mind churned with anxiety. What if the information were true, and if so, why in heaven's name hadn't Julius fled while he had the chance?

"Now that you're here, my lady, I'm even more convinced he's close by," the Runner said. "He's sent to you secretly, asking for aid, hasn't he now? I'm sure of it, just as I was sure you were lying when you swore you didn't know where he had gone."

I managed a languid sigh. "What *is* the world coming to, when the word of an anonymous correspondent is believed rather than that of the daughter of an earl?"

"My good man," Lord Cyril put in, "your responsibilities do not include addressing a lady in such an insulting fashion. I shall have to report you to Bow Street."

The Runner paled a little but stood his ground. "My lord, as an officer of the law, I am obliged to take lies and evasion seriously."

I patted Lord Cyril's arm. "Please don't be unkind to poor Mr. Linehorn. He is only doing his duty." I turned to the Runner. "I wish I knew where to find my brother, but even if he were nearby, he wouldn't ask me for help, particularly not whilst with his doxy. He would summon one of his friends. Not only that, I'm a mere female, likely to blurt out any secrets the instant I hear them."

He snorted. "That won't fadge. In my line of work, we come across plenty of females that know how to keep mum."

"You do? How wonderful! I expect they are the criminal sort of women, but still, what a compliment for the distaff sex. Seemingly some of us *are* capable of holding our tongues. But in this instance, alas, I know nothing of my brother's whereabouts."

He eyed me. "Then why are you here, if I may be so bold as to ask?"

"You are impertinent, Mr. Linehorn, but I suspect that refusal on my part to answer your question will only make you more suspicious. If you must know, I'm on my way to visit friends in Hertfordshire. I intend to spend a day or so here in Barnet. Lord Cyril has kindly offered to show me about. Such a lovely little village; I may buy some property here for a pied-à-terre."

"For a what?"

"A house close to London, yet far enough away that I shan't be plagued by nosy friends and importunate suitors," I said.

"I apologize for Brill and Charting's presence," Lord Cyril said with a grimace. "If I'd known you were trying to escape them, I would have found a way to refuse them houseroom."

"What a pity the Red Lion couldn't refuse to lodge Sir Pinkerton Jones-Worthy," I grumbled.

"Indeed," Lord Cyril said. "We shall simply do our best to avoid him. Now, be off with you, Mr. Linehorn. Lady Rosamund has been most forbearing, but I daresay her patience is wearing thin—as is mine."

The Runner bowed and went away, muttering. Shortly afterward, Lord Cyril took his leave, after making an appointment to drive me about in his curricle the following morning. I went into the inn to inspect our rooms—which were low-pitched but adequate, each with a dressing table, a chair, and a sofa with rather pretty embroidered cushions in each, and a small private parlor between them—and ponder my next move. I was in a fever to visit the stables and question Hanson's nephew about whether Derwent had come this far, and if he really were here—but that would make the Runner even more suspicious. Not only that, there was likely at least one more Runner hereabouts, which meant one must be doubly cautious.

Perhaps I could ask John Coachman or the groom who had accompanied him, or my own coachman and groom. Or young Ivan. Definitely not Hamish. I was gazing out the window onto the quiet lane in front of the inn, trying to decide which of my five servants was best suited to do as I asked without arousing suspicion, when the door of my bedchamber opened, and Pinched Expression marched in.

Chapter Twelve

He shut the door and glared at me, McBrae's angry eyes in a peevish face that wasn't his, and in a low growl said, "Well now, my lady, are you satisfied with what you've just done?"

I'm sure I stood there gaping for at least three seconds before I summoned the wits to say, "How dare you enter my chamber without so much as a by-your-leave?"

"You invited the newsman to speak with you, did you not? But you needn't fear scandal, for Corvus won't caricature this, and I no longer have any designs on your virtue, such as it is." He clamped his mouth shut, as if he suddenly regretted those last words.

I should hope so—for what an insult!—but at the time, I was too shocked to be offended. Before I could get a word out (for I hadn't the least idea what to say; I rather felt like shrieking at him, but my upbringing stood me in good stead), he got on with scolding me.

He lowered his voice to just above a whisper. "You should have stayed home, where you would have been safe. If you couldn't stomach that—" Here he paused, reminding me unpleasantly of an earlier insult in Lord Baffleton's study. "You should have gone straight to your father. You damned well shouldn't have nosed your way in to see that corpse."

"I feared it might be my brother's body!" I cried.

"Hush!" he snarled. "Have you no sense? The Runners—there are two of them here—may be eavesdropping."

I bit my lip and said nothing, determined to remain calm and aloof despite his horrid, unkind behavior. *I am the daughter of an earl*, I reminded myself.

He is a nobody.

"Very well, you wanted to make sure it wasn't Derwent's corpse," he said, softly now. "That's understandable, but why stop in Barnet, and at the Robin and Worm, of all places? Do you *want* your brother to be hanged?"

It took every ounce of control not to slap him. "Must you insult me in every single sentence?"

"Listen to me. The Runners were already nosing about because of an anonymous letter saying Derwent is here, and the fresh corpse convinced them that Derwent is indeed lurking nearby. Now you have confirmed their suspicions."

"How was I supposed to know the Runners were here?" I hissed at him. "Or that there would be another anonymous letter and another murder?"

"You weren't, I'll grant you that."

"How *very* kind of you." I forced myself to glare right back at him, despite feeling queasy at the facial features that weren't really his.

"Why wasn't one murder enough to make you cautious?" he said. "You should have stayed away. You should have gone directly to Lord Medway, as you said you would, instead of trying to take matters into your own hands."

"I might have done so if you had included me in your plans." Actually, this probably wasn't true, but I wasn't about to stop and ponder. "If you had told me what was going on. If you had given me some useful information. Instead, you obliged me to seek it myself! And don't tell me it's unladylike of me to do so, or—" I clenched my fists.

Again, I wanted to scream, but I restrained myself. Not that I cared if he were found in my bedchamber, but...

Actually, perhaps I *should* scream. It would serve him right. He would have to leave the inn in a hurry—but then he would be even less use to me than he was now.

He said nothing, and all at once, I knew. Hope suffused me. "Derwent really *is* here?" I whispered.

His features relaxed, and suddenly he was McBrae again. "I believe so—or at least nearby. His horse, Thunder, is here. The stable hands are close-mouthed about it, unwilling to admit anything, even though I was being

132

myself when I spoke with them, and told them I'm Derwent's friend." He rubbed his forehead as if to erase the peevish lines of the man he'd been playing. "Why do you think I rode up here in such a hurry after seeing you? I had to warn them to disguise the damned horse, so your coachmen and grooms wouldn't give him away the instant they arrived. Now at least they'll have a chance to warn them to keep quiet."

"I'm sorry," I said, "but I wish you had told me."

"How, may I ask, was I supposed to do that?"

I threw up my hands. "Perhaps it was impossible at the time, but if you hadn't stormed out a few days ago, without even allowing me to explain myself—"

His expression turned stone-cold.

"We might have pooled our resources," I continued, but it was clearly so useless that I gave up and sank into a chair, suddenly overwhelmed. I covered my face with my hands, tears seeping unchecked between my fingers.

"I don't wish to discuss this right now," he said, pressing a handkerchief into my hand. "Surely we can deal with personal matters later. For now, I have to make a plan to get rid of the Runners."

I took a deep breath, sniffled hard, and blew my nose. "You may leave if you choose, or you may listen to what I have to say." He didn't move. Staring down at my hands, I said, "I do not find you disgusting in any way, Gilroy McBrae, whether physically or morally." Although he'd come close in his latest guise earlier that day, but I set that down to acting a part. "The problem—the barrier between us—has nothing to do with you. It's because of *me*."

He made a rude noise. "How would you feel, my lady, if you tried to seduce me, and I spurned you with a feeble excuse like that?"

I couldn't imagine trying to seduce anyone, even McBrae. I wouldn't even know how to begin. But I did know how I'd felt the last few days.

"I expect it would hurt like the devil," I blurted. "I expect I would feel utterly bereft. The way you have treated me for the last two days has certainly had that effect on me."

He was silent.

So much for my so-called pride. I had just humiliated and abased myself—I, the daughter of an earl, et cetera—before an inconsequential Scotsman. Surprisingly, I didn't care. In for a penny...

I raised my eyes and said, "If you cannot bear to speak to me anymore, I shall eventually become accustomed. I don't have many true friends, though, so I shall miss you."

"You will?"

"Of course I will," I said crossly. "I realize now that I shall have to explain my—" Heavens, what to call my strange marriage and consequent virginity? "My difficulty to you or suffer the loss of your friendship—and that perhaps I shall lose your friendship regardless."

"Why, for God's sake?" he retorted.

"Because I am not what I seem," I said. "I am trying to gather the courage to tell you, but ..." I was too afraid of saying the wrong thing. I knew, somehow, that another insult now, however unintentional, would drive him away forever. "Please, might this conversation wait until my brother is safe once more?"

He bowed his head and blew out a long breath. "Aye."

I took a deep breath of my own. "You spoke of a plan," I ventured.

"Later," McBrae said shortly. "I have a room here as well. It will appear natural if we encounter one another in the coffee room." He reassumed his pinched face and bowed himself out of my bedchamber, thanking me volubly for the truth, which, he said, would make his reputation as a newsman *extraordinare*. Needless to say, I was looked at askance from then on, not only for speaking to a newsman, but for doing so unchaperoned. No one was openly rude to me—they wouldn't dare, because of my status—but the maids were wide-eyed and the landlord awkward. His daughter, who ruled the inn's kitchen, slammed things about and loudly grumbled about preferring good, honest, common folk as customers rather than the Quality.

I don't care what the lower orders think of me, but I hoped the fact that I had voluntarily spoken with a gossip hound wouldn't reach my mother's ears. She would see it as yet another sign of incipient madness.

Fear of being locked up coupled with distress about McBrae swept over me. I lay down on my bed, which was unexpectedly comfortable for such a mediocre sort of inn. Shivering (although it wasn't cold), I pulled the blankets over myself, closed my eyes, and tried to think what to do next. I couldn't afford to give in to either 1) fear or 2) sorrow whilst my brother's life was at stake. There would be plenty of time later to give unpleasant emotions free rein.

Why in heaven's name would Derwent stay here in Barnet? He must know by now that Worsten was dead. He must have heard that the Runners were after him. Why hadn't he left while he had the chance?

I woke with a headache and a decision. Once again, I would take matters into my own hands. My grooms and coachmen must by now be aware of Thunder's presence in the stables. I was willing to bet that at least some of the grooms belonging to the inn knew the secret of my brother's whereabouts—in particular, Jacky Hansen. I couldn't risk going directly to him, but I could have John Coachman summoned to speak to me, ostensibly to discuss our plans.

If McBrae stormed at me again for doing something which made complete sense, now that I was here, he could (insert expletive, using your imagination, for I refuse to write it) well go to Hades.

That thought was pure bravado on my part, as the last thing I wanted now was to anger him. He was right about not discussing personal matters. We could have settled my next move before he left, if we hadn't become embroiled in emotions.

On the other hand, at least he had more or less agreed to listen to what I had to say. He didn't really want to, though—he'd made that clear. He would rather be rid of me for good.

Fortunately, John Coachman arrived, obliging me to pull myself together.

"You wanted to see us, my lady?" John Coachman asked, and Ivan slipped into the private parlor after him. This was unexpected, but John wouldn't have brought the young man if he hadn't had something important to contribute.

"Yes, about our plans for tomorrow." I motioned to Ivan to shut the door and beckoned them to the middle of the room. I lowered my voice. "We must speak softly, as the Bow Street Runners may be trying to eavesdrop."

"Aye," John said. "You'll be wanting to know about Lord Derwent."

"Yes!" I said, grateful for his instant comprehension. "What have you learned? I know Thunder is here and hope that means my brother is nearby."

"Aye, my lady, Jacky Hanson whispered to me that his lordship was wounded in a fight but is healing nicely."

That certainly explained why he hadn't left in a hurry. "Thank God!" I whispered. "I've been so worried about him."

"Indeed, my lady, so have we all."

"In a fight with whom? Lord Worsten?"

"He had no chance to say more than that, for we don't know who we can trust." He grunted. "There's a wench been lingering at the stables, flirting with the lads. Fortunately, Jacky's no fool. He told the lass to go away, as she was keeping the lads from their work—but she came back just now. A good thing, too."

He motioned to Ivan, whose excitement gleamed in his eyes. "She's the same girl what brought the message to Medway House, my lady," the footman said. "The message what sent his lordship riding away in an almighty hurry that day."

My mind hummed with conjecture. "You're sure?" He nodded. "Thank you, Ivan. That's very helpful."

I dismissed them, asking them to learn where I could find the girl if I wished to speak to her, but not to let her know of my interest. Then I went straight to Miss Concord's room—remembering at the last moment to omit McBrae from my tale, for she didn't know he'd been here in disguise. I relayed the news as if it came directly from John Coachman.

"Julius was wounded?" she whispered, tears springing to her eyes. She set down her stitchery and stood. "How? Where?"

"I don't know anything except that he is healing well. Jacky Hanson, whose uncle is head groom at Medway House, couldn't say more for fear of being overheard, so we don't know with whom he fought."

"I must go to him." Miss Concord stood. "I should be there to nurse him back to health."

"I agree, but until we get rid of the Bow Street Runners—and perhaps also the flirtatious maid from your house—we can't risk it. She may have been sent by your father or your suitor, if they somehow learned that Derwent intended to go in this direction. In fact, you'd best keep to your room, for what if she recognizes you?"

Her brows knit. "Which flirtatious maid?"

"You would know that better than I, wouldn't you?"

"I only have two maids, and I wouldn't call either of them flirtatious," she said. "Doris craves attention, but she's plain and awkward, and the other maid is far too old to dally with young lads."

"This one certainly did. She flirted with Ivan when she delivered the note, and she's been flirting with the stable hands here as well."

"But...how would one of my maids get all the way up here?" It was a good question. "How did Ivan describe her?"

I tried to recall his words. "Pretty, I think. Fair and...ripe as a peach, or something of the sort."

Miss Concord shook her head. "None of my servants fit that description. I hope Ivan's head wasn't turned by the girl, seeing as he is about to marry Joan."

"No, he seems to have disliked her." I pondered. "This means the message didn't come from Kensington after all. It came from someone who knew that Lord Worsten had abducted you—someone who hoped Derwent would follow."

"Someone who hoped he would save me?" she asked. "Perhaps because he would lose a wager if Lord Worsten succeeded."

"It's the only explanation that makes sense. I don't think Derwent's cronies are the chivalrous sort, particularly when it comes to mistresses." I paused. "I learned that Mr. McBrae has a room here. Hopefully, he will return soon. We must discuss this with him."

"If he agrees to speak with you," she said.

Once again, I was obliged to mind what I said. As if it wasn't already difficult enough being acquainted with 1) Gilroy McBrae, the expert in sick-making disguise, and 2) Corvus, the odious caricaturist, I now had to ponder every word.

"We may be at odds, but he's not a fool," I said with an imperious sniff. "He'll listen to useful information." She looked dubious, so I added, "Why wouldn't he? He was rude at Lord Baffleton's, but he did listen—and if necessary, *you* may speak to him instead."

Fortunately, that wasn't necessary. McBrae returned as himself and coolly invited Miss Concord and me for a stroll before dinner. One on each arm, we meandered along the lane.

It was frightfully awkward, at least for me. Surprisingly so, for it is commonplace to walk with one's hand on a gentleman's arm. Perhaps it was the feeling of an invisible barrier between McBrae and me—one which had not existed before. I couldn't take comfort from the strength of his arm under my hand, knowing he would rather I weren't there at all.

Best to get it over with quickly, I decided. The moment we were out of earshot of the inn, I murmured, "My coachman brought me the news that Derwent was wounded in a fight and is recovering nearby."

"Excellent!" he said. "I wonder if he is well enough to be moved."

"Moved to where?" I asked. "We dare not bring him home until we have identified the true culprit."

"An injured man should not be made to travel," Miss Concord whispered. "The jolting might reopen the wound."

"True," McBrae said. "If we can rid ourselves of the Runners for a while, we'll have a chance to assess his condition."

"I don't think the Runners are the only problem." I told him about the flirtatious girl who wasn't from the Kensington house after all.

"Which goes to show the danger of making assumptions," he muttered. "I wonder who sent her to Medway House, and why she's here in Barnet now."

"It must be someone who wagered Lord Worsten wouldn't succeed in abducting Miss Concord," I said, and then clamped my mouth shut on a question. I feared I would lose my temper if he refused to divulge who had made such wagers.

"Sir Pinkerton Jones-Worthy, for one," he said—without me asking!

To play fair, I volunteered some information. "Mr. Brill is also in Barnet, as is Mr. Charting. They are both staying with Lord Cyril Telfrey."

"Ah," McBrae said dourly.

"Ah, what?" I demanded. "Surely Lord Cyril didn't make such a horrid wager!"

"Not that I'm aware," he said stiffly. "However, there are betting books in other clubs to which I don't have access."

"I doubt very much that you will find Lord Cyril did any such thing," I said. "He's a consummate gentleman."

"Perhaps," McBrae said, "but as I said a moment ago, assumptions can be dangerous."

"Lord Cyril is taking me for a drive tomorrow. I'll ask him if he has seen anything pertinent in other betting books. He has the entrée everywhere."

Oh, God—how rude and stupid of me to stress McBrae's lowly status, particularly under the circumstances, but I was perilously close to giving up on him. Not only that, facts are facts. He was a relative nobody, relying upon friendships within the *ton*, whilst Lord Cyril's position in society meant he was accepted virtually everywhere without question.

There was a simmering silence. McBrae blew out a breath. "Lady Rosamund, much as I hope you are correct about Lord Cyril's character—"

Aha. He *was* jealous.

No, impossible. He couldn't be fed up with me and jealous of another man at the same time.

"—It would be unwise to assume that anyone is innocent—particularly those in Barnet at the moment."

I sighed. "Yes, you're right." (Not that I was the least bit suspicious of Lord Cyril, you understand.) "Did Mr. Brill place one of those bets? Or Mr. Charting?"

"Brill didn't, as far as I know."

"And Mr. Charting?"

He sighed. "Yes, I believe so, although not for a large amount—but since being deprived of his allowance, it may seem large to him."

"How about people who may have owed Lord Worsten money?"

"Baffleton has his man of business looking into that. It takes time." A pause. "In the meantime, it behooves us to find out who brought or sent that flirtatious maid here."

"The same person who sent the note to Derwent, I suppose—to try to find out what happened to him—but why would he assume that Derwent is here, unless everyone is getting anonymous letters like the Runners did, or unless he somehow knows that Thunder is here in the stables, or unless...." A ghastly thought occurred.

McBrae completed my thought. "Unless he knows that Derwent is injured and likely couldn't get far."

"A—a witness to the murder, who knows Derwent was a witness, too?" I asked.

"Or the murderer himself," McBrae said. "We must speak to Derwent and learn what he saw."

"I asked John Coachman and my footman to make discreet inquiries," I said.

"Tsk." He shook his head. Drat the man, must he shoot down my every suggestion?

"Why shouldn't they?" I hissed. "She was hovering near the stables, so why wouldn't they flirt a bit, see what they could learn?"

"Because your footman has a pregnant bride-to-be, and John Coachman is too old for such foolishness."

"Oh? I thought everyone suffered from carnal urges until they die—or so you told me, once upon a time." On the day we first met, to be exact—at which time I decided I disliked him. Perhaps my first assessment was correct. "I think they're the perfect choice, neither of them being stupidly vulnerable."

He said through gritted teeth, "I believe that to ensure success, this particular enquiry will require both freedom from entanglements and relative youth."

"Ah. Now I understand." He couldn't have said more clearly that he considered himself free from any sort of entanglement with me. "You're eager to employ your vaunted charm of manner." He actually was an accomplished flirt, as I had learned this summer.

"It comes in useful," he growled, "but obviously not with everyone."

"Will you two stop it?" Miss Concord cried. She lowered her voice again. "You may carp at one another all you want later. For now, a man's life is at stake."

I don't know how McBrae felt at that, but my face flooded with shame. "I beg your pardon, Miss Concord."

"As do I," McBrae said. "We must work together for the safety of all. It's entirely possible that others, apart from Derwent, are in danger. Whoever killed Worsten and that coachman will not hesitate to kill again if he fears exposure."

That sobered me even more. Nobly, I offered an olive branch. "Mr. McBrae, what do you suggest we do?"

He outlined his plan, which was actually rather fun, although Hamish didn't agree when he joined us a minute later—for he was to take the role of decoy.

"What if they arrest me, Young Gil?" he demanded. "I've no mind to be thrown into the lockup."

"They're not fools," McBrae said. "You're obviously not Derwent, and if necessary, John Coachman will threaten them with Lord Medway's wrath."

Hamish muttered something under his breath and glowered at me, which made McBrae chuckle. A swift exchange between them ensued. I understood not a word of it. (Nor, judging by her blank expression, did Miss Concord.) Perhaps they were speaking Gaelic, of which I naturally knew nothing. I bit my tongue on a disparaging remark about heathen languages, because 1) when the Scots speak Scots, which is in many ways similar to English, it's almost unintelligible, so perhaps I was wrong about the Gaelic, and 2) I was determined not to insult McBrae.

(This despite the horrid insults he had tossed my way. Spitting in the presence of a lady! Maligning my reputation, much of which was his fault! But I believe he was as upset as I, in his own way. Either that, or he wanted to show me how it felt when I insulted him, or how very rude he could be if he chose. However, I couldn't afford to be affected by a few insults, what with 1) my brother in mortal danger, and 2) the many, many slights I had dealt McBrae.)

Hamish left us, still scowling, to join the lesser sorts in the taproom and glean what information he could.

"He says you're stubborn and disobedient, my lady," McBrae said with a slight curl of the lip. He wasn't sufficiently in charity with me to smile properly. A pity, as I had become rather fond of his smile.

Well, I would just have to become un-fond. "He is the most pigheaded, disrespectful servant I have ever had the misfortune to deal with," I retorted.

"Aye, he's not entirely a servant, you see. He's some sort of cousin of mine as well."

How unexpected—and strange. "But not a gentleman!"

"We're a sizeable clan. We can't all be gentlemen."

"He says he needn't obey you if he doesn't wish to."

"That's more or less true. I can't sack him, but I can send him home to Scotland. He'd rather be with me, despite despising the English, so usually he does as he's told."

"Are we all so ignorant and proud?" I asked, for his remark of a few days earlier still stung. I sucked in a breath, wishing I had bitten my tongue on that as well.

He just shrugged. "No more so than many Scots, my lady, but there's a long history of mistrust between our two peoples." Which also expressed the current state of our friendship, alas.

We returned to the Robin and Worm, where we took a table in the corner of the coffee room. I am not accustomed to dining amongst my social inferiors in a common inn, but needs must. Our aim was to appear to be plotting the escape of a desperate criminal, so we spoke in low voices and cast furtive glances about from time to time. Mr. Linehorn was nowhere to be seen, but McBrae pointed out his cohort, a short, sturdy fellow who ate alone while pretending to read a book. (Since the coffee room was nowhere well-lit, he could not possibly be doing so.)

The fare, at least, was delicious, if plain—ragout of rabbit with cabbage and carrots, a salad of young greens—the last of the season—and rustic bread. This was followed by coffee, apple dumplings, and a delicious plum cake.

Under the influence of good food and polite conversation, guided by Miss

Concord, some, at least of my anger dissipated. (Although not my chagrin; a member of the House of Medway should not be outshone in the excellence of her manners by the daughter of a Cit.) McBrae seemed abstracted, but although our relationship was strained, it was necessary in the interest of saving my brother. At least we were united in that common goal.

A little before dawn the next morning (after a restless night despite the comfortable bed), I crept down to the coffee room with Ivan and Joan. They were to leave at first light, conveying a letter to my father. John Coachman and the groom were already out and ready to go, the team hitched and impatient.

I wished I knew whether the Bow Street Runners were keeping watch on us. We would foil them either way—whether they set out in pursuit now or later, when they realized one of the Medway coaches had gone—but what fun to put on a little charade!

Ivan loaded the baggage and helped Joan into the coach. They seemed to be getting on well; Joan glowed with happiness and Ivan with pride. They, like John Coachman and the groom, were excited at taking part in a plan to foil the Runners and keep Lord Derwent safe.

The inn was still quiet, save for Hamish creeping down the stairs, dressed rather more smartly than usual. John Coachman drove the team as close as possible to the front door. "Goodspeed, my dear," I said to Hamish, and kissed his cheek in a very sisterly way. He put up with it, climbed quickly into the coach, and they were off.

The remaining grooms planned to be extraordinarily slow in providing horses for the Runners, thus feeding their suspicions. By the time they set off in pursuit, the coach would be miles ahead along the Holyhead Road, on the way to my father. With luck, the Runners would take the Great North Road, which would delay them even more. I didn't see McBrae either on the way down or back up to my bedchamber, but he surely lurked somewhere nearby to see who went in pursuit of the coach.

Miss Concord and I helped each other dress—which was rather fun, as she didn't fuss over me as Mary Jane does—and breakfasted together in our private parlor. Whilst I drove about the town with Lord Cyril, Miss Concord planned to walk to the shops in search of colored silks for her embroidery. McBrae, meanwhile, would attempt to discover more about the flirtatious girl, as well as anyone else who might have been suborned to the murderer's cause.

"What a pity I had to send Ivan in the coach," I said to Miss Concord. "You shouldn't walk unescorted."

"I shall be perfectly fine," she said. "I cannot possibly sit here and gnaw on my fingernails. I'm aching to go to Julius, but since I dare not risk exposing his hiding place, I must be up and doing something else. Not only that, I may happen upon some useful gossip. Shopkeepers are an excellent source of news."

Not in my experience, but that was probably due to my exalted position in society. Most of the time, all I got was bowing, scraping, and 'yes, my lady,' 'no, my lady,' and 'as you please, my lady." The few times when I had ventured out alone, my reception had proven to be far different—annoying in some ways and refreshing in others. Whatever people may commonly believe, there are certain disadvantages to status and fame.

I watched her trip away down the lane with some misgivings and went up to my bedchamber to empty and refill my reticule several times. I didn't even bother to try to stop myself from doing this. No one was there to see and judge me mad, and the ritual of checking things over and over felt almost normal and comfortable compared to everything else that was going on.

I had just finished the seventh time—seven is a lucky sort of number—when Lord Cyril drove up in a natty curricle pulled by a pair of shiny chestnuts. I checked my reticule once more, and then once again. Suddenly, it wasn't ordinary or comforting anymore. "Stupid, stupid!" I berated myself, and hurried downstairs before I had a chance to check it all over again—and who should emerge from the inn like a disapproving brother, but Gilroy McBrae.

Chapter Thirteen

Rat. If I hadn't checked my reticule those last two times, I might have escaped without encountering his scowl. Not that he was scowling in actuality, but I'm sure he was grumpy inside. What a pity I couldn't simply put my nose in the air and ignore him, but Lord Cyril nodded cheerfully. "Good day, McBrae. Didn't expect to see you here. Come, Lady Rosamund, let's be off on our hunting expedition." He handed me up into the curricle, and we were off.

He took a different direction to the one Miss Concord had taken, heading us away from the main road and out into the countryside, where we bowled along past fields, most of which had already been harvested, others not. For the first several minutes, I was occupied with fidgeting with my reticule, feeling the lumps and bumps to assure myself what I knew was in there really *was* in there—without looking as if I were doing so, of course. Finally, I got fed up with myself and asked, "Where are you taking me?"

"Around the outskirts of the village, where there isn't much traffic, but we'll have to go via the main road on our return."

"Isn't it always busy with traffic from London?"

"Yes, but most vehicles pass through. Still, I'm considering selling my cottage and finding peace and quiet elsewhere. Perhaps you'd be better off seeking a pied-à-terre elsewhere, too."

"Yes, indeed," I said with a sigh. "I have no idea why my horrid suitors are here, but it's enough to make me continue to my father immediately."

"But you won't," he said, casting me a sideways glance. "What is your real reason for stopping here, if I may ask?"

Drat. I had expected a pleasant drive through the countryside, and now...

"It has something to do with Derwent's disappearance, I assume."

"Is it so obvious?" I asked, dismayed. Perhaps I truly had done more harm than good by coming here.

"To me, yes," he said. "You are unusually calm and clever for a female, never allowing gossip—or the caricatures of Corvus—to discompose you. The way you turned it all to jest this spring, remaining friendly with Lady Benson, was most admirable. As for your good sense and consideration of the lower orders, despite that corpse—quite astonishing."

"How—kind of you, Lord Cyril," I said, although I wasn't sure whether he approved of my actions vis-à-vis the corpse. Still, such an encomium couldn't but warm my heart. "I am more accustomed to meeting with stern disapproval. The innkeeper and his daughter fear for the reputation of the Robin and Worm, thanks to me."

"I don't suppose it's quite that bad," he said. "There was some gossip in the taproom of the Green Man last night about your private meeting with a vulgar newsman, but I did my best to make light of it."

"Thank you," I said. "He was a dreadful man, but I couldn't think of a better way to get rid of him." I paused, pondering what to reveal. "Before continuing to my father, I hope to glean news of Derwent, perhaps to find out whether he passed through here with Miss Concord and which direction they took. We must find him before the Runners do and perhaps get him out of the country."

"Assuredly—but for a lady of your stature, surely the Robin and Worm is an inferior choice?"

"Yes, but it's a little out of the way, and is known to Derwent because of one of the grooms there —the lad I mentioned yesterday. Therefore, he was likely to choose it for Miss Concord's sake. My brother has always been respectful of her privacy. He would not expect to meet any acquaintances there."

"You have no news of him so far?"

I shook my head, gazing down at my gloved hands for fear the lie would show in my eyes. "Alas, no, but perhaps Mr. McBrae will succeed where I have failed. He can chat with the common people in a way that I cannot."

"That explains his presence. Are you on terms of close friendship with him?" He sounded surprised, and no wonder. McBrae is a gentleman, but far below me in degree.

Fortunately, I had an answer ready, and it wasn't entirely untrue. "No, but he is acquainted with my father, as they share an interest in Scottish folk tales and such." I gave what I hoped passed for a light, charming chuckle. "And whisky. Mr. McBrae's father has invited Papa to visit his estate in Scotland and sample the best there is."

He grinned. "It's certainly a beverage of kings." He paused, knitting his brow. "I agree that we must ensure Derwent's safety, but surely it would be better for all concerned to find out who murdered Worsten."

"Yes, but how?" I cried. "Everyone assumes my brother is the culprit." I decided to risk McBrae's wrath. "I have heard...that there may have been some wagers as to whether Lord Worsten would succeed in stealing Miss Concord from my brother."

Lord Cyril sighed. "A few."

"What if—what if one of those who stood to lose if Worsten succeeded, decided to make sure he did not?"

"Murdered him rather than lose a wager?" Lord Cyril sounded appalled.

"If it were a large wager that he couldn't pay," I said. "I believe murder is often done for material gain—or perhaps to stave off material loss." I took a breath. "Can you tell me who made such wagers?"

"Sir Pinkerton Jones-Worthy did. Unpleasant fellow—a bit of a mushroom, in my opinion, although he's accepted everywhere. Charting wagered as well, but I don't recall how much in either instance."

"Mr. Brill?"

He shrugged. "Not that I'm aware, but I was in bed with the grippe for a few days, so I didn't even know about these wagers until I happened to go to White's and glance through the betting book."

"Perhaps there were other wagers entirely, in which someone stood to lose a great deal to Lord Worsten."

He said nothing, and when I turned to look at him, he appeared to be concentrating on his pair. Why, I had no idea, for they were trotting sedately along an empty country road. He gazed for a while at the fields and hedgerows, coppices, and tracks leading to this farm and that. Leaves were turning on the trees and twirled down in the delicate breeze. Murder and horrid wagers seemed so far away—and yet they were not.

At last, he said, "Perhaps there were other wagers, but surely, Lady Rosamund, you don't suspect any of these men—or other men of our sort—of murder!"

"There are those who believe my brother capable of it!" I retorted hotly. "I don't know what to think—but I do know that the Runners are acting on information received in anonymous letters. Surely these letters must have the air of coming from an educated, well-placed individual. If the letters were badly-written or on cheap paper, would the magistrates have sent Runners to Medway House and my house, and now two men here? I don't believe so."

"One would think they would require more evidence to pursue the son of an earl. However, circumstances are not in Derwent's favor."

I sighed, for this was true. My brother shouldn't let his temper get the better of him. (And nor should I, I reflected; I ripped up at McBrae without even the excuse of intoxication. Not that I have or ever will become addled with drink, I hope you understand.)

"I wish I knew why so many of my suitors are here," I said. "None of them seem to have a convincing reason to kill Worsten. Not only that, if they had committed the murder, surely they would stay far, far away. On the other hand, whoever did it must be nearby, for now, another man is dead."

"We don't know for sure that there is a connection between the two killings," he said.

Actually, I did know, but just in time, I had the good sense to keep that to myself.

We rounded a bend in the road, and he gestured to a house off to the right. "That's my pied-à-terre. It's not much to look at, but it's quiet and cozy, which is all I care about, and there's a pond on the property, which I've had stocked with fish."

Actually, it was a charming brick building with room for quite a number of inhabitants, but compared to the estates of most of the nobility, it was unassuming. And rather cheerful-looking, with a garden sporting the last flowers of summer. "It looks peaceful," I said.

"Often it is," he said, and soon we found ourselves on the busy main road. "Perhaps your suitors are here to compete for your hand, although they should know better than to do so whilst you are in mourning."

"None of them have the slightest chance of winning it," I said tartly. "In any event, how could they have known I would stop here? I only decided on it myself yesterday, after seeing that corpse. I *knew* Derwent hadn't killed that coachman. It had to be someone else."

"Your faith in your brother is admirable, but even if he didn't kill the coachman, it doesn't absolve him of the first murder. Do try to think logically, my dear."

He probably didn't mean it as an insult, but— "Oh!" I cried. "Can that be the girl?"

"I beg your pardon?"

We were almost at the Red Lion. I indicated (circumspectly, as it is vulgar to be obvious about it) a saucy-looking female with blonde curls tumbling from a familiar yellow bonnet, her violet fichu not quite concealing a shockingly low decolletage, and a bevy of ostlers vying for her attention.

"She was amongst those who saw the coachman's body," I said, although I wasn't sure whether that fact had any significance. Lord Cyril still seemed all at sea, so I gave up on good manners and pointed at her. "That woman who's flirting with the ostlers. Could she be the one who's been hovering at the Robin and Worm, making a nuisance of herself?" I hastened to explain. "My coachman was quite incensed about it yesterday, saying she was keeping the young fellows from their work, and—"

I glanced up in alarm at a strangled sound from Lord Cyril. He had grown extremely red in the face, which rather marred his handsomeness, but... Good Lord, he was blushing!

"My dear Lady Rosamund," he began, then stopped, clearly at a loss.

The girl looked up as Lord Cyril's curricle approached. She cocked her head, smiled, and gave him a flirtatious little flutter of the fingers.

Lord Cyril ignored her and drove past. If I hadn't been there, I'm sure he would have sworn under his breath. Or perhaps he was upset precisely because I *was* there.

"Dear me," I said. "Are you acquainted with her?" When he didn't respond, I said, "You needn't be embarrassed, Lord Cyril. I do know that gentlemen consort with women of easy virtue."

"Not I," he said in a growl, "or at least not often, and definitely not indiscriminately."

Ah. "Well, but you're wealthy and good-looking, and she's the sort of girl who flirts with every man who crosses her path. Does she dwell hereabouts?"

After a silence, one bitter word exploded from his mouth. "Temporarily." He paused. "This is an unsavory subject, my lady, and I'd much rather not discuss it."

"Temporarily?" Was she in Barnet for a specific purpose to do with Lord Worsten or my brother? I couldn't imagine Derwent dallying with such a brassy sort of female, but men are incomprehensible. (Poor Miss Concord, if he had indeed done so.) "Temporary in what way? Where is she staying?"

"It's not appropriate subject matter for a lady," he said. "I cannot in good conscience discuss this matter with you."

"For heaven's sake, I shan't become hysterical over a little impropriety."

"I'm aware of that," he said. "You're a courageous lady, and you have borne your burdens well, but I refuse to add to them."

We approached the Robin and Worm. A brilliant but extremely annoying notion assailed me. It wasn't fair, but my brother's life mattered far more than my pride. "But you would be willing to discuss it with another man," I said.

"I imagine so, but—"

"Then you must and shall discuss it with Mr. McBrae."

"Why would I want to do that?"

"Because I'm almost certain her presence here has something to do with...I'm not sure what. Either Lord Worsten's murder, or my brother's disappearance, or the other murder, or...I don't know what, but I *cannot* leave any stone unturned."

Drat, he wore an expression that was all too familiar—as if he feared I were mad. "Please, Lord Cyril, out of kindness to me—for I am quite overwrought and perhaps a little hysterical after all—please, *please* discuss it with Mr. McBrae."

I believe he would have refused, but luckily McBrae was loitering by the door of the Robin and Worm, speaking to the landlord. "Perfect," I said. "There he is." I beckoned, as Lord Cyril pulled his pair to a halt.

"Mr. McBrae, Lord Cyril wishes to speak with you privately on a subject which he cannot discuss with me, because it is far too improper for a delicate lady. I believe it's important, or I wouldn't trespass on your time."

I would have laughed at McBrae's expression—as wary as Lord Cyril's was annoyed—if I hadn't been so anxious, and so sure it was important to learn more about the flirtatious wench.

"Certainly, my lord," McBrae said with a polite bow. "It would be my pleasure." He reached up a hand to help me down from the curricle, whilst an ostler ran up to take the reins.

I turned to Lord Cyril, who had descended as well. "Thank you for a charming drive, my lord. What a shame if you must sell your cottage and find a pied-à-terre elsewhere, given the unpleasant company frequenting Barnet."

"Indeed." Lord Cyril sounded frightfully grumpy, poor man.

McBrae raised his brows. "That bad, is it?"

"Lord Cyril will tell you all about it." I smiled at them both and trod with ladylike languor into the inn—after which I raced upstairs, hoping against hope that McBrae would bring Lord Cyril to his own room for privacy. If they chose to stroll along the lane, as we had done last night, I would—

There wasn't much I could do, except beg McBrae later to tell me what had transpired. I tossed my reticule onto my bed and hastened down the corridor to McBrae's room, which was just past Miss Concord's. I slipped inside, shutting the door as footsteps sounded on the stairs, and crawled under the bed. It was up against a wall, so perhaps if I slid as far back as possible, I could remain unseen.

Ugh! It was dusty under there—a sign that the inn had lazy servants. I sneezed, blew my nose on my skirt—frightful, I know, but my handkerchief was in my reticule—and brushed the dust away.

"Care for a taste of my father's whisky?" McBrae asked as they entered the room. "It's not his finest, but it's close."

"I should be delighted," Lord Cyril said. "Lady Rosamund tells me your father has invited Lord Medway to Scotland to taste the best he has."

"Aye," McBrae said, "and to hear Scottish tales from the folk round about." Next came the sound of whisky being poured, followed by sips and sighs of appreciation.

"If this isn't the best your father has, the finest must be pure ambrosia," Lord Cyril said.

McBrae chuckled. "I'm sure my father would be happy to welcome you at any time." I heard the sound of whisky being poured again. Perhaps McBrae was attempting to relax Lord Cyril—an excellent notion, for although his lordship is always proper, I had never before known him to be grumpy or ill at ease.

"What does Lady Rosamund wish you to discuss with me?" McBrae asked.

"Lady Rosamund is a most estimable lady," Lord Cyril said, "and extraordinarily courageous in the face of gossip and caricature, but there are lines which a gentleman cannot and must not cross in conversation with a lady."

"Understood," McBrae said, and I rolled my eyes, which was completely acceptable since no one could see me. McBrae has crossed a great many lines with me, and crosses even more in his caricatures. Lord Cyril would no doubt shun him if he knew.

"Nor should she concern herself with murder," Lord Cyril said. "She showed great composure when confronted with a corpse yesterday, but it would be preferable for her delicate, feminine nature not to see such a thing."

What nonsense. In the ordinary course of life, women deal with illness and death far more than men.

"I believe she feared the body would be that of her brother," McBrae said. "She was far too worried about him to wait patiently for news."

"Understandable. Nevertheless..." He tsked. "Is it true that you wish to locate Lord Derwent to ensure his safety, and that you also hope to prove his innocence of both murders?"

"Precisely," McBrae said. "I must investigate every avenue, and although Lady Rosamund should avoid direct participation, she is intelligent and often has useful ideas about which path to take."

Gentlemen are so very adept at delivering compliments and insults to us ladies in almost the same breath!

"She asked me about wagers that depended on whether Worsten succeeded in stealing Derwent's mistress," Lord Cyril said, "the assumption being that the possibility of substantial loss might be a motive for murder." His tone was frankly dubious. "Why make a wager if one can't pay?"

"Why indeed," McBrae said, "but it's done all the time, and murder is often an act of desperation. Unfortunately, I haven't learned of any wagers that seem sufficient reason for killing Worsten."

"What wagers I've seen lately are nothing but muck," Lord Cyril said. "I find myself more and more disgusted by my fellow man. It's bad enough betting on mistresses, but bandying Lady Rosamund's name about, wagering on her, is more than I can stand."

"Yes," McBrae said, "they deserve to be thrashed." Heavens! I'm used to my name being bandied about a bit (largely thanks to Corvus' caricatures), but this sounded serious. I would have to insist on an explanation.

"Quite right," Lord Cyril said starchily. My, my, these two were getting along like winking. "What a pity some of them are here in Barnet—the unpleasant company to which Lady Rosamund referred. Sir Pinkerton is vulgar, and young Brill is a bore, but I am thoroughly incensed with Charting."

"He's staying with you as well, I hear."

"Yes, and he had the infernal gall to bring a doxy to my house. Lady Rosamund saw the wench on the village street and immediately demanded to know more about her—something to do with distracting the lads at the Robin and Worm. I fail to understand why Lady Rosamund believes the girl's presence is related to the murders, but she was almost hysterical in her demand that I discuss it with you."

"She fears for her brother's life," McBrae said, "and as I said, I must investigate every avenue. The girl has been seen hovering about the stables here, as well as the Red Lion and Green Man, flirting and asking questions about both the guests and the horses."

"What does that have to do with Derwent?" Lord Cyril sounded exasperated. "Most likely she's a thief, looking for her next victim. Or she's seeking a better protector. Charting, even when he had money, wasn't known for generosity."

For a brief moment—very brief—I felt for the girl, then reminded myself that she was likely in Barnet for far more nefarious reasons.

On the other hand, why had she been so upset by the coachman's corpse? I could understand being sickened, but sobbing afterward did seem a bit much.

"You're probably right, but to calm Lady Rosamund, I'd best find out what I can about the wench," McBrae said.

Calm me? Oh, how *kind* of him. (In case you didn't notice, that was my sarcastic comment to myself on his infernal gall—although perhaps that was unfair of me, and he was actually placating Lord Cyril.)

"Is she a local girl?" McBrae asked. "It seems she was in the area before Charting and the others arrived."

"I'd never seen her before last evening," Lord Cyril said. "Charting cavorted with her half the night. My housekeeper is threatening to leave. She tolerated the occasional couple visiting without me in the past—perhaps she didn't even realize there was any impropriety—but this is too much for her."

After a silence, during which I expect McBrae and I were thinking the same thing, he asked, "You've allowed other gentlemen to use your cottage for private trysts?"

Lord Cyril cleared his throat. Poor man, he sounded so awkward—quite unlike himself. "Occasionally, I've permitted a friend to use my cottage for a few days' privacy with a lady of the respectable sort, a widow, perhaps, who doesn't wish her romantic entanglement to be known, or a mistress of respectable appearance. Definitely no common trollops—but I daresay Charting doesn't know any better. It's damned embarrassing."

"Am I correct in assuming that Lord Worsten was headed for your cottage on the day he met his demise?"

"Yes," Lord Cyril said miserably, "but had I known with whom he intended to dally, I would never have allowed it. Unfortunately, I was in bed with the grippe and hadn't heard the latest gossip, so when he wrote asking to use the cottage, I replied in the affirmative and thought no more of it." He groaned. "And now—and now I feel in some sort responsible, for had I only known...."

"You're not responsible for Worsten's bad behavior," McBrae said. "Nor for his death."

"I wish my conscience would let it go so easily," Lord Cyril said. "In any event, I intend to tell Charting to leave immediately and take the girl with him."

"Don't do that quite yet," McBrae said. "I believe we should let matters develop a little."

"Develop into what?"

"That remains to be seen," McBrae said. "Why are three men, all of whom were involved in the wagers we discussed, suddenly clustered here in Barnet, not far from where both Worsten and a coachmen met their end?"

Which wagers? I asked myself. As far as I knew, only two of the unexpected arrivals in Barnet had wagered about Worsten's chances at stealing Miss Concord. Did he mean the wagers about me—in which Brill, Charting, and Sir Pinkerton had all participated?

"Very well, I'll hold off for the moment," Lord Cyril said, "but I can't see any of them as murderous sorts—just fools and lechers." He sighed heavily. "I wish you luck, McBrae. Lady Rosamund seems to think the same person killed both Worsten and the coachman. I find that hard to believe, unless the coach he drove was Worsten's, but even so, why kill the coachman, where is the coach, and where is the groom who came with it?"

"That's another avenue I'm following," McBrae said.

"Regardless, there is at least one murderer about, perhaps two," Lord Cyril said. "I hope you can persuade Lady Rosamund to continue onward to Lord Medway. She isn't safe here."

"Agreed," McBrae said. "I'll do my best, but her ladyship is stubborn and disobedient. That's a direct quote from my servant, Hamish, who made the arrangements for her journey. He left again this morning and fervently hopes never to be obliged to work for her again."

I ground my teeth. Not only should he have kept that comment to himself, he had just indicated a far closer relationship to me than actually existed. I had perfectly good servants of my own to make arrangements for me.

Lord Cyril laughed, thanked McBrae for the whisky, and the two parted amicably. McBrae waited while Lord Cyril descended the stairs, then shut the door.

"You may come out now, Lady Rosamund," he said.

Chapter Fourteen

Crawling out from under a bed is an undignified procedure at best. If that wasn't bad enough, McBrae burst out laughing at the sight of me.

On the other hand, laughter meant he was smiling. In other words, neither scowling nor giving me that stone-cold stare. "Lord Cyril's not such a bad fellow," he said after his guffaws became chuckles and finally died away.

"He's a very good sort of man," I retorted, brushing dust and cobwebs off my pelisse, "if a little too conventional, but he means well."

"You may be right," he said. "However, we cannot afford to trust anyone at this point."

Ah. Time for the scold. Very well, I would spike his guns by changing the subject. "What are the wagers about me that you both find so unpalatable? Should I demand a caricature in which the men are all suitably punished?"

"No." He clamped his lips shut, all smiles and laughter gone.

"You'd better tell me," I said. "Better than bottling it up inside. You look as if you are about to spew out a great deal of bad language. Perhaps you'll even spit."

"I apologize for that," he said. "I was angry, and it fit the part."

"I forgive you. In fact, I think we should forgive each other for everything and get on with it—but I shall find it almost impossible to do so if you don't tell me what they were saying about me."

He threw up his hands. "It had to do with their reasons for wanting to wed you."

That was a surprise. "My money, of course. My lineage as well." I shrugged, unable to think of anything else.

"If only that were all," he said. "Not only are you wealthy and well-connected, you're attractive and very desirable, barren and therefore unlikely to saddle anyone with a pack of brats, and also conveniently lacking in the moral standards usually—"

One of these days I would tell *him* to beware of assumptions. "I am not lacking in—"

"Standards usually looked for in a wife," he continued relentlessly. "In consequence of which, they assume they'll be able to have their cake and eat it, too."

Innocent though I am, I caught his meaning. I couldn't get a word out.

"Not only that, with more than one mistress. They're placing bets about how many ladies of easy virtue (and which ones) they can squeeze into bed with you at the same time—no common strumpets, of course, all very ladylike. Jolly friends frolicking together."

Heavens, they had extrapolated my friendship with my dead husband's mistress into orgies in which I would willingly participate!

I could have blamed McBrae for this, as his caricatures had made the situation between Albert, Cynthia, and me the subject of widespread speculation, but he wasn't responsible for their disgusting imaginings. Besides, he was already upset, whereas I wasn't—or at least, not much.

I took a breath. "How frightfully sordid, but since there's not the slightest chance that I'll wed any of them, I don't see why you're so perturbed." Actually, furiously angry would have been a more appropriate description, judging by his demeanor, but I hoped to calm him down. (Ha! Who was calming whom?)

"Because they can't see past their revolting fancies," he growled. "They don't see your intelligence, your kindness, your courage and beauty and perseverance and sense of humor and any number of other delightful qualities."

How does one respond to such a compliment? "You're too kind to me," I said at last.

He snorted. "No, I'm telling the truth. I'm not a kind sort of person."

"You have been *extraordinarily* kind to me," I said. "You helped me when I was desperate. You saved my life. You even promised to rescue me again in the future. Do you realize how much that matters to me?"

"At the time, it seemed to disgust you."

"No, it frightened me," I said, "but I can't afford to be frightened anymore."

"Frightened of what? Not of me, surely."

"Afraid of being...exposed for what I really am, but I feel safer with you than with anyone, except maybe my father, but that's a different kind of safety."

For a while, we were silent. I fidgeted. Should I confess *now*? I didn't want to—not yet, not while my brother was missing and a murderer was somewhere nearby. Which was just an excuse, perhaps, but I knew that soon my time would run out. Why not get it over with?

I turned away and went to the window, steeling myself to confess—and Fate came to my rescue.

Miss Concord hobbled toward the inn, one of her feet swathed in bandages. She clung to the arm of a stout lady in a Pomona green gown with too many flounces and a straw hat with violet ribbons. (Why do so many people with no sense of dress choose violet? It goes with so very few other colors. I'm not the least bit interested in clothing, but at least my garments match.)

(Although come to think of it, if I felt free to be entirely myself, I might choose mismatched items just for the fun of it. It would drive Mary Jane to distraction.)

(Poor, dear Mary Jane. What was I to do about her? But that was a matter for later.)

Bostock, the landlord, bustled out, exclaiming, and McBrae went out to assist. I followed, after carefully checking that no one was in the corridor to see me leaving his room, and opened her bedchamber door to prepare for her arrival.

Bostock and McBrae assisted Miss Concord up the stairs, with the newcomer taking up the rear.

By the time they got Miss Concord settled in a chair, it was clear to me that 1) her rescuer was a lady of sorts, or at least well-to-do and respected by the community, 2) Miss Concord was not in any great pain, and moreover, 3) she was in a highly emotional state. McBrae must have been dying of curiosity, but of course he couldn't remain in her room. I felt a shameful little jolt of pleasure at excluding him. Not that I truly intended to do so, but all too often, he tries to keep information from me.

The instant the door was shut behind the men, Miss Concord whispered, "I found him. I saw him!" Tears rolled down her cheeks.

The stout lady introduced herself as Mrs. Pearl. "As you certainly know by now, for you must have seen me taking my constitutional on the lane, and everyone greets me, such a friendly little village is Barnet." She settled Miss Concord into a chair, clucking and soothing. "There, there, Miss Evans," she said softly. "All will be well. I have his lordship safe."

She set Miss Concord's basket, which contained one of her half-boots, on the floor next to the chair.

Miss Concord dabbed at her eyes. "I'm so grateful for all you did for him."

"Think nothing of it." Mrs. Pearl turned to me and confided in low tones, "It was the sweetest thing you ever saw, my lady. They were both limping, she from her turned ankle and he from his wound, but they went straight toward each other as if no one else existed in the world, and he pulled her into his arms, just like in a novel. 'Esme darling,' he said, 'you're safe. *Safe!*' and she said, 'Oh, Julius, I was so worried about you.' '*You* were worried?' he cried. 'I feared for you at the hands of that—that *blackguard*.' So romantic!" She clasped her hands to her Pomona-encased bosom.

This was unexpected. Usually, a lady wouldn't consider the embracing of a mistress a romantic gesture.

"How delightful," I said, feeling my way, "and how marvelous of you to take care of him. Is he well enough to be moved?"

"Not quite yet, my lady. His fever's gone, and he can walk again, but only a few steps, and too much jolting might reopen the wound. Now that he knows his dear lady is safe, he'll stay still and heal better."

His lady. Had my idiot brother finally realized how he truly felt about Miss Concord?

"He was that afraid for her, raving in his sleep, poor boy, and then to learn

160

that he was wanted for murder! What nonsense that is, but he understands that his only chance of recovery is to rest and be patient."

Well! This certainly absolved him of the murder of the coachman—but not of Worsten, alas.

"Never you fear," Mrs. Pearl said. "I've an old house with hiding places aplenty, going back to Restoration times. Those dreadful Runners won't find him, and nor will anyone else. Two murders, and the villain still loose! I hear the Scottish gentleman who's staying here is trying to catch him."

Her eyes glowed with excitement. She had definitely read too many novels.

"Where did you hear that, Mrs. Pearl?" I asked.

"I overheard Jacky telling my groom, but word has got about, the way it always does—although it wasn't I that spread it. I know when to speak and when to keep mum."

I thanked her and tried to phrase my next question in a flattering way. "Are your servants as trustworthy as you?"

She beamed. "Indeed, they are! But just to be sure, I promised them a generous recompense for their silence, and so I told Lord Derwent. He said he would repay me, but I told him that's nonsense, I've plenty of brass and happy to do my share."

"So very kind," I said. She was frightfully vulgar, but she meant well.

"His lordship was that put out to learn that you are here in Barnet, my lady, and even more so today, when he realized the friend with you was Miss Evans." She lowered her voice even more. "Yes, I know she's really Miss Concord—I've read the new sheets—but I adore keeping secrets."

"That's fortunate," I said, "because you're in possession of quite a few."

She chuckled. "Yes, and it's such fun, but I do understand that there's also a lot of danger. Lord Derwent wishes you both to return to London. He fears for your safety."

"So does Mr. McBrae," I said. "I don't understand why. The murderer has no reason to harm either of us."

"Maybe not, my lady, but think about your dear mother. She must be prostrate with shock and desperately in need of you."

Sometimes I wish I were a rude sort of person who says precisely what she thinks. I was about to open my mouth on a modified version of my thoughts—but probably not modified enough—when Miss Concord forestalled me.

"I told him we're first going to Hertfordshire to get Lord Medway's help," she said.

"Yes, but we're not going anywhere until I have spoken to Derwent," I said. "Has he told you anything about what happened to him, Mrs. Pearl?"

She tutted. "He doesn't seem to remember much, poor lamb."

That sounded to me like Derwent being evasive. "If he doesn't wish to go into permanent exile, he must tell us everything he can recall, no matter how irrelevant it may seem. A pity he cannot speak with Mr. McBrae, but I can't think of an excuse for him to visit your house. However, it would be perfectly appropriate for you to invite me and Miss Evans to dine."

Naturally, she was thrilled at the prospect. She would be able to boast about it for years. There is an advantage in being the daughter of an earl, granddaughter of a marquis, and cousin of a duke, and this was an appropriate moment to exploit it.

After a great deal of exclaiming, she left, chuckling and rubbing her hands, and loudly announced to the innkeeper that Lady Rosamund and her friend were coming to dine. The instant I shut the door behind her, Miss Concord said, "What am I to do? He told her we are betrothed!"

"You'll marry him, of course," I said. "Finally, my brother is showing some sense."

"He was only being chivalrous," Miss Concord said. "He knows he must marry a lady of his own degree."

"Nonsense," I said. "You're an heiress, so it will be considered acceptable, and besides that, who cares? You're just what he needs."

"But what about Lady Medway? She'll never agree to it."

"She can go to the devil, for all I care," I said. Miss Concord's pained expression reminded me that she only knew Derwent's version of our mother. "She doesn't have to agree. You're both of age, and if you're worried about my father, don't be. He'll be relieved Julius is untying the apron strings."

"Truly?"

"Yes, of course. You're doing a great service by rescuing poor Julius from the tedious sorts Mother tries to foist onto him." She still looked dubious, but I would pursue that subject later. "Does he truly recall nothing of what happened to him?"

"I don't know. Mrs. Pearl didn't leave us alone for long, and he wanted to know exactly what had happened to me. When I told him you had saved me, he was completely taken aback. He is torn between gratitude to you for saving me and annoyance that he has to be grateful."

"That sounds like him. I can do no right in his eyes."

"I told him how wonderful you are, how kind you've been to me, and how courageous you were to do what is right regardless of what others may say, but Mrs. Pearl had told him about your tête-à-tête with the newsman, so all he could think of was the scandal."

"That's my stiff-rumped brother." The one who wants me locked up. It was kind of her to try to make Derwent see I'm not so very bad, but I doubted it would help much. "What about the scandal surrounding *him* just now? It's ten times worse."

She sighed. "Yes, and he cursed his own bad temper, which started it all. Try to be kind to him. He's not well, and I think he is ashamed of himself but too proud to admit it."

McBrae sidled into the room. He moves far too silently. I mightn't have noticed if I hadn't been eyeing the door. "He's at Mrs. Pearl's, I take it?"

I frowned. "Don't tell me you already knew where he was."

He shifted a shoulder. "No, but it had to be close by, and although Jacky's mother's cottage seemed the most likely, it was also too obvious. Mrs. Pearl lives just down the lane from the inn. She's the widow of a wealthy merchant, and has servants enough to spurn the Runners if necessary—but I gather it wasn't."

"He was at Mrs. Hanson's the first night, but there isn't much room there, and the next day the body of Lord Worsten was found, and rumors began to fly," Miss Concord said. "Jacky felt he would be safer at Mrs. Pearl's, because Lord Derwent has no connection with her, while he does with Jacky, and his horse is in the stables at the Robin and Worm." Her voice caught. "He moved him at dead of night with a raging fever."

"Jacky's a good lad," McBrae said. "How did you find Derwent?"

"I was walking down the lane toward the village and happened to glance at Mrs. Pearl's house—it has such a pretty garden—and who should I see at one of the upper windows but Lord Derwent! In my shock, I tripped, lost my balance, and turned my ankle. I stood and brushed myself off as slowly as I dared, pretending I was hurt worse than I was, while I tried to decide what to do. Then Mrs. Pearl came bustling out with her footman, and between them, they helped me indoors. Mrs. Pearl bound my foot to make it appear that I had sprained it badly."

"Did he say anything of what happened to him?"

She shook her head, and I said, "I invited Miss Concord and myself to dine there tonight. I don't believe it will seem suspicious, for it will be quite a social coup for her. My brother introduced Miss Concord as his betrothed—so she will be able to boast of acquaintance with both the daughter of the incumbent earl and the wife of the future one."

"Felicitations, Miss Concord," McBrae said. "An excellent notion, Lady Rosamund. I hope you can pry some useful information from your brother. Perhaps a request to speak privately with him would be best." His lip curled in the beginnings of a smile. He knew perfectly well I had expected him to protest being excluded. He was ready to trust me to handle this particular matter.

Gratitude, absurd but nevertheless powerfully moving, flooded my breast. "Did you find out any more about the flirtatious maid?" I asked, to cover my confusion.

"So far, she has eluded me—while at the same time, someone else is following me about."

"What?" I cried. "Who?"

"I don't know yet, as I have only caught glimpses of the fellow. I don't know whether he means me harm or is merely reporting my movements to someone else. Everyone seems to know why I'm here in Barnet, so I decided to be frank and open about my enquiries."

"Please be careful," I said. "What if he's the murderer?"

"I don't believe he is, but I expect I can handle him if it comes to a fight." How like a man to be so carefree about the possibility of a vicious attack. "Meanwhile, I shall seek out the visitors to Barnet. They can't all have just happened to come for a visit."

"No, but what is the connection?" I asked. "And don't say it's because they're all my suitors, because that is completely irrelevant."

McBrae shrugged, which made me wonder immediately if perhaps it wasn't—not that I could imagine in what possible way it might be significant. "Unless Mrs. Brill sent her son here to follow me to Papa. When we met in Hatchard's, he did say he wished to speak to him. But that doesn't explain the other two."

"It should be easy enough to worm an explanation from young Brill," he said. "I'll tell him he's wasting his time, shall I?"

"Tell him to stand up to his mother," I said grumpily. "Yes, yes, I know I must learn to stand up to mine."

I ordered tea and a slice of the excellent plum cake we'd had the evening before, and retired to my room to 1) try to rest, 2) try not to worry about McBrae's safety, and 3) try to work out who the murderer might be.

I began a list, which I find is the best way to organize my thoughts. I might have done so much earlier, if I hadn't been distracted by my dispute with McBrae. I was both appalled and ashamed at the effect it had on me, which wouldn't matter so much in everyday life, when there is time for such emotions to pass naturally, but it mattered a great deal when someone's life (perhaps his!) was at stake.

Item 1: Avoid further dispute with. (Yes, it looks like I didn't finish that sentence, but I had good reason. What if someone, such as a nosy servant, peeked in my journal? How mortifying to write my thoughts for anyone to see. I knew what the last word in the sentence should be, which was plenty good enough.)

Item 2: What did that shrug mean? That he knew something about the suitors that I didn't, perhaps. (A definite possibility, which made me want to dispute with him!) On the other hand, perhaps it meant he was as perplexed as I.

Item 3: Instead of thinking of the visitors as my suitors, maybe I should see them as friends of Lord Worsten, nobly banding together to identify the murderer and save his good name. Oh, very well, stop laughing. They're far too selfish and too concerned for their own skins.

Which, in turn, reminded me of Corvus' caricature in which various gentlemen wondered who would be murdered next, whilst I simpered at Lord Cyril. I had never looked at it this way before, but what if my suitors also coveted Miss Concord for their disgusting orgies?

Absurd! None of those idiots would commit murder to a) bed Miss Concord or b) wed me. Lord Cyril would make a far better choice of victim, as his birth matches mine—but he wasn't a suitor. Lord Worsten had never been one of my suitors, either; he had several nephews to ensure the succession and was as averse to marriage as Derwent had been until just lately. (In fact, I sometimes wondered if Derwent persecuted me to placate Mother for not wedding one of the ladies of her choice.)

Therefore, Worsten was killed for another reason entirely. How were we to identify the murderer without knowing his motive?

Item 4: What if one of the visitors was actually the murderer, here to make sure the others didn't identify him? And to ensure McBrae didn't identify him, either. My stomach twisted at the thought—for McBrae was acquainted with all those gentlemen and wouldn't expect them to attack him. I sprang up, intending to go straight to his chamber and warn him—and then I recalled that he'd gone out. Not only that, he had no doubt thought of it himself. Anyone in the vicinity might be the murderer. We knew this because he had killed the coachman (or so one assumed; two murderers seemed unlikely), which in turn reminded me:

Item 5: Where was the groom from Lord Worsten's carriage? Would he be the next to lie dead in a ditch?

Writing all this down got me exactly nowhere, except to worry about McBrae's safety. I loathed feeling so helpless. I have enough of that in everyday life, thanks to the threat of confinement which always hangs over my head—bearably so at the moment, but it's always there in the background, and its fangs and claws show themselves whenever my mother is mentioned.

Dear me! How childish of me to imagine that my fears are like monsters under the bed. I am long past such foolish fancies. What I needed was a useful role to play.

The last time McBrae and I had attempted to identify a murderer, I'd gossiped with the ladies as a way of identifying a likely suspect. This time, all the suspects were gentlemen. It would be dangerous—and highly improper of me—to call on any of them, and I couldn't seek them out in the inn taprooms in the evening. Ladies do not frequent such places. What a pity I couldn't pretend to be a tavern wench and garner gossip that way. It must be fascinating to eavesdrop on the men's conversations. On the other hand, I'm sure tavern wenches suffer a great deal of annoyance and worse.

I dreaded my upcoming conversation with Derwent. He is almost as intolerable as Mother and wouldn't take kindly to his mad little sister questioning him. I was likely to fail utterly this evening. For once, I wished McBrae could take on this particular task.

Mrs. Pearl kept country hours, which meant my humiliation loomed all the sooner. After hiding my notes in my secretaire, then removing them and putting them under the mattress, then pouring water over them so the ink would run and dropping them in the wastebasket, I checked my reticule a full seventeen times.

Furious at myself, I marched down the stairs, intending to wait for Miss Concord in the coffee room, where I wouldn't dare check anything for fear of being seen. Except that after ordering a pot of coffee, I dug through my reticule once again, trying to check it without removing the contents.

"Lose something?"

I started, almost dropping the reticule in my dismay. McBrae stood in the doorway, eyeing me quizzically. He smiled and asked if he might join me.

I waved him to a chair and retorted, "What I'm *losing* is what little composure remains to me." I tugged shut the strings of my reticule. "Did you learn anything yet?"

He shrugged. He was doing too much of that for my taste. "Can you describe the missing groom?"

I pondered. "Shorter than you, wiry, and verging on elderly—at least fifty years old, I would say. Nondescript clothing, and I hardly saw his face. He was too occupied with the horses to spare more than a glance for us."

"That fits the description of the fellow who is following me. We shall see." He beckoned to the waiter for another cup, and silently poured for himself. Softly, after glancing about to be sure no one was near, he said, "Don't let Derwent intimidate you, my lady. You're the stronger and wiser, whilst he is barely beginning to learn to stand up for himself. He is doubtless ashamed of what happened lately—and perhaps humiliated as well."

"You don't understand," I began, and clamped my mouth shut. I knew what his response would be.

"I understand that he treats you as if you are foolish and irresponsible," he said, surprising me. "However, you know that isn't so, so why let it bother you? It's his problem, not yours."

"He could easily make it my problem, if he chose to. He wants me to—" How might I phrase it and not give myself away? "To live quietly in the country where I can't cause any scandals."

McBrae snorted. "That's absurd. Scandals are unavoidable in the countryside, where everyone knows what everyone else is doing."

Not if one is locked up and declared too ill to receive visitors. But I couldn't tell him that.

"In the city, one has more leeway." His lips twitched. "More opportunity to be scandalous undetected."

I glared, and he put up a hand. "Don't fly at me, Lady Rosamund. I am not suggesting anything untoward, or at least not any more than I have already done. It's the wrong moment for that in any event—and judging by what I don't understand in the least, it may never be the right one." For a long moment, he said nothing. I sensed that he was seething inside, and far too willing to be annoyed at me or worse. Finally, he said, "If Derwent proves stubborn and evasive, I suggest you tell him you are questioning him on my behalf."

"I am planning to do so," I grumbled. "It will waste less time, and perhaps I can avoid a barrage of reprimands." I took a deep breath, which proved useless. My indignation demanded release. "But it's so *unfair* that he won't take me seriously. That I have to call on the—the word of a man to gain credibility."

"Yes, it's unfair, but it's the way of the world. We cannot reform it in an afternoon, and—" Miss Concord came into the coffee room, and he rose, smiling at her. "I have a strong feeling Derwent's wife will be instrumental in making a new and better man of him."

I surely hoped so. Miss Concord blushed, and I took a last bracing swallow of coffee and stood. "Good evening, Mr. McBrae. Pray have a care for yourself. Don't forget even for a moment that there's a murderer out there."

"I'll walk you to Mrs. Pearl's," he said. Miss Concord had acquired a stout stick, and she hobbled without much difficulty the hundred yards or so to Mrs. Pearl's house. There McBrae left us in the direction of the main road, after admonishing us to have a manservant escort us back to the inn.

The butler, a cheery individual, showed us into a paneled drawing room with plaster strapwork on the ceiling, an Axminster carpet, and an unfortunate grouping of chintz-covered sofas, chintz-covered chairs, and chintz curtains. "How cozy," I said faintly.

Mrs. Pearl greeted me with a grin. "I do like chintz, my lady, but I think I may have gone a little overboard this time. I'm tired of it already. I think if I'd had only one sofa and a couple of chairs done, it would have been plenty. You'll like my dining room chairs, though—I embroidered the seat covers myself. Now, you sit down, Miss Evans, and put your foot up. Lady Rosamund must go to her brother directly, for it won't do for her to be seen in an upstairs window once the sun goes down and the candles are lit."

"He can't come down to dine with us?" Miss Concord asked, a little forlorn.

"Twouldn't be safe," Mrs. Pearl said. "Upstairs, he's close to a priest's hole and can slip inside if there's any danger. I'm not expecting any, but it won't do to be careless. I understand the Runners were tricked into leaving, but they will most likely return." She directed the butler to show me to his lordship's bedchamber and was still talking as I left the room. "We'll have a comfortable coze, my dear, and then you may slip up and see him for a few moments, too."

The butler led me up a flight of stairs to a room at the back of the house. The rays of the late afternoon sun fell on my brother as he lay asleep in a large four-poster.

I glanced about the room. "Where is the priest's hole Mrs. Pearl spoke of?" I asked.

"Beside the chimney stack." The butler showed me how to turn a boss in the wainscoting and next pull a chain in the fireplace, which then opened a narrow door in the wall. "That's one of them. The other is behind the cupboard."

"How marvelous," I said. "Two in one room! Surely that's unusual."

"I daresay it is, my lady," he said. "There's a dozen all told, some fit for a big man, others just enough for a child. As boys, my brother and I had a deal of fun in them."

"You lived here as a boy?"

"Aye, my lady. My father was secretary to the previous owner, and I belong with the house, you might say. Worked my way up from boot boy to butler and stayed when Mrs. Pearl bought the place." He glanced over at the bed. "Well now, his lordship's awake and in the nick of time. I'll leave you to a happy reunion, shall I?"

I thanked him, trying to look pleased to see my brother, but it was with trepidation bolstered with annoyance that I walked over to the bed. I looked down at his wan and anxious face, and to my horror and dismay, tears filled my eyes.

It seemed that in spite of everything, I loved my brother.

Chapter Fifteen

"For God's sake, Rosie, don't go all weepy," Derwent rasped, dragging himself to a sitting position.

"Very well, I shan't." I wiped my eyes and positioned several pillows behind him. "I'm just relieved to find that you're alive and on the mend."

"Yes, well, it was a close-run thing, I tell you." He stopped, as if he shouldn't have said as much to a delicate female. He cleared his throat and began again. "I owe you a debt of gratitude for rescuing Miss Concord. For taking her in, despite such a course of action being entirely improper. She is—she is very dear to me." He swallowed and added defiantly, "I intend to marry her."

"Good," I said. "She's a lovely girl. I look forward to having her as a sister." He gaped at me. "You do?"

"She's just what you need. She's sweet and kind and well-mannered, and more to the point, she loves you. Mother won't like it, but since Miss Concord is an heiress, she'll have to take it with a good grace, and Papa will be pleased at the prospect of an heir."

"What prospect? If I can't get out of this accusation of murder, I'll have to go into exile. I can't ask that of Miss Concord."

"Fustian! She would happily go with you to the ends of the earth, Julius—but I hope that won't be necessary. Mr. McBrae is doing his best to catch the murderer."

"Yes," he grumbled, "for what it's worth."

"It's worth a great deal," I said, incensed but hastily stopping myself from flying to McBrae's defense. I didn't wish Derwent to know the extent of my friendship with McBrae—particularly as I didn't know the extent of it yet.

"Why should he do anything for me? We've only been acquainted a few weeks."

"True, but both Papa and I have known him for longer, and Papa plans to visit his father, the Laird of Loch Tarlaid, in Scotland."

Derwent grunted, which could mean anything from approval to disdain.

"He has a strong sense of justice, too, but he needs your help."

"My help! In what possible way can I be of use to him or anyone else, stuck in this damned house, barely able to stumble across the room to a priest's hole?"

"By telling us absolutely everything that happened, from the time you received the message that Miss Concord had been abducted, until you arrived in Barnet wounded. Any clue to the murderer's identity, however small, will help."

"It was dark," he muttered. "I was stabbed. I have no idea who he was."

I suppressed a sigh. "That's why we have to start at the beginning. Mr. McBrae believes that if we knew why Worsten was killed, we might also know who did it."

"What possible reason can there be? Worsten was an excellent fellow—until he abducted Esme, that is."

"Abducting other men's mistresses is not *de rigueur*?" I couldn't keep a sarcastic note from my voice.

He scowled. "Of course, it isn't, and that's exactly the sort of subject a lady shouldn't discuss."

"What nonsense," I said. "Ladies can't help but be aware of mistresses, so why should they have to pretend they are not? There was certainly no pretense between Cynthia and me." I put up a hand. "Let's not argue about it. I hear there were several bets made as to whether he would succeed in stealing Miss Concord. Did he perhaps feel obliged to try?"

"No!" he scoffed, but then hesitated as if he'd had an unwelcome thought.

"What?" I demanded.

"Nothing." He pouted, or as close as makes no odds. "We'd had a bout of fisticuffs because of that stupid caricature, but we were both foxed at the time. They all know a drunken brawl means nothing."

I have heard that this is the case with men, which I find incomprehensible. If I had a dispute with one of my female friends—particularly if it came to blows—I would likely be estranged from her for days, if not months. Or forever.

"He could have laughed it off. He could have said he wasn't about to steal a mistress he didn't even want," Derwent said.

"Then why didn't he?" I asked. "Was he upset with you about something else?"

Derwent shrugged. "Perhaps," he muttered, "but what does that have to do with anything?"

"I don't know," I said, struggling for patience. "That's why I'm asking you."

"Why can't McBrae come and speak to me? He wouldn't waste my time with irrelevant questions."

"Because I can come here to dine with Mrs. Pearl without exciting suspicion, but he cannot. Everyone knows that Mr. McBrae's reason for coming to Barnet is to identify the murderer. Someone has been following him about, for what purpose he is so far unsure." Exasperated, I said, "What if it's the murderer? He has already killed two people. Mr. McBrae may be in grave danger, all for trying to help you."

Derwent groaned and clutched his head in his hands. "I won't be able to bear it if yet another man dies because of me. And what about you and Esme? It's not safe here. Not safe for anyone until that fiend is caught."

"Miss Concord and I intend to continue on to Hertfordshire to join Papa, who is staying with the Elderwoods. We'll be perfectly safe there."

He let out a sigh of relief. I had no need to let him know precisely when we would leave Barnet. Perhaps tomorrow...perhaps not. I didn't think I could just leave McBrae here on his own. Absurd, perhaps, but...

However, on with my purpose. I reached into my reticule for pencil and paper. "Tell me everything that happened."

"It's not a pleasant story, Rosie. Not suited to the ears of a lady."

"I'm not an innocent," I said, which was only partly a lie, "and this is an emergency." He didn't respond, so I added, "Stop thinking of yourself and

LADY ROSAMUND AND THE PLAGUE OF SUITORS

consider Miss Concord's situation. What will she do if you are arrested and hanged?" I would find a way to take care of her if that happened, but he didn't need to know that.

He took two shuddering breaths. "I shan't let that happen. As you said a moment ago, we'll leave the country."

"Hopefully so, but think about the effect on the whole family," I went on. "You're not a common criminal, but the heir to an earldom. The scandal will be...cataclysmic." Actually, it already was rather ghastly.

"Don't you think I know that?"

"I'm used to scandal, and Papa will shrug it off, but what about our sisters and their families? Our brother?" Exasperated, I played my best card. "And our poor mother?"

"She can go to Hades," he cried, and let out a harsh, racking sob. "I've done my damnedest, but I'll never be able to please her."

Miss Concord's steps sounded—soft, uneven thumps—and she entered. "Julius, dearest." She hobbled to his side and took his hand. "There, there. All will be well, you'll see. Mr. McBrae is very clever. If anyone can save you, it is he."

Derwent got ahold of himself, while I sat frozen with astonishment. I often wish my mother to Hades, but I thought Derwent adored her. Perhaps he had at one time, but evidently not so much anymore.

Miss Concord sent me an inquiring glance.

"He doesn't want to tell me what happened because it's unsuitable for a lady's ears," I said. "Since in many ways he finds me unladylike, I don't see why he's making such a fuss. Either I am a fragile, delicate lady or I'm not."

She gave a tiny laugh. "You're definitely a lady, but not at all delicate, fortunately for me. I might have been dead by now if not for you. I'm not even a lady, but I'm far more fragile."

I was tempted to disagree—she wasn't the least bit fragile—but I held my tongue.

"You *are* a lady." Derwent raised her hand to his lips. "And you will be my wife and a countess someday." He let out a long sigh. "You'd best leave, my darling. I must overcome my revulsion and speak to Rosie about what happened, but I refuse to sully your ears."

I suppressed a snort. Miss Concord limped to the door. "Thank you, Julius. I'll come see you again afterwards, shall I?" She left.

"Isn't she wonderful?" he said.

I nodded. "She is perfect for you. Now, let's get this over with before Mrs. Pearl decides to butt in."

He grimaced. "There's not much to tell. One of the footmen brought me a note saying Worsten had abducted Esme, and I left immediately in pursuit."

"Who was the note from?" I asked.

"It wasn't signed. An educated man, judging by the well-formed hand and clarity of expression. He said we were not well acquainted, and that he did not like to interfere in matters that were none of his concern, but at the same time felt it to be his duty to let me know that Lord Worsten had just abducted Miss Concord by force from my Kensington house. That he did not approve of such behavior and hoped I would do my best to retrieve her."

Another anonymous letter from an educated man! Or rather, that was the first, followed by one written to the magistrates at Bow Street accusing Derwent of murder, and another saying Derwent was in Barnet.

I didn't mention any of this to my brother. I was beginning to have a disturbing inkling of what was going on, but I would have to think it through first.

"We know who delivered it to Medway House—a young woman who is now here in Barnet, flirting with every male in sight," I said. "We think she was sent by someone else to gain information about your whereabouts."

"Why? Whoever advised me to pursue Worsten must assume that I did just that—and killed him."

"Perhaps he cares about your welfare," I suggested, although I was beginning to believe just the opposite. "However, since he said you were not well acquainted, it seems unlikely he would go to such lengths. What happened next?"

"I rode in this direction, asking everyone I encountered, as well as at every inn, if they had seen a fleeing couple. Or a gentleman in unusual haste. Or a lady being constrained to accompany him."

Heavens! He couldn't have done a better job of spreading scandal if he'd planned it. "No wonder no one believed my story that you had left town with Miss Concord, after learning that a suitor of her father's choice planned to abduct her the following day."

He grunted. "Apparently, the Kensington servants are all traitors except the butler, who was conveniently out of the way. Esme should have told me."

"She wanted to spare you worry," I said. "Now, what happened next?"

"Darkness fell, and I hadn't found them yet. I was determined to pursue them all night if I had to, but then I heard an altercation off to the side of the road. There was a coach, and a groom lighting the lantern, and then I saw Worsten. He was having words with a big fellow. He shouted, 'You lost her?' and the big fellow, likely the coachman, was frightfully rude to him in return."

"He was rude to my coachman, too, when he offered help."

"He made the usual excuses—it wasn't his fault and so on, saying she must have escaped while they were trying to get the coach wheel back onto the road, and they didn't know where she'd gone. And then Worsten, damn him, said to forget the wench, as she could be anywhere, and ordered them to return him to town." He clenched his fists. "Meanwhile, Esme could have been all by herself in the dark, the prey of any ruffian who happened along!"

"So you attacked him."

"I wanted to kill him—not to say I would have, though. I wasn't thinking clearly, to tell the truth, but I didn't mean to do more than land a few good punches, because I had to go find Esme."

"Naturally," I said. "Then what happened?"

"We fought, of course, and he was as bad as the coachman, saying it wasn't his fault either, that I'd driven him to it by telling everyone a damnable lie, trying to force him to—" He stopped short. "Oh, (excrement)!"

"To do what?" I demanded. Something he didn't want me to know. "Tell me, Julius."

"It's nothing. Nothing at all." My, was he anxious! Nothing but extreme uneasiness would make him use such vulgar language in the company of a lady. "At least nothing relevant to the case at hand," he added.

"Tell me," I repeated. I can't say I had a premonition about exactly what he was hiding, but I had a strong feeling that 1) it mattered very much, and 2) that it had to do with me. "Or I shall bring Mr. McBrae here to choke it out of you, and your safety be damned."

"Rosie! Profanity is unbefitting a lady."

"You can't curse Mother in one breath and scold like her in the next. Just tell me, Julius!"

He hunched an offended shoulder. "Oh, very well. I'd had enough of stupid fellows coming to me for permission to marry you—far too early for one thing, as you are still in mourning, and for another, none of them were acceptable, so I told them Worsten had already been approved, but that nothing would be announced until your period of mourning was over."

I stifled a shriek. "How dare you! Approved by whom?"

"I didn't exactly specify, although when Worsten found out, he accused me of colluding with his mother and ours to force him into marrying you. He already has heirs, so he doesn't—didn't—mean to get leg-shackled, no matter how conveniently lax you may be."

I did not intend to get into a discussion of my behavior. "Not only have you no right to approve or disapprove my choice of spouse—if I ever choose to wed again, which is unlikely—but how horrid of you to do that to your friend."

"I was trying to protect you, Rosie," he said. "You must wed again for your own safety, and Worsten wasn't such a bad fellow. He would have treated you decently enough, as long as you stayed out of trouble."

Out of trouble—in other words, safely at home doing stitchery. Being an obedient little madwoman. Had he planned to spring the fact of my madness on Worsten immediately following the wedding ceremony, just as he'd done with Albert Phipps?

Julius went blithely on. "He wasn't one of the idiots who—"

"Who wagered about how many strumpets they could fit into bed with me? Yes, I heard about that. I suppose I should be grateful you didn't promise me to one of them." I glared, as sudden understanding dawned. "Now I know why you tried to marry me off. It was to please Mother, to make up for your decision to marry Esme."

He shrank against the pillows, pouting. "Perhaps, but something has to be done about you, Rosie. It was bad enough when you were married to Phipps, but now, without a controlling hand, who knows what folly you'll commit?"

"Such as rescuing Miss Concord?" I shot back, and took a breath. I wasn't here to dispute with my brother. "You fought with Lord Worsten. Then what?"

I think Derwent was relieved to avoid further discussion of my flaws. Why waste time arguing with a madwoman? "I don't rightly know," he said. "Someone else arrived, for one of the fellows said, 'It's the guv'nor!' and started whining about how it wasn't their fault they hadn't made it all the way to Barnet. The new man cut him off and told them to take the coach and go. 'You did well, but I'll handle these fools now,' he said, and 'You'll get paid, never fear.' They drove off, and without the lantern, it was pitch dark. I had a grip on Worsten, and I was about to land one last punch when he made a queer groaning sound, and suddenly he was gone."

"Gone where?"

"He fell into the ditch, but I didn't know it at the time. Suddenly my leg hurt like the devil, and I found myself fighting off a man with a knife. Somehow, I managed to stun him. I ran away, which may seem cowardly, but I was wounded, and I couldn't defeat the fellow if I was bleeding to death."

"It wasn't cowardly," I said. "You were unarmed and would shortly have been helpless."

"I staunched the blood with my cravat and tied it as tight as I could, listening all the while in case the man had followed me, but I heard nothing until the sound of hoofbeats told me he was leaving. I was most of the way back to the road when Thunder returned. He must have spooked during the fray."

His chest rose and fell. After a long moment, when his thoughts seemed to be elsewhere, he continued.

"Fortunately, I keep a tinder box in my saddlebags. I struck a light and...and found Worsten. He was lying in the ditch where he had fallen—but that fellow must have jumped in and finished him off after I escaped. There were a dozen stab wounds in his chest."

"And one in his back," I said. "Or so Mr. McBrae told me, for he rode up to see the body."

"That one must be what felled him in the first place," Derwent said. "It was horrible, but there was nothing I could do for him, and I was well-nigh fainting by then, so I dragged myself onto Thunder and rode to Jacky's cottage. Luckily, I asked him to doctor me himself and tell no one I was there."

"You did admirably, Derwent—and you were wise to keep your presence a secret. Otherwise, you would be in Newgate by now."

He reddened a little, as if gratified by my approval. This was completely unprecedented—and unlikely ever to recur, so I made a point of enjoying it.

"I knew something was amiss," he said. "They weren't ordinary ruffians. The coachman and groom had been hired by Worsten, but the other fellow knew about it, for he promised to pay them."

"And the coachman recognized him," I murmured. "Called him his gov'nor." What if the groom was following McBrae at the murderer's behest?

I was tempted to run and find McBrae, but that would be foolish. It was already evening, and I didn't know where he had gone. *He'll be fine*, I told myself. *He's bigger and younger than the groom.* Fretting wouldn't bring him back. My role was to learn what I could from my brother.

"And then he killed Worsten in such a brutal fashion!" Derwent said. "He must have had a dashed good reason to hate him."

Or to hate you, I thought, but again, I didn't say so. Time was running out. "Was there anything familiar about the murderer?"

"It was pitch dark, Rosie. I never saw him properly, even when he was talking to the servants. The lantern didn't give much light, and the brim of his hat covered his face—not that I got more than a glimpse, because I was occupied with Worsten. I had the impression he was a little taller than I, but that's all."

"What about his voice? Was he a gentleman? Was there anything distinctive about his speech, anything you would recognize if you heard it again?"

"He spoke like a gentleman. His voice didn't strike me as unusual—in fact, it was quite pleasant—but I heard only the few words he spoke to the servants." He sank against the pillows. "I'm too tired for any more questions. Please send Esme to me."

The meal was plentiful and well-prepared, and Mrs. Pearl was no more tedious than many of my London acquaintances. In fact, she was rather better, for her kind heart shone through everything she said.

We were just saying our goodbyes when there came a sharp rap on the door. Panic surged in my breast, and Miss Concord paled.

"Never you fear," Mrs. Pearl said and sent her footman to see who was at the door. At the sound of Lord Cyril's voice, I let out a breath of relief.

Mrs. Pearl had never been introduced to Lord Cyril, being so far below him socially, but of course she had heard of him. She was thrilled to number the son of a marquis among her acquaintances. She tried to herd us all back into the drawing room for another pot of tea, but Lord Cyril politely declined.

"I have a message for Mr. McBrae," he said. "Bostock at the Robin and Worm said he'd come up here with you." I sensed his anxiety, but he was far too well-bred to show it.

"Yes, but only because it was on his way into the village," I said. "I'm not sure exactly where he went."

"I'll walk you to the inn and wait for him," Lord Cyril said, and we once more made our adieux. He was too polite to comment on my condescension in dining with such a woman, or perhaps he was distracted by his own concerns. More than halfway to the inn, he said, "Perhaps I shouldn't wait, but rather try the Red Lion or the Green Man. I'm concerned for his safety."

"What is the message?" I asked, and when he hesitated, I assured him that Miss Evans was in my confidence. What a pity I couldn't reveal who she really was, but I was trying my best to heed McBrae's concerns. I didn't for a moment suspect Lord Cyril, and in any case, he was hardly likely to harm two ladies in the short distance between Mrs. Pearl's and the inn.

"I received a most unexpected letter this morning," he said, "and should have received it earlier, but my correspondence was only just brought to me from town. It's a plea for help from—"

A shot rang out, cutting him off. From down the road came a shouted curse—it was McBrae! "Gil!" I cried, and picked up my skirts and ran.

Chapter Sixteen

"Lady Rosamund, wait!" Lord Cyril called, but I was halfway to McBrae as he staggered out of the hedgerow, clutching his left arm.

"Winged, by God," he muttered. "And I didn't get a glimpse of the bloody fellow."

I fetched up beside him. "You're bleeding. Come into the inn."

"It's just a scratch," he said. "What the devil are you doing out here? Have you no sense?"

"You were shot at!" I retorted. "Did you expect me to stroll blithely past?"

By this time, Lord Cyril and Miss Concord had caught up. Lord Cyril hustled us into the inn, calling for Bostock. A number of men crowded out of the taproom to see what was going on, but Bostock ordered them back and ushered us into the empty coffee room. Lord Cyril helped McBrae out of his coat and pulled out a bench for him to sit on.

(For once, Lord Cyril didn't let propriety rule. It is improper for a gentleman to leave his chamber without a coat. I'm not certain why, for laborers are often seen in their shirtsleeves, and no lady faints from the impropriety of it. In fact, I believe many of us enjoy the sight of a brawny man. Women of the lower orders plainly do.)

But I digress, perhaps because I am loath to admit how shaken I was. McBrae didn't look at all well. "Please fetch one of my clean shifts," I told Miss Concord, my voice wobbling unbecomingly. "It will do to bind the wound."

Lord Cyril ripped the sleeve open to expose the shallow furrow the bullet had made in McBrae's arm. It was far more than a scratch, but at least it wasn't bleeding much anymore. "Bring me some spirits," Lord Cyril ordered the innkeeper. "I don't think there's any danger of infection, but may as well be careful." McBrae clenched his teeth as Lord Cyril trickled brandy over the wound, then dabbed the liquid away.

By now, Miss Concord had returned with not only the shift but her scissors as well. Efficiently, she cut the shift into strips, and Lord Cyril bound the wound tightly.

You may have noticed that I did almost nothing at all.

"Stop looking at me like that," McBrae scolded me. "It's nothing. The devil of it is I made another foolish assumption. If anything, I was expecting to be attacked with a knife, not a gun."

"You expected an attack?" Lord Cyril asked.

McBrae shrugged, and winced. "It was a possibility. Everyone knows I'm here to identify the murderer, so it's to his advantage to get rid of me."

"Then why didn't you keep your purpose here a secret?" Anger gave me control of my voice. "Was it you that spread the word?"

"Let's say I didn't try to stop it. I hoped to flush him out, thinking that if he attacked me, I might recognize him." He shook his head. "I didn't see him at all. I should have heeded the groom's advice." He paused to down a swallow of brandy. "That's who was following me today. I waited for an opportunity for private speech and grabbed him, poor fellow. He swears he and Ribbs—that's the coachman—had nothing to do with Worsten's murder, that he wasn't too keen on abduction either, but the money was good—although they didn't get the rest they were promised. No surprise, he said, as it was a gentleman that hired them."

Lord Cyril bristled, as if he were about to object to this slur against gentlemen as a whole, while Bostock, the innkeeper, looked as if he agreed with the slur, but couldn't risk saying so.

"Who was this so-called gentleman?" I asked, to placate both sides.

"The groom said he doesn't know—never saw him, and Ribbs, the coachman, said it was more than his life was worth to tell. Ribbs went to meet the fellow and collect the balance owed them, but he never came back."

"Murdered only a few miles from my inn," Bostock said. "I don't know what the world is coming to."

"What was the groom's advice?" I asked.

"To beware, because anyone who could overpower Ribbs was mighty dangerous. Ribbs was a former bruiser, just as we surmised." McBrae slumped against the back of the chair. "But anyone can be fooled by trickery. I should have been more careful. I should have kept out of sight."

"It's late," I said. "You'd best go up to bed now and get some sleep."

He eyed me, said, "Very well," and stood. There was something aggressive in his manner, and immediately, my suspicions were aroused. He didn't intend to rest.

Meanwhile, this discussion should be continued—in private. "Bring ale to Mr. McBrae's room," I told the landlord. Bostock left, muttering under his breath.

"Lord Cyril, please come along as well," I said. "Mr. McBrae's man isn't here, and he may need assistance preparing for bed."

McBrae's glance shot daggers. "I do not need—"

"Lord Cyril has information for you," I whispered, and he subsided. We all trooped upstairs, and when McBrae tried to bid me and Miss Concord good night, I told him not to be absurd. "I refuse to be dismissed. Miss Evans and I have the right to know what is going on."

(Another dangerous moment, in which I remembered to use her assumed name. Perhaps I was getting better at subterfuge.)

Miss Concord cast me an uneasy glance. "I'm sure the gentlemen will let us know...."

"Nonsense. They have every intention of doing something dangerous, or at least Mr. McBrae does." Not only that, I had to tell McBrae what Julius had said—but not, I realized with annoyance, until Lord Cyril left. (Despite how entirely certain I was of Lord Cyril's innocence, may I remind you. I suppose I wanted to avoid further annoying McBrae.)

"Very well," Miss Concord said. "We'll chaperone each other. Ah, here comes Mr. Bostock with the ale." She took the tray from him and carried it into McBrae's bedchamber.

Fortunately, there were both a chair and a bench in the room, for I'm sure McBrae would have insisted on standing whilst we ladies seated ourselves. As it was, I had to insist that he sit down.

"Why was the groom following you about the village?" I asked. "How do you know he was telling the truth, and not luring you into the path of the murderer's gun?"

"I don't," McBrae said, "except that he is clearly a frightened man who wants to make sure he's not implicated in the murders. He's from Islington and wants to stay there, not spend the rest of his life on the run. He says Worsten got a knock on the head when their wheel went off the road, and didn't wake up until dusk. He was berating them when Lord Derwent arrived. The two of them traded angry words and then came to blows. By then, it was dark, and the groom had just lit the lantern when the gent who hired them arrived and told the coachman and groom to take the coach and leave, that he would pay them later. Meanwhile, he would deal with Worsten and Derwent."

The groom's story agreed in essence with what my brother had told me, but again, I couldn't say so, despite my confidence in Lord Cyril's innocence. "Are we to assume, then, that the gentleman who hired them killed Worsten?"

"Unless Lord Derwent did," McBrae said, "although in that case, why didn't the other gentleman prevent it?"

"Lord Derwent would never do any such thing!" Miss Concord blurted.

"My brother couldn't have done it," I added, giving McBrae a glare to say I thought better of him. "He doesn't carry a knife. He fights with his fists. He would never stab anyone. In any event, wouldn't the other gentleman have interfered? No one has found *his* corpse."

"I agree. Lord Derwent is an honorable man." Lord Cyril cleared his throat. "I believe the gentleman who hired the coach must be the murderer. That explanation hadn't occurred to me until this very moment, but now it makes an unpleasant sort of sense." He removed a folded paper from his pocket. "I received this letter this morning. I should have had it earlier, but my secretary—not the most efficient of fellows, but he's a good sort—forgot it and didn't send it on until today. It's from someone purporting to write on Derwent's behalf, asking me to help him."

Miss Concord muffled a squeak of surprise. I snatched the letter, not just because I wanted to see it, but because it would embarrass Lord Cyril to have to choose between me (delicate female) and McBrae (to whom he wished to show it). It was written in an untidy hand. I shall not attempt to reproduce the many errors which revealed the writer to be more or less illiterate, but here is the gist of it: *Lord Cyril, I am in Barnet, wounded and in desperate need of help. My nurse is writing this for me. I must flee the country before the Runners catch me. In the name of old friendship, please come to my aid. I shall reward you with regard to the personal matter we discussed not long ago.*

"What personal matter did you discuss?" I asked, passing the missive to McBrae.

"I haven't the slightest notion what he means," Lord Cyril said. "I've hardly seen him lately, beyond the occasional nod."

"You're not on terms of 'old friendship' with Derwent, are you?"

He shook his head. "We're acquainted, of course, but I'm closer to your other brother, as we were in the same year at Eton. Why would Derwent write to me?"

I was almost certain he hadn't done so. He hadn't mentioned it, and in any event, he wasn't too ill to write it himself. "He wouldn't," I said firmly. "Someone else must have written it." I turned the paper over, but found no postmark. "It must have been written and hand-delivered soon after the corpse became common knowledge, perhaps before the hunt for Derwent began."

"Perhaps written—or at least dictated—by the same person who wrote to Bow Street, claiming to have witnessed the murder," McBrae said. "Someone who wishes Derwent to take the blame."

"How *dastardly*," Miss Concord said. "But why would someone purporting to be Lord Derwent write to Lord Cyril for help without saying where he is to be found?" She was pale in the candlelight.

"Because," McBrae said, "he doesn't know where Derwent is. Perhaps he attacked both Derwent and Worsten."

I gave McBrae the faintest of nods, hoping he realized that I had learned precisely the same from my brother.

"But Derwent escaped, perhaps with Miss Concord's help," McBrae went on.

Good Lord, I had almost forgotten that for all Lord Cyril knew, Miss Concord had witnessed the fight as well. Eventually, Lord Cyril would learn what we had kept from him, and he would be justifiably annoyed. Well! I intended to blame that on McBrae.

"Most likely, he was injured, and the murderer knows this," McBrae said. "Since Derwent's corpse has not been found, it stands to reason he is hiding in the vicinity. Lord Cyril is familiar with Barnet and therefore has a better chance of locating him than the murderer does."

"But if Lord Cyril finds my brother, surely Derwent will deny having sent this missive," I said. "Also, he may be able to identify the murderer."

"The murderer doesn't seem to fear that, does he?" McBrae said.

"Perhaps it was dark by then," I said, again giving McBrae a confirmatory nod.

"It seems likely," McBrae said. "I think there may be a more sinister implication to this letter. If Derwent is alive, he may be able to exonerate himself. He may have a credible witness who can vouch for him. But if he is found dead...."

"The Runners will continue to assume that he killed Worsten, and the murderer will be safe," I said.

Miss Concord tried, and failed, to muffle a sob. I put an arm around her. "Don't worry, my dear. I'm sorry your visit has been spoiled by such horridness, but I'm sure my brother and his mistress, poor girl, will be safe in the end."

She took out a handkerchief and dabbed at her eyes.

"Terribly sorry," Lord Cyril murmured, adding something about an improper subject and not wishing to distress a lady.

"Even if Lord Derwent flees the country," McBrae said, "the murderer won't be completely safe. He is playing a dangerous game. He must be nearby, watching to see if Lord Cyril locates Derwent, so he can move in quickly for the kill."

"We already know he's nearby," I said. "He shot at you."

"Aye, so he did," McBrae grinned. "There are three other gentlemen in Barnet now, all friends of a sort with Derwent. Is one of them the murderer? If so, why are the other two here?"

His eyes sparkled. Damn the man, he was enjoying this.

"I wonder," he said, "if any other of Derwent's friends received such a letter."

Lord Cyril and McBrae left soon after, despite my attempts to stop them, or at least to convince McBrae to remain at the Robin and Worm. "He won't risk shooting Lord Cyril," McBrae said. "He's the son of a marquis, and besides that, he wants his help. I'll be with him the whole time."

"My brother is the heir of an earl, and someone stabbed *him*," I retorted, but it was no use. Miss Concord and I decided on an early night, but we had scarcely reached our rooms when Mr. Bostock called up, "There's a gentleman to see you, my lady. Shall I send him up?" There was quite a sneer in his voice.

"Certainly not!" I retorted. Such impudence! How dare that horrid landlord suggest that I was in the habit of entertaining men in my private rooms?

McBrae would say I deserved it, but where else could I have a quiet conversation in this woefully inadequate inn? "What is his name?"

"His name," came a voice I detested, "is Pinkerton Jones-Worthy." He began to ascend the stairs.

"Don't you dare come up," I said. "I haven't the slightest notion why you're calling on me at this time of night, Sir Pinkerton. It's most improper."

Miss Concord peeped out of her room and whispered, "Do you wish me to chaperone you?"

I shook my head and told Sir Pinkerton, "I'll see you in the coffee room, and if it's empty, Mr. Bostock must stay to chaperone us. Better yet, Miss Bostock. Would your daughter be willing to do so, Mr. Bostock?"

After a surprised pause, the landlord said, "I reckon so."

"Bring us wine, please." I proceeded down the stairs. As I expected at this time of the evening, the coffee room was unoccupied, so I stood in the doorway, in full view of the merry-making patrons of the taproom, to wait for my chaperone's arrival.

Sir Pinkerton kissed my hand and held it. "Why is there no welcoming smile on your lovely face? I am here on a charitable mission, and yet you frown at me. I am positively broken-hearted."

"What charitable mission?" I recovered my hand, tempted to wipe it on my gown, but that would be frightfully ill-mannered. (Not that he had a sloppy, wet kiss, you understand—he's not that sort—but nevertheless, I find him repulsive.)

"The same as you, my dear: looking for your absent brother, in the hope of aiding him to flee the Runners. Have you found him?"

Heavens, did he really think I would blurt out my brother's whereabouts? For all I knew, he had come to finish him off.

It wasn't too terribly difficult to see Sir Pinkerton in such a role. He's what Mary Jane would call a nasty piece of work, if he were of a lower class. However, he is not physically robust, and I couldn't imagine him overpowering that huge coachman.

"If I had found him, would I be lodging here?" I demanded. "It is not what I am accustomed to." Mr. Bostock came in with two cups of cowslip wine, followed by his irritable daughter, and I wished I hadn't said that.

Bostock set the wine on one of the tables, but I remained standing. The last thing I needed was Sir Pinkerton sitting down and making himself comfortable.

"Then why not move to the Red Lion?" Sir Pinkerton asked. "My rooms there are excellent—most commodious, and the servants are polite."

I shrugged. "The Red Lion is such a bore. The Robin and Worm is a much friendlier place, preferred by my coachman, and in any case, I prefer sincerity to obsequiousness." This was a meager attempt to placate the Bostocks, or rather to prove to myself (since I had no need to prove anything to McBrae) that I have come to understand that even the lower orders have their pride.

I offered a cup of wine to Miss Bostock. "Please take a seat on the other side of the room and enjoy some of your delightful wine. I'm sure you're weary from your day's hard work. We shan't keep you long."

She eyed me as if I were mad, but she didn't refuse the wine. She sat, albeit warily, for it was unheard of for such a woman to sit at her ease in the presence of the daughter of an earl.

"You seem to have developed a taste for the inferior," sighed Sir Pinkerton. "Not only did I learn, upon coming here earlier, that you were actually dining with the relict of a Cit—how outré—but that McBrae is here. Surely that nobody isn't one of my rivals for your affections."

"There is no one in the running for my affections," I said. McBrae, drat him, had already won that race without the slightest competition, drat him again. "Allow me to remind you that I am in mourning, and that Mr. McBrae is Derwent's friend—which you are not, Sir Pinkerton. Nor are you competent to judge the quality of my acquaintances." I shouldn't have said that; it was an entirely unnecessary insult. Well, in for a penny... I narrowed my eyes at him. "Why are you really here? Ah, I suppose you asked Derwent for my hand, and he refused."

"Indeed he did, and in the most insulting way. My lineage is impeccable."

There are many who would disagree, but when one is alone with a possible murderer, one hesitates to insult him further. I had already done enough of that, as I was too annoyed to entirely hold my tongue.

"But now he is in difficulties and willing to change his mind," Sir Pinkerton said. "How the tables do turn!"

I widened my eyes as if in sudden comprehension. "Did Derwent write to you as well, asking for help?"

"As well as whom?"

"Lord Cyril," I said coyly. "Who really is my brother's friend." I didn't specify which brother. "You needn't scowl at me. I don't intend to marry anyone, nor does Derwent have any say in the matter. Let me see the letter he sent you." I put out an imperative hand.

"I didn't bring it with me," he said.

I huffed. "Did it say where to find my brother?"

"No, it merely said he was in Barnet and needed help, so of course I came here *ventre à terre*, for your dear sake as much as Derwent's."

Persistent, wasn't he? Fortunately, we were interrupted by another unwelcome visitor.

The Bow Street Runners were back.

Mr. Linehorn stomped into the coffee room, fuming, but quickly recovered his poise. After the briefest of bows to me and Sir Pinkerton, he said, "Lady Rosamund, might I beg a word with you?"

"Who the deuce are you?" Sir Pinkerton examined the Runner through his quizzing glass. To his credit, Linehorn didn't quail in the slightest, despite being disheveled and travel-weary—which was his own fault for sticking to the stupid notion that Derwent was a murderer.

"Mr. Linehorn is a Bow Street Runner," I said, "and entirely respectable, I assure you. You may leave me without any gentlemanly qualms."

Sir Pinkerton sniffed. "Runner or not, he should not impose himself upon a gently-bred lady."

Nor should you. What a pity one cannot say such thoughts aloud.

"Let him speak with that McBrae fellow," Sir Pinkerton said.

"I expect he shall, but Mr. McBrae isn't here at the moment." I gave Sir Pinkerton my hand. "Thank you so much for dropping by. I expect we'll see one another tomorrow. Good evening!"

Sir Pinkerton had perforce to leave. I didn't relish the expression on his face. If he had no chance of winning me, he also had no longer any reason to control his sharp and bitter tongue.

Not to mention that he might be a murderer—but I had my doubts.

I offered the remaining cup of wine to the Runner and apologized as kindly as I could. "I'm so sorry, Mr. Linehorn, but we had no choice." I told Miss Bostock that she need no longer stay, and gave her a shilling from my reticule. If these rustics looked askance at my private conversation with a Bow Street Runner, they could go to the devil.

"Murderers should be brought to justice," he said, "not aided to escape the consequences of their actions." His disapproval of me didn't stop him from accepting the wine and downing it in one gulp.

"Which is why we had to get you out of the way," I said. "It was difficult, if not impossible, to concentrate on finding the real murderer whilst you dogged our every footstep." I sat and waved him to a chair. "I suppose you intend to do so once again."

He remained standing. "Aye, for we have received another communication proving that Lord Derwent is in Barnet."

"A communication from whom?" When he hesitated, I asked, "Anonymous, once again? What sort of proof is that, except that the writer wishes my brother ill?"

"The proof, my lady, is that it informs us that Lord Derwent wrote to several friends saying he is injured, and asking them to come here and help him escape."

"Some aspects of this information are correct," I said. "I know of at least two such letters. Sir Pinkerton Jones-Worthy, who just left us, received one of them, and Lord Cyril Telfrey received another."

"Aha! You admit, then, that Lord Derwent is nearby?"

"I'm beginning to think it may be possible," I said, "although it doesn't explain what happened to his mistress. In any event, Mr. McBrae has gone to ask Mr. Charting and Mr. Brill—who also suddenly arrived in Barnet, but are not close friends with my brother—if perhaps they also received such letters. I expect he is at the Red Lion, or perhaps the Green Man, if either you or your helper wish to eavesdrop on them." Which was catty of me, I admit, but duty or not, this Runner was a nuisance.

Mr. Linehorn rightly ignored my last comment. "By this, you contend that Lord Derwent would not have asked these particular gentlemen for help?"

"Certainly not," I said. "Nor would he have promised my hand to whichever of them helped him first—for that is what the letters imply. Not only that, he would have given some clue as to his whereabouts, or the name of someone to contact. As it is, all he asked for was help in escaping."

I bade the Runner good night and returned upstairs. Miss Concord and I helped each other undress, but I don't suppose either of us slept well. I didn't even doze until I heard McBrae return. I wouldn't have heard him at all if Mr. Bostock hadn't greeted him in a low voice.

I leapt out of bed, donned a dressing gown, and hurried to my door, but by the time I turned the key and opened it, he had shut his own door behind him.

Chapter Seventeen

"Damnation!" I muttered, and went back into my room.

A moment later, there was a soft tap on my door. I opened it to find McBrae standing there, a full glass of whisky in his hand. "Such language for a lady."

"I want to know what happened," I whispered grumpily.

He slipped into my chamber and shut the door. "You've become mighty cavalier about your reputation."

"I don't c—" I'd been about to say that I didn't care what a bunch of rustics thought of me, but McBrae respects the lower classes to an exaggerated extent. "I can't afford to care about what Bostock and his daughter think of me. My brother's life is at stake." And so was McBrae's every time he ventured out of doors.

I took a chair and waved McBrae to the sofa. He looked exhausted, and no wonder. No doubt his arm was painful, but he wouldn't want me to fuss over him.

"The Runners are back," I said. "Has Hamish returned as well?"

"No, I told him to continue to your father, to explain the situation and tell him, on your behalf, that you hoped he would find an appropriate solution for Ivan and Joan. They were somewhat fearful of being obliged to explain themselves."

Trust McBrae, in the midst of trying to unmask a murderer, to remember the sensibilities of a few foolish servants.

I suggested that he ask Bostock to help him remove his coat—and left it at that. He was a grown man, stubborn like all his countrymen and most

Englishmen too, and arguing with him would make no difference.

"The groom's account tallies with what my brother told me," I said. "In the darkness, he didn't recognize the murderer. All Derwent said was that he was a gentleman, perhaps slightly taller than himself, and had quite a pleasant voice."

"Not terribly helpful." McBrae sipped at the whisky.

"Mr. Linehorn tells me another anonymous letter was sent to Bow Street, revealing that Lord Derwent wrote from Barnet asking friends for help. I told him Lord Cyril and Sir Pinkerton are not his friends, but—"

"Sir Pinkerton?" Did that sudden frown indicate jealousy? No, more likely his arm was throbbing badly.

"He called on me this evening, gloating because earlier, Derwent refused to give him permission to court me, but now he needs his help." I huffed. "I reminded him that I am in mourning, and that in any event, my brother has no say in the matter."

McBrae's frown eased, and he even gave me a hint of a smile. "We found young Mr. Brill nursing his chagrin in the taproom at the Green Man."

"Chagrin about what?"

"He's either a complicated young man or an excellent actor." He sat back, crossing his legs. "He feels obliged to help a friend but doesn't want the prize that is offered."

"Just tell me," I retorted.

"He received a similar letter to Lord Cyril's—the essential difference being that he had indeed discussed a personal matter with your brother. Unlike Sir Pinkerton, though, he doesn't wish to wed you."

"Thank heavens for that," I said. "Then what—?"

McBrae's lip quirked up. "He hopes to marry Miss Trent."

"Heavens! I wonder how Miss Trent feels about that." She'd certainly clung to his arm the other night. "Why doesn't he just ask her?"

"Because his mother prefers the candidates that she herself has chosen. Brill says the only way to deal with his mother is in a roundabout way. She is horrified at the thought that you might snatch up her darling son. He knows this and believes that when, after being refused by both Derwent and

195

Lord Medway, he is obliged to give up hope of winning you, she will be so relieved that she will accept Miss Trent."

Which was as bad as my brother agreeing that I needed to be confined, in order to gain Mother's acceptance of Miss Concord. I had a feeling Mrs. Brill knew exactly what her son was doing and might have something horrid up her sleeve, but that, thank God, was not my problem.

"Perhaps Mr. Charting was another," I said. "Derwent let something slip this evening, and I insisted on an explanation. He told several gentlemen who approached him that I was promised to Lord Worsten, who learned of this and was infuriated at being trapped into a marriage he didn't want. That's what led to the estrangement between them, and I believe Lord Worsten abducted Miss Concord for revenge, or perhaps even to cause a scandal that would release him from any obligation toward me." I rolled my eyes; there is no point in being polite with McBrae. "If I had known, I would have told Lord Worsten not to worry, for I hadn't the slightest intention of marrying him or anyone else."

"Never?" McBrae said softly, almost wistfully, which was absurd. He certainly didn't wish to marry me. He downed half the whisky in one gulp. "I wonder if Mr. Charting received a letter, too."

"Or if he sent all the letters and one to himself as well," I muttered. "We know he's short of money, since Sir Devlin withdrew his allowance. Not only that, he's a rough sort of man, who talks constantly of sport. He's probably a good shot, and perhaps is acquainted with bruisers like the coachman. You didn't see him in the village?"

He shook his head. "Unfortunately, he seems to be occupying himself otherwise."

"By shooting at you?"

"Or bedding his wench," McBrae said, which verged on crude and just went to show how our relationship had deteriorated—although I appreciated his frankness. At least he didn't treat me like a delicate ninny.

"Which is stupid of him, if he still hopes to wed me," I said. "Possessing a mistress is one thing. Cavorting publicly with a low woman is beyond unacceptable to a well-bred lady."

He opened his mouth and shut it again, evidently too tired to berate me for condoning the indecent behavior of gentlemen of my class.

"One can't expect much of a murderer in the way of scruples," he said at last. "As far as I am aware, he's the only other visitor in Barnet who has a connection with you and your brother."

"I should have asked Derwent for a list of suitors," I said grumpily. "I've been thinking. Why does the murderer not fear being recognized? My brother didn't recognize him, but he can't know that for sure. What if Derwent accuses him?"

"It's a possibility, and it explains why he is trying to find Derwent and kill him." McBrae leaned his head on one of the embroidered cushions. "Tidies up the loose ends."

"Maybe—but the more I think of it, the more I wonder if this is all part of a plot."

"Like one of your stories?" He yawned.

"Yes," I said crossly, "just like a story. If the murderer is also the letter writer, which seems likely, he is the sort of person who plans things in advance. Maybe he didn't mean to kill Worsten. Maybe what he really wanted was to get my brother away from Town and into the countryside where he could murder him unseen and make it look as if he'd been robbed."

"Worsten wasn't robbed." McBrae eyed the whisky, then downed the rest. I wondered if he was drinking to dull the pain.

"So…maybe the murderer stabbed the wrong person in the dark, and on realizing that he'd killed Worsten instead of Derwent, he stabbed him several times out of frustration and rage."

"Slightly more plausible," McBrae muttered. "Or maybe it occurred to him that Derwent would likely be accused of the murder, which got rid of him another way."

"Maybe this whole horrid affair has nothing to do with me and my suitors after all."

"Or maybe," McBrae said, "he wanted them both dead. Worsten because he was supposedly already betrothed to you, and Derwent because he refused him permission."

"Nonsense," I said. "That's even more unlikely."

"Not at all. Once they are both dead, leaving you grieving for your brother, your late husband, and your prospective one, he will take advantage of your weakened state and sweep you off your feet."

I made a rude noise. (I simply couldn't remain polite and proper with him anymore.) "No, because I would simply take refuge with my father, who is perfectly capable of driving unwanted suitors away." Oh, God, what if the murderer decided to kill Papa, too?

No, that was stupid. This wasn't a Gothic novel. Nobody could possibly want me that badly. I'm wealthy, but not extremely so, and I'm sure there are fast widows who are much better prepared than I to participate in orgies.

An unpleasant thought occurred. "When you drew that caricature of all the men clustered like vultures around Worsten's body, were you referring to Miss Concord or to me?"

"Both," he murmured, closing his eyes. "I knew people would assume I meant Miss Concord, but it was really more about you than her. Drawing helps me express unpleasant emotions. I was angry and upset with you—while at the same time, I would gladly have killed all those men who wanted to take advantage of you in such a foul manner."

I stood and walked to the window. This was too much emotion for me.

"Loving you is a damned nuisance," he said.

I stared into the darkness. I knew he liked me sometimes, and that he lusted after me...but love was such a heady notion. "I wish I knew what that means," I said softly. "I wish I knew what to think."

He didn't respond, and when at last I turned, he had slid down on the sofa and lay curled up on his side, his head on a cushion. He gave a soft snore.

I stood there, watching him sleep. He looked vulnerable in repose, and yet contented to be that way. Without really intending to do so, I perched on the edge of the sofa, my hip almost toughing his thigh. He slept peacefully on (at least, I assumed he was asleep. He has so much control over his features that I couldn't be completely sure). I couldn't resist laying a hand gently on his side, just next to where his injured arm lay.

What a pleasure to touch him, to feel and hold him, without sensual desires (his for certain; mine uneasily emerging) getting in the way. I might not get another chance to do so, for once I told him the sorry story of my marriage, he would leave me be. He might think he loved me, but he didn't know the real me.

I'd said I didn't know what to think, but that was a lie. What I thought was: I'm in love with him. What a pity the realization had come over me, because it would make our inevitable parting so much more painful.

I shivered drowsily. He was so peaceful, so tranquil, there on my sofa. I couldn't bring myself to wake him. How much simpler if we could sleep (and only sleep) together, cuddled close.

Impossible! I covered him with one of my blankets and went to bed.

I woke in the morning to a soft tap on my door. I sat up in sudden panic, for I had woken twice during the night to find that McBrae was still asleep on my sofa—but he was no longer there. "Who is it?"

Miss Concord opened the door that led to the private parlor, carrying a steaming jug of water. "I'm sorry to wake you, Lady Rosamund, but there's a gentleman here to see you."

I groaned. "Who is it this time?"

"It's your neighbor, Sir Devlin Curtis."

"What?" Why was he in Barnet? Annoyance, with a touch of dread, uncurled within me. "Did he happen to say why he wants to see me?" What if Mother had sent him?

"No." She chuckled. "He looked down his long nose at me as if I were little better than a servant—which isn't surprising, I suppose, as I was in the coffee room, having just changed the dressing on Mr. McBrae's arm, and was helping him into his coat."

I felt myself reddening.

"I found Mr. McBrae in our private parlor this morning, cursing under his breath, and smuggled him out when no one was looking," she said primly.

"I didn't—we didn't—" What was *wrong* with me? It was none of Miss Concord's business if McBrae spent the night in my room. In fact, it was no one's business but mine and McBrae's.

She laughed. "Of course not. He was injured and exhausted, and he fell asleep on your sofa."

"He shouldn't have been in my bedchamber in the first place, but how else were we to find the privacy to discuss the murders? In any event, I didn't have the heart to wake him. How is his arm?"

"Doing very well," she said. "A little red and sore, but there's no sign of infection."

"That's good news." I threw off the covers and got out of bed. "But the arrival of Sir Devlin probably isn't. I don't like to be rude to him—he is my mother's favorite cicisbeo—but if he has come from her..." Well, there was no point in speculating.

Miss Concord stirred the banked fire into life and helped me wash and dress. I would have liked to empty and refill my reticule several times, but she didn't give me the opportunity, and I couldn't order her to leave as if she were my maid. Drat! Yet another reason why I could never share my bedchamber with anyone else, in this instance meaning McBrae.

Feeling rather like a martyr on my way to torture and execution, I made my way downstairs. I did my best to sweep into the coffee room in my most imperious manner, but this was difficult to achieve because 1) Sir Devlin has known me since I was a child and would recognize this attempt to copy my mother, and 2) McBrae.

(Surely, you need no further explanation of the complexities of my relationship with McBrae—particularly after he'd spent the night in my room.)

The two gentlemen were seated at a table with a coffee pot and several cups. They rose as I entered. Sir Devlin smiled kindly. "There you are, my dear! I apologize if my message woke you. I've never known you to sleep late into the morning."

As if he knew my sleep habits—which he most certainly did not! I expect he was trying to make the point that he had known me forever, whereas McBrae was an encroaching nobody, but how dare he!

"Dear me," I said vaguely, looking about me as if for a clock (there wasn't one). "Is it so very late? Perhaps I was overtired; the last few days have been trying."

Drat! I shouldn't have said that, for it gave Sir Devlin the opening he wanted (not that he wouldn't have brought up the subject of my mother anyway).

"Perfectly understandable, dear child, which is why I have come to fetch you home."

Dread seized hold of me. "To Kent?" I squeaked, and shut my mouth, aghast. A lady's voice should never squeak. It must be melodious to the ear.

Sir Devlin's eyebrows climbed a fraction. "If you wish, my dear, but only to town for now. I expect your mother to arrive any day, and although I know you find her difficult, she will need you. Upon hearing that you were in Barnet, what else could I do?"

I scowled. "Who told you I was in Barnet?"

He frowned as if in thought. "Does it matter? I can't say I recall, but it may have been Lady Danby. She demanded my assistance, as she fears for your state of mind in such distressful circumstances."

"My state of mind is perfectly fine," I said, a lie which was no doubt as obvious to him as it was to me. Meanwhile, McBrae watched us both in speculative silence. "It's kind of you to offer your help, but I don't plan to return to town just now. I'm going to my father."

"So why are you still here in Barnet? A charming village, I daresay, but frankly, I am appalled at your choice of accommodations. The company in this rustic hostelry is far beneath you." He didn't quite sneer in McBrae's direction, but close enough. He can be such a horrid snob—although I doubt his birth is much better than McBrae's (if one accounts for the differences between English and Scottish precedence, of which I know almost nothing).

McBrae pulled out the only other chair for me. I sat, and the gentlemen followed suit. With a tiny quirk of the lips, McBrae served me a cup of coffee.

"The company is unassuming, the accommodations are adequate, and the meals are delicious," I retorted. "Lord Cyril Telfrey himself is acquainted with the landlord and asked him to take special care of me."

"Lord Cyril should know better," Sir Devlin said with a disapproving frown.

"He knows I don't wish to encounter my annoying suitors—such as Sir Pinkerton Jones-Worthy, who is at the Red Lion."

"Good God," Sir Devlin said with a snort, "surely he doesn't deem himself *worthy* of you, dear child."

I didn't even smile at this quip; I was too annoyed to do so.

"My nephew is equally unworthy," he said, "and so I told him. I hear he's in Barnet, too."

"Yes, at Lord Cyril's," I snapped. "So is Mr. Brill."

"Calm down, child, and have some coffee," Sir Devlin said, and I sensed McBrae rolling his eyes. Now, that almost did make me laugh.

"Why didn't you simply continue on to Lord Medway, as you were supposed to do?" Sir Devlin probably thought his smile was kind and forbearing.

"Because the Bow Street Runners are here," I said, "and for some absurd reason, they believe Derwent is here too, in hiding."

"With good reason, my dear. I have it on the best of information that the Runners have received letters not only accusing Derwent of murder, but revealing that he is hiding somewhere in Barnet."

"Anonymous letters, by what I hear," I retorted, "evidently written by someone who wishes to harm my brother, for it is obvious to me and to any person of sense that Derwent is not a murderer."

"My dear, don't delude yourself. I understand that you love your brother, but he is as capable as any man of acting rashly in anger."

"He wouldn't stab his friend. He would challenge him to a duel. Not only that, if he had killed Worsten, why would he hide in Barnet? He wouldn't just wait here for the Runners to catch him!"

"Perhaps he fought Worsten and was injured," Sir Devlin suggested gently.

"Perhaps, perhaps not," I said, "but I have a horrid feeling the murderer himself wrote those letters, because if Derwent is caught and hanged, or if he flees the country, thus appearing to be a murderer confessed, that will be the end of it. No one will look for the real culprit after that."

Sir Devlin gaped as if he couldn't believe his ears. "My dear girl, this is precisely why you should not be here. This is not the sort of matter about which a lady should concern herself. Without proper guidance, you have allowed your imagination to run amok."

"No, I am putting my imagination to good use." I shouldn't have allowed my fear of Mother to rile me. Sir Devlin couldn't help his stupid views, which were also those of most gentlemen.

"I fear for Derwent, truly I do," Sir Devlin said, "but in the meantime, my child, you mustn't fret over something about which you can do nothing. Allow me to counsel you on the best way to go on."

"Lady Rosamund is not a child," McBrae said softly. "She's a grown woman and can make her own decisions."

Sir Devlin drew himself up haughtily. "You, sir, are presumptuous."

"That isn't so," I said. "Mr. McBrae is very kind to me and helpful in this trying time. Sir Devlin, I know you mean well, but I was married for four years and am now a widow—hardly a child—and if I do need counsel, I shall seek it from my father."

"Then do so," Sir Devlin said impatiently, "and if you need help, ask it of your tried-and-true friends, not this Scottish interloper, who, I hear, is in Barnet solely to interfere with the Runners in the execution of their duty."

"Mr. McBrae is here to identify the real murderer. We believe he is in Barnet, for he shot at Mr. McBrae yesterday."

He pursed his lips. "My dear child, that makes no sense at all. It must have been a poacher, for they are often about at night." He threw up his hands. "Bah! We already know who killed Worsten and a coachman as well, by what I'm told." He paused. "My dear, I should like to have a word with you in private."

"About what?"

His gaze flickered in McBrae's direction and back again.

"Whatever it is, you may say it here," I said. "Mr. McBrae has my full confidence."

Sir Devlin huffed. "I see that matters are worse than I believed. I prefer not to be impolite, but I feel obliged to say that both your mother and Lady Danby believe that this McBrae person is not an appropriate acquaintance for you."

This was his way of not being impolite? "They may believe what they choose, but my father disagrees."

"Lord Medway means well, but he buries himself in the country and knows nothing of what really goes on in the world." He stabbed an accusatory finger at McBrae, who cocked his head and eyed Sir Devlin as if he were some strange sort of insect. Was he envisioning a caricature? I hoped so.

"This fellow is a fortune hunter, preying upon you in your time of distress and sorrow."

I sprang up. "That's not true!" Suddenly, I realized we had an audience, including the landlord, his daughter, Miss Concord, and both the Runners.

"He knows it's the truth. He won't even try to stand up for himself," Sir Devlin scoffed, rising as well. What a relief he hadn't discarded quite all his good manners. He must be excessively concerned for me to allow himself the slightest deviation from propriety.

Drat, what a *nuisance*. Fortunately, he couldn't force me to go with him.

McBrae laughed, sounding almost joyful. "I have no need to when Lady Rosamund is doing such a fine job on my behalf." He stood as well, taking his time—to emphasize, no doubt, his disdain for the hypocrisy of customs followed merely for show.

"Thank you, Mr. McBrae." I turned to Sir Devlin. "I'm very sorry, sir, but I do not intend to return to London now."

"What a pity," Sir Devlin said. "My dear child—and you are a child to me—we shall speak of this later, after you have breakfasted and are feeling rather more yourself." He pulled on his gloves. "In the meantime, I must relieve Lord Cyril of my fool of a nephew, who had the infernal gall to bring his doxy here."

He left, and I watched through the window as he mounted his coal-black stallion and tossed a coin to the lad who'd been holding him. I turned to address our audience. "Might I have some breakfast, please? And fresh coffee."

Bostock and his daughter hurried away to attend to my request. The Runners went into the taproom, and Miss Concord joined McBrae and me.

"When he returns," McBrae said, "let it be known that you are ill with the

204

migraine or some such, and are not seeing visitors. Also, set preparations in train for departure tomorrow morning." He put up a hand. "Whether you actually leave is entirely up to you, my lady—and it may not be necessary, if Lord Medway comes here—but it may be easier to get rid of Sir Devlin if he knows you mean to leave Barnet tomorrow."

"I shan't receive him. I wish I could leave the inn to avoid him," I said grumpily, "but where would I go?"

"You may drive into the village with Mrs. Pearl and me," Miss Concord said. They had made a plan to shop together for embroidery silks this morning—not my idea of a good time. She lowered her voice. "Or perhaps you could go to her house and wait there."

I shook my head; I would rather not draw attention to Mrs. Pearl's house, for I had no idea who might be watching and wondering. "Thank you, but I'll write letters, I think—to my mother and Lady Danby, trying to sound completely calm and composed."

McBrae stood. "I'll leave you now. I intend to speak to the Runners. I think our best hope at this point is to work *with* them instead of against them."

"How do you plan to do that?" I asked.

"I don't know yet, but I hope I can convince Mr. Linehorn to look at the crime from a different angle. He's not making any progress with his approach, so why not try mine?"

Chapter Eighteen

I t didn't take long to dash off a note to Lady Danby, thanking her for her concern, and reassuring her that I had stopped in Barnet to take advantage of Lord Cyril's kind offer to show me about.

Gloomily, I pondered my future. It seemed my only options were marriage or a chaperone. Since marriage was impossible, I pondered elderly relatives. Where would I find the unlikely combination of a lady who would be content to leave me be while at the same time intolerant of interference by my mother, brother, Lady Danby, et cetera. (The et cetera refers to my sisters, one of whom bids fair to become as difficult as my mother. Another has immured herself in rural fastness with her husband and children and never comes to town. The third is soon to give birth to her fourth child and hopefully will be unable to get in my way for some time to come.)

Sighing, I wrote that my father had asked one of his spinster cousins to spend the season in London with me. I didn't specify which cousin or which season, so it wouldn't stave Lady Danby off for long.

Now for my mother. I was in the first throes of composition when I suddenly remembered the letter she had written to Derwent, which I hadn't finished reading. I had stopped because there was a pause in the letter itself—she had maundered on and on about controlling me, et cetera, and then set it aside and began again a week later. Her handwriting in this second portion was even more difficult to read than is usual with crossed and recrossed letters. This meant she had written it in great agitation—doubtless about something to do with me. Not that I wanted to know any more about what she thought of me, but needs must if I were to compose something that would satisfy her.

Satisfy my mother? Ha!

My dearest Derwent, she wrote, *I just this minute received a letter from Sir Devlin Curtis. I am extremely vexed with you. You have mortally offended him by your tactless refusal to entertain his suit—which I had already approved!*

Sir Devlin writes that you have arranged for Rosie to marry Lord Worsten once her year of mourning is past. Impossible! In the first place, she cannot be left to her own devices for over six months. Secondly, Lord Worsten and his mother—a friend of mine—would never forgive us when they realized we had duped him into marrying your mad sister. I know you meant well, dearest, but you may easily release Worsten from this foolish arrangement by explaining that I had already promised Rosie to Sir Devlin.

Go immediately to Sir Devlin and beg his forgiveness. His offer comes in the very nick of time. He is a dear friend, mature and capable, and entirely willing, for my sake, to take on the burden of a mad, barren wife. Not only that, he is devoted to me and will do precisely as I say. Once Rosie is under his control, we shall no longer fear any scandals.

Dearest, please turn your mind to your own marriage. There are a number of lovely young ladies on the market this year, and I know of a few more who will come out in the spring. It is the wish of my heart to see you wed and setting up your own nursery!

With fondest love,
Your Mother

As you can well imagine, I was shaky and ill by the time I finished reading this letter. How dare she! As if Derwent's scheme wasn't bad enough, she must needs betroth me to a man as old as my father. Not only that, she had *told* him about my supposed madness and counted on him to keep me safely tucked away from society. No wonder his manner this morning had been so falsely soothing. It was a ruse to get me under his control.

So much for McBrae's promise to save me (which I had so unkindly spurned). He wouldn't be able to rescue me from such a fate. A husband has complete dominion over his wife. Fortunately, I didn't intend to marry Sir Devlin, so I would have no need of rescue.

I tore the letter up and fed it to the flames.

I wondered when Sir Devlin meant to spring this horrid betrothal on me. Was that why he'd wished to speak with me in private, and why he intended to return here today?

More important, why would he agree to wed me? He is a longtime widower and seems content that way. Surely, he's not quite *that* devoted to my mother. Yes, he is her cicisbeo, most likely because it's socially useful—but if anything, he has cause to resent her. She refused his proposal of marriage in favor of my father, because she fancied being a countess. At the time, Sir Devlin was a mere mister, but even a knighthood cannot compete with an earldom, and although he can trace his ancestry back to the Conqueror, his estate is relatively small. He's not the sort to disregard a slight, and nor is he kindhearted—witness his callous treatment of Mr. Charting, who depended on him for an allowance. Although, come to think of it, such a step was not quite what one would expect from Sir Devlin, who took pride in appearing magnanimous toward his nephew.

A startling thought occurred. What if Sir Devlin had stopped Mr. Charting's allowance because he could no longer afford to pay it?

A commotion below roused me from this unpleasant notion and what it might mean.

"This is a respectable hostelry," Mr. Bostock said. "We don't allow your sort here. Out you go!"

"But sir, I've a message for Lady Rosie Mund." (Yes, that's how she said my name.)

"A likely story," Bostock retorted. "Lady Rosamund is poorly today, and even if she weren't, she wouldn't receive a message from the likes of you."

"But sir, it's life or death!" the girl cried.

"I said *out!*" Bostock shouted, and I threw open my door. There, at the foot of the stairs, the flirty blonde wench struggled with the landlord, shrieking.

"Release her, Mr. Bostock," I said. "If this woman has a message for me, I wish to receive it."

You may wonder (quite rightly) why I allowed this treacherous trollop into my presence. It had little to do with my attempts to impress McBrae with my newly-acquired appreciation of egalitarian values. No, I was frightened by the horrid notion which had just seized my already confused mind. I needed to learn whatever I could from whichever source presented itself.

His grip loosened, and the wench flew up the steps toward me.

"This ain't right, my lady," Bostock cried. "You're ruining the reputation of my inn!"

"Nonsense, my good man," I retorted. "She's not going to *stay* here, for heaven's sake. I'll send her away as soon as she has spoken with me. Continue to deny all visitors, please."

The landlord subsided, grumbling, and I motioned the girl into my bedchamber. She was trembling, disheveled, and pink from exertion, her yellow bonnet askew, and her shoes coated in mud. She glanced about the room. I hoped she hadn't come at the murderer's behest to try to kill me.

She gave a shaky curtsey. "I ain't got long, milady," she said in a voice husky with fear. "That devil is after me, and I wouldn't give much for me chances." (She spoke with the accent of the London working class, which I shan't attempt to reproduce here. Consider every initial h to be dropped, and go from there.) "Or anyone else's, once he has his evil eye on them, and when he's done, he'll kill your brother to lay all the blame on him, poor lad."

"You're acquainted with my brother?" I demanded frostily.

She snorted. "Not that way, milady. He don't want no common wench like me. But I seen him afore with that Lord Worsten. They was friends! He can't help being a fool, but he didn't kill no one, and he don't deserve to swing."

"If you believe that, I don't understand why you have come to me," I said sternly. "You're aiding and abetting a murderer."

She put her hands on her hips. "No, I ain't!"

"You carried a message from him to my brother," I said with the scowl my mother gives a sloppy maidservant, "to induce him to follow Lord Worsten."

"Aye, to save his mistress! I didn't know he meant harm. Leastways, not then. I thought he was doing him a good turn."

"Later, he sent you here to find if my brother is close by in hiding. You flirted with the grooms at all the inns."

"Luckily, that didn't get me nowhere. If I'd found your brother, he'd be dead by now." She was trembling again, and wrapped her arms about herself. "I left, 'cause nobody would give me a room. I may be common, but I ain't no tavern wench neither, so I bedded down in a barn near Highgate. Then I—" She stifled a sob.

"You came upon the coachman's corpse," I said. "I saw you there. You were ill and weeping."

"He was my friend," she said simply. "I'm not as stupid as I look. I worked out what was really going on, and I come back to Barnet to *warn* your brother. Henry Charting was here by then. We've had some good times together, so he let me stay with him."

"You're not the least bit stupid," I said. She'd worked it out long before I had. She'd also just exonerated Mr. Charting.

She shrugged. "Listen, milady. The devil gent hired the coach for that lordship, and then he killed him, and he killed me friend, and he shot at that Scottish gent what fancies you, and next he'll kill me uncle and me."

"Your uncle?" I asked idiotically. Was it obvious to *everyone* that McBrae loved me?

It didn't matter. I mustn't allow myself to be distracted.

"Me uncle Charlie, the groom." She clutched my arm. Her nails dug into my flesh. "Ain't you listening? Mark my words, milady. That devil gent wants to wed you, but one day he'll kill you, too. I seen that sort afore. Cross them, and you're for it. Don't wed him, milady, no matter what he says."

"Who?" I asked at last, although I already knew the answer.

"Sir Devil with the black horse," she said. "He comes and he goes, and nobody don't see him in the dark."

From below came a dreaded voice. "Lady Rosamund is expecting me."

"Oh, no!" the wench squeaked. "He'll kill me!"

210

"No, he won't. You're going to leave by the back stairs." I motioned her toward the private parlor, and when she didn't move, I grabbed her hand. "I can keep him busy for a while, but I need your help. Go find Mr. McBrae, the Scottish gentleman, and tell him to come, and to bring the Runners with him."

"Her ladyship has a headache," Bostock said. "She told me no callers, only messages." He made a vulgar noise. "She already took one from a doxy, if ever I saw one."

The wench moaned. "He'll find me, and I'll go to Hell for me sins!"

"Hush!" I towed her into the parlor.

"I am not a caller," Sir Devlin said. "I am soon to wed Lady Rosamund. She will welcome me."

I opened the door to Miss Concord's room and pushed the woman through. "I'll handle him," I said. "He won't see you if you go out the kitchen door. Quickly! Find Mr. McBrae."

"Remove yourself, fellow," Sir Devlin said. "If she is too ill to come to the coffee room, I shall go up to her."

I dashed to my door and opened it, intending to hurry down, but he was already on his way up the stairs. "I'll come straightaway, Sir Devlin."

"No need, child." He continued up. "In any event, I wish to speak to you privately."

Short of pushing him down the stairs, there wasn't much I could do. (Imagine the scandal if I had, for I was already believed to have killed a footman in that very way. And it would have served no useful purpose, for if I had succeeded in killing him—by no means a certain outcome—my brother would still be at risk of hanging.)

"Bostock, bring us coffee, please," I said, while frantically trying to decide how to deal with the situation.

"Tsk." Sir Devlin shook his head. "No, coffee will excite you, my dear. That is what brought on your migraine. You must rest."

"So far, resting has only made it worse. Bring the coffee, Bostock, and some of Miss Bostock's delightful plum cake." I stood back to let Sir Devlin in, hoping desperately that Bostock would obey me rather than Sir Devlin. I didn't think Sir Devlin would murder me—that was counter to his goal, as far as I understood it—but how could I help but be afraid?

And furious! He had killed two people, tried to kill my brother, and seemingly now planned to kill two more. A devil indeed!

He shut the door behind him, surveyed the room, glanced into the private parlor, and turned, knitting his brows at me. I scowled back at him, allowing my anger to take hold. "This is most improper of you, Sir Devlin. The landlord is already annoyed because I let that horrid newsman into my chamber. He says I am ruining the reputation of the Robin and Worm."

He snapped his fingers. "*That* for the Robin and Worm. I am far more concerned about *your* reputation. Who is the doxy that brought you a message?"

"A young woman in a yellow bonnet," I said. "She wanted the Runners, but they're not here, and the landlord was being frightfully rude to her."

"A doxy wanted the Runners? Unlikely."

I felt my cheeks heating; did he know I was lying? "Why wouldn't she? She was terrified, in fear for her life. I felt it to be my duty to calm her."

"Unwise. Such low persons should never be encouraged. They only take advantage."

"You're as bad as my mother," I retorted, "completely lacking in sympathy and understanding for those less fortunate." How could he so calmly pretend that nothing was wrong? "She did no such thing. She said the devil who killed the coachman was after the groom now, and that he would come after her next."

He tsked again. "If this is the slut who has her claws into Henry, she's a common thief. I warned Henry to spurn her, but he bedded her instead." He put up a hand. "I beg your pardon, my love. I should not speak of such improper matters in your presence."

I shuddered at this endearment. "I am not your love. How dare my mother betroth me to you without my consent?"

He eyed me, saying nothing for a while, and I quaked inside. "How did you learn of your mother's plans? She promised to keep silent, so as not to upset you."

"Since she knew it would upset me, she shouldn't have done it!" I raged and stomped across the room and back. (A lady should never stomp—rather, she should glide—but if I didn't shake from rage, I would do so from fear, and he would know it. Not that I thought all this through at the time, but I pondered it deeply afterwards.) I glared at him. "If you must know, she wrote to my brother, and I found the letter and read it. She was furious that he had promised me to Lord Worsten—again, without my consent."

I plopped myself into the chair by the dressing table—to Hades with ladylike grace—and waved him to the sofa.

He sat and leaned back, crossing his legs, completely at ease. "Most unwise of Derwent, as it has led him to this present fix. If he had approved my suit, Worsten would still be alive, and all would be well."

"Except that I do not wish to remarry," I said.

"Unless to that upstart McBrae, I suppose." He gave a derisive laugh.

I rolled my eyes. Vulgar, yes, but one doesn't fret about propriety when speaking with a murderer. "I don't know why everyone thinks I want to marry Mr. McBrae. I like him, but I don't want to marry anyone."

"But you must, Rosie dear, for your own safety," he said softly.

"I have not given you permission to use my given name," I said, which was pointless, but I didn't know what else to do. Should I try to send him away? Judging by his demeanor, he intended to stay as long as he chose. Not only that, if he left, he might get on with committing a few more murders. It was my duty to keep him here. Surely McBrae would return soon.

"Come now, Rosie, I have known you from the time you were born. I have always been a sort of uncle to you."

"And it shall remain that way, Sir Devlin." (Heavens! They say novels are unrealistic, but he was proving to be a genuinely wicked uncle, just like in a stirring romance.)

He tsked again, making me long to snap at him—and said indulgently, 'Foolish child. You really have no choice. Without a husband, you are alone and prey to fortune hunters, such as McBrae."

"And such as you, perhaps?" Oh, dear. I shouldn't have said that, judging by the way he straightened, narrowing his eyes. "I beg your pardon, sir, but it seemed unlike you to cut off Mr. Charting's allowance. I wondered if perhaps you were in financial difficulties."

After a pause, he said, "I admit, your money would come in useful, but never doubt my affection for you."

Ha. He had no affection for anyone but himself. He didn't even love my mother, despite professing undying devotion. (Come to think of it—and I couldn't help but do so under the circumstances—undying thirst for revenge was more likely. Killing her son or forcing him into exile seemed rather vengeful, while as for marrying me... I suppressed another shudder.)

Miss Bostock came in with the coffee and cake. "Please pour for us, Miss Bostock," I said hurriedly—for I feared that if I did so, my hands would tremble. We waited in silence while she slopped coffee into the cups and left again, slamming the door behind her.

"These rustics have no manners," he said, "but what else does one expect in such an inferior inn?"

I gazed unhappily at the cake. I am inordinately fond of sweet treats—perhaps because my mother deprives me of almost anything tasty—but now, my appetite had deserted me. "The plum cake is quite good. Do try some."

He sneered. "I think not. Tell me, my dear. It seems unlike you to read another's private correspondence. Where did you come upon this letter of your mother's?"

"In Derwent's study. I found it when I went to Medway House to ask where he had gone."

"Ah. So you have known of my intentions since before you left London?"

I wished I had. Perhaps it would have made muddy waters a little clearer. "No, I didn't read it until just now."

After another horrid pause, he made a rude noise. "I don't believe you."

Taken aback, I said, "Why not? It's true! I'll show you the letter." Maybe he would read it, which would keep him occupied for ages. I sprang up and fetched my reticule, opened it and dug inside—and then remembered that I had burned the confounded letter. I looked hopefully at the fireplace: nothing but ashes. "Drat—I forgot. I was so furious with her that I burned it."

What I did remember, though, was that my little pistol was in the reticule—fortunately, for I feared I might need it. I sat again, reticule in my lap, withdrew a handkerchief, and dabbed at my eyes. Not that I was weeping, you understand. I was far too angry to weep, but the handkerchief gave me a reason to keep my reticule open.

"I haven't the slightest wish to read your mother's maunderings," he said. "I rarely spend more than fifteen minutes with her, for the spoken version is even worse." Ordinarily, I would have sympathized, but this confirmed my feeling that not only did he not love her, he despised, even hated her. "But you, my child, would be eager to read such a letter the instant you found it, to learn what she was planning. You are rightly afraid that your mother will have you confined."

He knew far too much about me, but worry about my mother's plans was nothing to my growing fear of Sir Devlin.

A member of the house of Medway does not show fear. I huffed. "My father won't permit that. If anyone in my family is mad, it's my mother herself. I started reading the letter when I first took it, but I was too tired, and later too concerned about Derwent, to spend my time deciphering her crossed and re-crossed lines. I wish I had, for it would have made some things much clearer."

Drat, I shouldn't have said that.

"Such as what?" he asked, far too calmly. The air was fraught with horridness.

What a pity one of my brilliant notions didn't descend on me. "Such as…as why Derwent was tenser than usual when he came to the Lakes," I explained feebly. "He'd had enough of Mother's machinations but didn't know what to do. I suppose that's why he told all my suitors I was promised to Worsten." Which didn't quite make sense, but I couldn't think straight.

"I agree that your mother is not in control of her faculties," he said, surprising me, "but she does know how to keep up appearances, whilst you, my love, although a clever little thing, have a tendency to flout society's rules. One can hardly blame her for wanting to control you. She will be most distressed when she learns you harbored Derwent's little strumpet."

I gaped like a fool.

He laughed softly. "Yes, I have known from the start. I recognized her because I have made it my business to know a little about Derwent's mistress, in case it should happen to prove useful…which it did, until you interfered with my plans."

Well. That explained why he'd gone back into his house the day I'd arrived in town, instead of mounting Fever and riding away. He'd probably been planning a ride in the park (for which one doesn't usually need a murder weapon), but my rescue of Miss Concord had necessitated a change of plans.

"You should have ignored her," he said. "An unknown wench running along the side of the road is no cause for a lady to concern herself."

"She wasn't unknown to me," I said. "I visited her once some months ago."

He tsked *again*. If I'd had any sense of humor at the moment, I might have giggled. "Even worse," he said condescendingly. "A lady does not visit her brother's doxy."

I should have retorted that she wasn't a doxy, but instead, I blurted, "A gentleman doesn't go about murdering people who get in the way of his plans!"

"Dear, dear," he said, and I almost wished he had just tsked. "You're a little *too* clever, aren't you, my sweet?"

I stood, fists clenched. He didn't move, but I had the horrid feeling he was tensed to spring at me.

"You *wanted* her to be abducted," I said.

"Of course, I did," he said. "Worsten would have taken her to bed whether she liked it or not—although being a strumpet, she would have at least pretended to—and Derwent, upon finding them, would have either killed Worsten with his bare hands or challenged him to a duel. Either way, Worsten would have been dead—my competition therefore removed—and Derwent hanged or in exile."

"Lord Worsten was never your competition," I said. "If you had come to me first, you would have known that I had no intention of marrying at all."

"True, but I need to marry you, and so I shall," he said. "Come to think of it, this unfortunate fiasco is all your fault."

"My fault?" I cried.

"Your interference, by succoring Miss Concord, meant I had to take care of matters myself—an entirely unnecessary inconvenience."

"In that you had to murder Lord Worsten yourself," I said.

"Precisely. I was unable to do more than wound your brother, and although it was dark, I couldn't be sure he hadn't recognized me, although I would have passed the blame to Henry, if the need arose—we're much alike."

"Poor Mr. Charting," I said, "stuck with an uncle like you."

"You needn't be rude to me, Rosie," he said. "In fact, I advise against it."

"You wrote horrid letters accusing my brother of murder," I said.

"Yes, which I admit to be an error on my part," he said, "but I hoped, if Derwent hadn't died of his wound, that he would hear of the accusation and flee the country. Meanwhile, I had to get rid of the coachman, who wouldn't hesitate to peach on me to save his own skin."

"And you wrote more letters pretending to be my brother, sending my suitors up here to look for him."

"Yes, but they haven't been much use." He sighed.

"Now that the coachman is dead, you mean to kill the groom and the girl. And you also shot at Mr. McBrae."

"Yes, for having the audacity to try to unmask me. Me! Can you imagine? What a pity he moved suddenly, or he would be safely dead by now." He must have seen the utter horror on my face, for he tsked *again*. "But he hasn't the faintest notion what I've done, so I needn't kill him, if it upsets you so very much."

"What upsets me," I retorted, "is your stupid *tsking* every second sentence. It is only one of the many, many reasons that I wouldn't wish to marry you, even if you weren't a murderer."

"Ah, but you *will* marry me, and if you do as you are told, I won't have any reason to tsk." He stood.

"I shall not marry you," I said again, standing my ground yet fearing his next move. I stuffed the handkerchief in my reticule but didn't remove my hand from it. "Even if you get away with murder and my mother is stupid enough to persist with her horrid plans, my father will never permit it."

"Tsk. Inconvenient fathers are easily dispatched."

"You would kill my father, too?" I shrieked.

"Only if need be. I won't even have to kill Derwent. He can go merrily off into exile; even if you tell him the truth, he won't accuse me. Imagine how the scandal would affect your poor mother." He snorted, went to the door, and lifted the latch, still facing me. "Come, Rosie, it's time to go. I've been patient, but time's a-wasting. I have a special license in my pocket and a cleric waiting for us in Highgate."

My heart thumped, and I trembled all over, but I could not let him prevail. "I am not going to marry you," I said with a surprising semblance of calm.

He tsked. Again! Can you imagine? If I'd married him, I would have been obliged to listen to numberless tsks a day. (If you feel that it is wrong of me to be flippant at such a tense moment in my tale, please bear in mind that it is distressing to relive these moments in writing, as I have already done over and over in my mind, awake and in dreams.)

He prowled toward me, and I backed away. "You can't escape me, child. Before you start raising an unnecessary fuss, consider your alternatives. If you wed me, I shall spare both Derwent and your father. I shall even spare McBrae, and it doesn't matter to you one way or the other whether I get rid of Henry's slut and the groom."

"It does so matter to me," I said. "They don't deserve to die." Where in God's name was McBrae? I didn't want to shoot Sir Devlin. I wanted him dead, but not by my hand.

He sighed. "My dear child, if you don't wed me, I'll have to kill them all."

I pulled out the pistol and cocked it. "I am *not* going to marry you."

He laughed as if the sight of the gun delighted him. "You'd shoot me?"

"I would prefer not to," I said, "despite the fact that you deserve to die. But I would much rather shoot you than marry you."

"Feisty, aren't you? Give me the gun." He put out his hand and took a step closer.

I gritted my teeth and aimed the pistol. "Don't move, or I'll shoot."

Chapter Nineteen

"No need," McBrae said. He strolled in from the private parlor, accompanied by Mr. Linehorn.

"What the devil are you doing here?" Sir Devlin snapped.

"Listening to your confession," McBrae said. Sir Devlin turned to flee just as the other Runner entered from the passageway and grappled him. He was no match for the two Runners.

As they disappeared down the stairs, I gave up every vestige of self-control. I fled to McBrae's arms.

They closed around me, holding me tight and safe. "Oh, Gil," I said, gasping into his coat. "Oh, *Gil.*"

He put his arms around me and held me tight. "That's my lovely, brave lass," he said and kissed the top of my head. I leaned into him, safe at last, and closed my eyes.

And then my father walked into the room. He was followed by Hamish, who took one look at us and gave a dour smile.

"What the devil is going on out there?" Papa demanded. "Where's my son?"

McBrae released me. "Well met, sir," he said without the slightest sign of embarrassment (although I felt myself blush). He removed the gun from my grasp and restored it to my reticule. "Lord Derwent was injured, but he's doing well, and your clever daughter provoked Worsted's murderer into confessing."

"There was nothing clever about it," I protested, hastening to hug Papa. "I was terrified. I almost shot him!" So much for the Medway dictum about never showing fear—although, come to think of it, I'd done fairly well in that regard.

"Sir Devlin's the murderer?" Papa gave me a quick squeeze. "I never liked the man, but I wouldn't have taken him for a villain. Too starchy for that."

I was about to try to explain, when McBrae said, "It's a long, complicated story. Perhaps over dinner—"

A commotion broke out below—Sir Devlin furiously protesting, Mr. Linehorn ordering everyone to make way, and Miss Bostock shrilly complaining about murderers in the Robin and Worm.

"Get your filthy hands off me!" Sir Devlin shouted. "It wasn't I—it was my fool nephew who killed him. There he is, with his thief of a doxy. Go arrest them, you blundering idiots!"

I hurried to the stairs. "That's what he said he would do—accuse Mr. Charting instead."

"It won't stick," McBrae said as he and my father followed. "You, I, and both Runners heard Sir Devlin's confession. Charting has plenty of people who can vouch for him at the time of the murders, while Sir Devlin has not. In fact, I dare swear there's a stable between here and Islington where he left his black horse after his jaunts up here at night."

"But the girl is just the sort the Runners will arrest with very little provocation." Sure enough, the Runners were hesitating, while Mr. Charting bellowed his innocence and his doxy wailed.

"That girl is my servant," I said in majestic imitation of my mother. "She has done nothing wrong. Leave her be."

That did the trick. The Runners shackled Sir Devlin and maneuvered him, still protesting, into a coach and drove away.

"Thank you, my lady!" the girl said. "You saved my life."

"Thank you for warning me," I said, "and for bringing help so quickly. You may well have saved mine, too."

"I didn't do much," she said. "Your Scottish gent already knew what was up. He were bringing them Runners. All I done was tell them to hotfoot it."

"Which I appreciate very much." I dug in my reticule which, fortunately, held a guinea coin and a few banknotes, which I passed to her. "I suggest you make yourself scarce for a while, just in case. If anyone tries to make trouble for you over this, send to me."

"And me," Papa said. "If my daughter is indebted to you, so am I."

She curtseyed low, awed, I assume, by having met an earl, and made her escape.

(Afterwards, I realized that I hadn't wondered, even for an instant, whether McBrae noted and approved the change in me, initiated by him some months earlier, that made it possible for me to deal appropriately with such a person. After that, I couldn't decide if I should be pleased with myself for having learned to be less proud and haughty, or annoyed for once again even *thinking* about wanting his approval.)

What I did wonder, and asked McBrae immediately, was, "How did you know what, er, was up?"

"Various things. His vague reply when you asked who had told him you were in Barnet. That he knew I had been shot at night. His proprietorial attitude towards you. A letter from Baffleton's man of business, mentioning as an aside that Charting had lost his allowance because Sir Devlin was short of funds. None of these were conclusive, but they added up."

Meanwhile, Papa and Mr. Charting were speaking softly together. McBrae and I approached them.

"It's an unfair law. Why should a man's family be penalized for his crime?" Papa said. "With any luck, no one will notice a missing horse, and if they do, we'll claim he disappeared in the confusion after Sir Devlin's arrest."

Heavens, he was suggesting that Mr. Charting abscond with his uncle's stallion, Fever, because of the law that everything owned by a murderer is forfeit to the Crown.

"I say, that's an excellent notion," Charting said. "Thank you, my lord, but where shall I hide the beast?"

"Far away," Papa said, "where no one is likely to recognize it."

"Ride him to Scotland," McBrae said. "Hamish here will provide you with introductions. You'll get good money for him. My mother's family were reivers for centuries and still deal in horseflesh."

How appropriate that Mr. Charting got a small inheritance from his wicked uncle.

"Now, where is my son?" Papa asked again. "And by the way, Rosie, you needn't fret about your weepy housemaid and her swain. After they're wed, I'll send them to the old hunting box. The butler's getting on and could use an energetic young fellow under him."

Isn't my father wonderful?

McBrae and I walked with him to Mrs. Pearl's. She and Miss Concord had not come home yet, but the butler led Papa upstairs to my brother's bedchamber.

Papa and Derwent spent a long time alone together.

Soon Mrs. Pearl and Miss Concord arrived—Mrs. Pearl in a paroxysm of delight at being visited by an earl, and Miss Concord pale with anxiety.

She needn't have been, of course. Papa came down at last, and after I performed the introductions, he smiled and took her hands. "So, you're the woman my boy has fallen in love with! Welcome to the family, my dear."

At which Miss Concord burst into tears.

Papa put an arm around her, gave her his handkerchief, and guided her to the sofa. "There, there," he said. "It won't be so very bad. I'm sure you have what it takes to whip Derwent into shape."

I sat next to her and whispered, "Told you so!" She gave a watery laugh and dried her eyes. I don't believe I've ever seen anyone so happy in my life.

Papa thanked Mrs. Pearl for her kindness to Derwent and graciously accepted her offer of a bed for the night, but when she invited us all to dine, he refused in his usual adroit manner. "No, no, you've already done enough, dear ma'am," he said. "We won't put you and your servants to any more trouble. I'll take this herd of people back to the Robin and Worm and return directly after dinner. Perhaps we can have tea together, eh? And some brandy wouldn't go amiss. It's been a long day."

Which was a sacrifice on Papa's part, for she would talk his ear off, but he is skilled at making—and enjoying—conversation with everyone he encounters. I wish I had inherited that ability from him.

Back at the inn, we dined in the private parlor, for Papa wanted to hear what had really gone on without any gossipy witnesses to our conversation.

McBrae, Miss Concord, and I recounted everything that had happened over the past several days.

Except why Papa had found me in McBrae's embrace. He didn't ask, either, which didn't surprise me. He approves of McBrae, although in what capacity I wasn't sure—and didn't wish to ask. Whatever happened, it would have to be between McBrae and me.

We walked Papa back to Mrs. Pearl's and returned to the inn. As we climbed wearily up the stairs, my promise weighed heavily on me. I had to tell McBrae the truth about myself, but must I do so *now*? It may seem foolish to you after what we'd just gone through, but I was horribly afraid. I had almost lost him once. What if I lost him again, this time forever?

We bade Miss Concord good night. Her door closed behind her, and McBrae said, "It's all right, Rosie. You needn't explain yourself to me now. I love you, and I always will. Whenever you're ready is fine with me."

I took a deep breath. "I'm ready now." I opened the door to my bedchamber, and he followed me inside.

About the Author

Winner of the Holt Medallion, Maggie, Daphne du Maurier, Reviewer's Choice, and Epic awards, USA Today bestselling author Barbara Monajem wrote her first story at eight years old about apple tree gnomes. After publishing a middle-grade fantasy, she settled on historical mysteries and romances with intrepid heroines and long-suffering heroes (or vice versa).

Barbara used to have two items on her bucket list: to make asparagus pudding and to succeed at knitting socks. She managed the first (don't ask) but doubts she'll ever accomplish the second. This is not a bid for immortality but merely the dismal truth. She lives near Atlanta with an ever-shifting population of relatives, friends, and feline strays. Learn more at www.BarbaraMonajem.com.

SOCIAL MEDIA HANDLES:
Facebook https://www.facebook.com/barbara.monajem
Twitter https://twitter.com/BarbaraMonajem
Bookbub https://www.bookbub.com/profile/barbara-monajem
Goodreads https://www.goodreads.com/author/show/3270624.Barbara
_Monajem

AUTHOR WEBSITE:
http://www.BarbaraMonajem.com

Also by Barbara Monajem

Thirty novels and novellas!

These include two mystery series:
  The Rosie and McBrae Regency Mysteries
  The Bayou Gavotte Mysteries